SAPPHIRE

MICHELLE ROSSA

Michelle Rossa

Sapphire

To the girls picking up this book solely because it involves a virgin who watches the fmc from afar, and wishes it were them instead being followed by a protective, dark-haired man who would kill anyone who laid a finger on them.

Also by Michelle Rossa

Shadows and Fire series
A Fate of Shadows and Fire
Guardian of Souls
Harbinger of Nightmares

Deal With A Succubus series
Cherry
Sapphire
Silver

Legacy of Cerasyn series
Captive to Twisted Torment

CONTENT WARNING

This is a *dark* romance. Themes in this book are for mature audiences only, and the content warnings should be noted prior to reading. This novel contains representation of sexwork (exotic dancing, camming), scenes of misandry and degradation of men, money laundering, drug use (marijuana), violence (not between MC's), death and disposal of bodies, mention of sexual assault, coercion (not between MC's), and explicit sexual content such as vore (imagined), masturbation, use of sex toys, masochism, voyeurism, snowballing, edging, and kink play.

It should also be noted that **both** the main characters are morally grey. And while there is plot to this storyline, there is a good deal of smut involved.

Michelle Rossa

CHAPTER 1

Cynthia

I watch as the crumpled one dollar bill lands on the stage, internally rolling my eyes at the stocky man who threw it. He lowers his hands back inside his dark navy jean pockets, cementing them there as he watches me with a hungry gaze.

Of course the man who smells like straight up garlic and onions is throwing me a single dollar bill while I'm putting on the best performance he's probably ever witnessed. Up here, looking like a seductive goddess with a leather thong hiked up my ass and my boobs on full display, and he has the nerve to tip me *one dollar*?

The audacity of men.

Gods, I hate them all—

Well, okay. Maybe not necessarily *all* of them. But about ninety-two percent? Yeah, that seems about right.

I lower my hand down the cool metal, releasing my grip from the silver pole as I step away from the center of the stage. His wild gaze trails up from my seven-inch heels to my breasts, and stays there as I lower myself down to my knees.

I pick the dollar bill up, fluttering my lashes as I lift it to my breasts, guiding his attention to where I want it. He takes a step closer to the stage as I tilt my head, moving the bill up until his eyes finally lift to meet my face. "What's your name, sweetheart?" My gaze flicks up to his greasy russet hair, the moving headlights above highlighting the dusting of dandruff he probably thought no one would notice.

It takes great effort to force the chuckle rising in my throat back down.

He works on a swallow before he answers, "Patrick."

"Patrick," I draw out as I rest my elbows on my knees. I exhale a long sigh, my bottom lip curling into a pout as I ask, "Are you struggling right now?"

His brows knit together as confusion splashes across his face, completely erasing the heated interest in his gaze. "I beg your pardon?"

My lips turn downward into a frown as I dangle the bill in front of his face like I'm waving a treat in front of a horse. "Are you throwing me a one dollar bill because you're poor, or because you're a prick?"

Patrick blinks at me, stunned into silence before a hint of anger surges into his expression. So, he's cheap and a prick? Got it.

I lower the dollar bill into the breast pocket of his beige button-down shirt. I pat the cheap polyester fabric against his chest, a light chuckle escaping from my red lips. "I think you need this more than me." I lift my hand beneath my nostrils, grimacing briefly.

Hopefully he uses it to get some fucking deoderant.

He takes a sharp inhale as his two friends beside him holler their amusement, their laughter ringing loudly above the club music. I stand myself up, my violet pleaser heels clicking against the stage floor as I turn around and make my way back to the pole. I notice a tall man at the other end of the stage throw a fifty dollar bill down, his thumb and index finger connecting in his mouth as he whistles.

Now that is a more respectable offer for my attention.

Though instead of giving him what he wants—coming straight over to him, I connect my right hand to the pole as I bring myself into a fireman spin. The bass of the song thrums in my chest as I slowly transition into a combination of twirls and spins as I finish up my stage performance.

It would be a lie if I said I didn't find myself looking over to that round-backed chair where *he* usually sits. The chair closest to the stage that has the best view of whoever is dancing on stage.

But he never sits there for anyone else. No one other than me.

He's been watching me for weeks—close to two months now. He never pays for a VIP room, never initiates conversation with me. He just tosses money on stage while I'm performing, and silently watches with a hunger in his eyes that smolders deeper than the fleeting lust of most of these patrons.

The song comes to an end as I slowly descend the pole, the small sea of men watching me with heated gazes as I lower myself down and collect my tips. Judging by the looks of it, I'm leaving the stage with about four hundred dollars.

Not terrible, but not the best.

I grab my matching leather halter top and descend the short set of silver steps. I walk across the main floor, heading to the women's locker room to put my money into my locker before fastening my top back on. After my top is secured and I've freshened up, I make my way back out to finish the rest of my shift.

But not before I have a shot first.

I approach the bar illuminated by the crystal chandelier above, the bartender pouring a draft beer into a tall glass for a man in a rich ebony suit. I take a seat in a black velvet stool, hooking a bare leg over my knee as I lean back. After the man pays and steps away from the bar, Ace walks over to me with a grin on his face. "I imagine he didn't expect you to give it back to him."

"Of course not." I say as he slides me my usual, a shot of tequila. "He probably thought I'd be desperate enough to hold onto it." I take it and slam it back, placing the emptied shot glass back onto the glass counter. "But I like to think I'm a generous gal. I see a man struggling to pay me, and think he needs it more than I do." I smirk at him. "After all, I'm always in the business of giving back." I wink.

Ace laughs as he takes my shot glass and pours me another. His perfect white teeth showing through his full lips, adding to his already handsome features. His golden-brown eyes lift to mine. "I would actually agree with you, *Virtual Vixen*."

I roll my eyes at him, taking the tequila shot and slamming it back. I guess that's one perk that comes with being a Succubus—other than having the very convenient ability to hypnotize others. I'd probably regret taking two shots if I were mortal, knowing I have one last stage performance for tonight. But with my tolerance, I could easily out-drink any man here. "At least that part of my *giving* nature is behind a paywall."

Outside of being a dancer at The Playground, I also operate a lucrative business. And—well, by lucrative business I mean posting pictures of myself in sexy lingerie and filming videos of me pleasuring myself with sex toys. The beauty of it is that it's all behind a paywall, so cheap bastards can't see my content for free.

I make more than enough money here to pay my way. Though as a Succubus, if I weren't for whatever reason, I could just compel a man to give me money. The beauty of having the power to enchant men to do what I want, out-dominating them at their own tactics. So being a spicy content creator is more for my enjoyment than anyone else's.

Besides, I love embracing my femininity by dressing up and I love having orgasms. Why should I ever let myself feel ashamed about either of those things?

I've found that the people who generally have the most to say about women doing sexwork are men—which ironically are the leading consumers who watch porn. Yet men who do sexwork for a living never get the same backlash. Sounds like a load of misogynistic bullshit to me.

"How many subscribers do you have now?" Ace asks as he leans his hip up against the counter. His arms fold over his chest as the black rolled up sleeves expose his umber, muscular arms.

I scrunch my lips to the side, shrugging my shoulders. "One-hundred thousand?"

"Gods damn." His brows shoot up as he chuckles deeply. "Sounds like you don't even need this job then."

"Yeah," I begin as I lean my head to the side. "But then who would be The Playground's new Pole Princess?" I wiggle my eyebrows.

Ace chuckles deeply, catching the attention from a woman down at the end of the bar. "I guess you're right."

At the smell of some strong cedarwood cologne and testosterone, I turn my head to look at the man inserting himself to stand next to me.

His voice carries a slight tremble as he speaks. "Sapphire, is it?" He looks to be in his mid-twenties, definitely no older than thirty.

"That would be me." I turn my seat until I'm angled to face him, watching as his gaze lowers from my rich blue hair down to my chest. "What's your name, sweetheart?" I purr.

I watch him work on a swallow, quickly lifting his round gaze up again. "Francis."

"Francis," I repeat slowly, watching his pulse on his neck begin to thrum faster. I quickly smell the nervousness seeping from his pores, a tinge of his desire slipping through. "That's a nice name."

He nods curtly. "Yeah—uh, yes." He works on another swallow. Gods, this must be his first time here. Poor thing is nearly trembling like a newborn fawn before me. It's kind of endearing. The men that frequent The Playground can be inconsiderate, thinking that they're owed our time. So it's nice to see a man getting this nervous in my presence for a change.

And thank fuck he doesn't smell like a bag of onions.

"I wanted to know if I could buy a dance?" His hazel eyes beneath light brown brows gaze up to meet mine. "Please?" He stammers out.

I lift my hand and lower it to his porcelain cheek, the tips of my pearl-white acrylic nails trail a mocha-colored strand behind his ear. I smile sweetly as his chest sinks suddenly at my touch. "Of course." I lower my hand as I nod towards the far left wall from the main stage. Round awnings travel along the entire wall with private rooms tucked within each space. Crimson velvet curtains hang above each section, parting open to show the unoccupied rooms within.

"I—I've never had someone give me a dance before."

Gee, I would've never guessed. "Well, there's a first for everything, isn't there?"

He nods his head curtly as I guide us away from the bar and towards an empty section, my fingers trailing along the velvet curtain pulled back as it exposes the single leather seat and small table inside.

I let the man take his seat and lower my hand from the curtain. But before I enter the room I feel an awareness wash over me. A set of eyes watching, assessing me from behind.

I look over my shoulder and lock gazes with piercing light blue eyes, nearly identical to mine. Jet-black hair that gradually fades from longer strands on top to a faded buzz cut on the bottom. Loose strands hanging loosely in front of his forehead above a chiseled, defined jaw.

He watches me as the breath I take falters, siphoning my attention for that split moment in the way I do with others so effortlessly. His gaze remains fixated on me as a man seated at his left with wavy, dirty blonde hair leans in to say something to him. I recognize his friend as the one who has been seeing Cherry—Amelia, as of late, a friend and another dancer here at the club. I don't know much about Levi, but I see them together often.

The handsome man with dark hair tracks his gaze over me as if he's been given the right to every inch of my body. Caressing my skin with his piercing gaze, lighting a flame to my heightened senses as he silently observes me.

His fixation with me sends a chill down my spine, watching me like I'm the burning sun and he's the moon.

Faithfully revolving his existence around mine.

I stare at the man for a moment longer before I step inside the private section, pulling the curtain closed behind me.

CHAPTER 2

In the last hour I've given a total of four lapdances, and only one of them I had to threaten his life because he couldn't keep his hands off my ass.

You'd think that men would know by now you aren't allowed to touch the dancers. But every now and then, I get one brave bastard that tries to test his luck.

And I always will it to end in my favor.

"You *want* to pay me an extra fifty dollars, Henry." I'd said to the man whose breath smelled like the bottom of a bottle of whiskey. Each word laden with that Succubus energy that no mortal can find themselves unaffected by.

He'd nodded his head slowly, overtaken by the power of manipulation through my words as he said, "Yes, I do." His eyes softened and his mouth partly hung open.

I'd retrieved my top and put it back on. "And you will be more respectful of women in the future."

As he reached into his pocket and pulled out an extra fifty dollars, he handed it to me as he repeated slowly, "I will do well to remember to be more respectful."

After I willed my energetic claws to release their grip from his mind, we both left the private section and went our separate ways.

I now sit on the armrest of a different leather seat, occupied by a patron who visits The Playground weekly. Renaldo, a tall hunk of handsome with a thick head of dark hair and tan, olive-toned skin. His charming demeanor and respect for women always gets him greeted warmly by the dancers and staff here, and always is the highlight of my Thursday night shifts.

He balances a glass of brandy on his knee, the lights on the ceiling high above giving his sharp black suit a faint pink glow.

"And you wonder why I am always planning getaways for us." His girlfriend Jessica says as she crosses her toned leg over her bare knee. Her long jet-black hair falls over her shoulder as she tilts her head. "You're always working and deserve to be rewarded."

Renaldo chuckles softly as he leans over and places a kiss on her cheek. "*You* are my reward." He pulls back as he smiles at her, his deep voice reverberating like a sensual touch. "But for you, we will go wherever you want. Just let me know the dates and I will step away from work."

Jessica gives him a smirk as he rests his free hand on her knee, slowly trailing his thumb over her tanned skin.

The two have been seeing eachother for just a little while, but I fucking love her. I remember the first time she came in with him. I had decided to keep my distance from Renaldo out of respect for her, but she quickly let me know that was unnecessary. That she was very accepting of the work us girls here do, and would probably do the same if she had the courage to.

It probably helps that her man isn't a starved animal groping on women here, too. And actually *loves* her.

He never asks the dancers for a lapdance. Never pays for a VIP. He throws his *generous* share of money for the dancers on stage but otherwise, he remains by his lady's side and just enjoys the night.

"Speaking of needing a getaway," Jessica begins, raising a dark brow at me. "You're here what...four nights a week?"

I laugh as I tilt my head. "Pretty much."

"Girl, I think *you* also need a getaway." A smirk plays up her red lips as she leans in closer. "Maybe that man who's always looking at you like you're the answer to his prayers will offer to pay for it." Her eyes flick to the right, past Renaldo.

I place a hand on my chest, grinning at her. "But then who else would you both talk to while I'm away?"

"Up next we have Starla!" Vinny's voice booms over the microphone at the DJ booth. The brief dim in the music subsides as the volume neutralizes back at the normal club level.

"Well, I hate to break up this little party here but I'm up next." I lower my feet to the ground, stepping in front of Jessica's seat as I lower down to give her a quick kiss on the cheek.

Her lips press against my cheek. "Get your money, girl." She pulls back as I stand fully up again.

She leans over to Renaldo, holding her hand out with a grin on her face. "Honey, where's your money?"

Without hesitation he goes into his pocket and pulls out a wad of cash.

I'd judge he has at least four thousand dollars there, and they're all in twenty dollar bills.

"Yes, dear." He says as he hands it to her, her face beaming as she holds the cash before tucking it into her purse for the time being.

"Have I told you how much I love you?" She says sweetly, his hand on her bare knee still trailing small circles over her tanned skin.

"You tell and show me everyday." He says in a sultry tone that edges to heated, wicked promises. He then looks up at me, flashing a handsome smile. "Have a good night, Sapphire."

I dip my head into a nod. "You as well, Ren."

I make my departure from the small section and head to the women's locker room. If Starla just got on stage, that means I have about fifteen minutes to freshen up and change my outfit.

As I step off of the main floor, a wide grin curves up my red lips. Knowing that the man with bright blue eyes will be sitting in the seat in front of the stage, waiting for me as usual.

CHAPTER 3

Dexter

She's been on stage for less than two minutes and I'm already reaching into my wallet to give her everything I have on me.

Showing her that she has my attention—has *always* had my attention, and that I'm perfectly content with watching her dance every single week. Being her disposable ATM just to even be in the same presence as her.

I've been content watching from the sidelines, observing the way her body gracefully moves like the fluidity of water. But my discipline and patience is quickly wearing thin.

I haven't made my interest subtle, either. I want her to know it's me watching her, like a moth swallowed by the light of a flame. A willing participant ensnared by the grace of her magnetism. I just need my initial approach to her to be right.

I might have gotten her attention with the way she lifts her lashes up at me, or the way she locks eyes with me as she takes her top off on stage.

Gods, she's fucking perfect.

But none of those things truly matter when at the end of the day, I'm still another customer here. And therefore, the very last message I want to convey is that I'm just another gropey dickhead that thinks of these dancers as just a piece of meat.

I doubt—or *hope*, rather, that she wouldn't think that as her friend Amelia is seeing my partner Levi. Whether she's aware that we're affiliated with The Deimari Mafia, and I'm the Don's close informant is still unclear. It's also unclear if she's aware that I know exactly what she is. It doesn't matter. Her being a Succubus wouldn't sway my interest in her.

Because I know what I want. Even if I've made no effort yet to actually talk to her. I might be confident in all other areas of my life, but actually *speaking* to her? Slightly terrifying.

And—well, there's also the fact that I'm still a virgin, and even just the thought of her being within five feet of me sends my heart racing and my words feeling like boulders on my tongue. Would she find the fact that I'm still a virgin intriguing? Lame? Regardless, I've had a few drinks tonight in hopes to loosen my nerves for when I finally do speak to her.

Because that desire to *know* her outweighs everything else.

Being a virgin at the ripe age of twenty-six is not something a grown man goes around loudly telling other people. Because if I'm not getting made fun of for my intentional abstinence, then I'm being pitied. And neither of those responses delight me.

Sure I've kissed girls, and gone as far as second base. But that's about it. It's not that I don't want to have sex, but I just—

I shake it off, not wanting to go there right now.

I pinch a stack of twenties in my fingers, lowering my wallet back into the pocket of my black pants. I lift my gaze back up to the stage as I stand up from the leather seat, walking the few feet to the stage.

Alright, here we fucking go. I'm finally going to say something.

She's currently doing some slow spin on the pole, gradually moving closer to the ground. Looking like some ethereal goddess in her hot pink halter top with her matching sequin mini skirt.

She notices my approach to the stage and slowly lowers herself down to her knees, widening her legs until she's seating herself down onto her ass.

I toss each twenty onto the stage, my gaze never leaving hers as she begins to inch herself over to me. By the time she makes it to kneeling in front of me, I've laid down two thousand dollars.

She lifts her long lashes as she looks up at me, her glacial eyes welding me in place. Twin pools of jewels lighter than the shade of her short blue hair. The ends brush along her collarbone as her bangs sway to the side.

"Thank you." She says huskily, the smell of jasmine wafting towards me. "Does this mean you're going to finally tell me your name?"

A light chuckle escapes me. "Dexter. But you can call me Dex."

She hums her appreciation before a breathy laugh slips through her dark-red lips. "Dex." She purrs. "And if I want to call you neither?"

She trails her hands up her waist until they're reaching around her neck, undoing the straps that keep her halter top in place. The pink strings around her neck fall down her chest before she begins caressing her bare breasts.

Don't look down. Don't look down.

I somehow manage to keep my eyes cemented on her face as I grin at her. My voice low and husky. "I don't care what you call me. Though my name sounds good coming from your lips."

Those shots of bourbon surely loosened up my tongue and boosted my confidence in talking to her.

She tilts her head as her brows raise slightly, a soft grin curving her lips. "He does speak." She lowers her hands from her breasts and moves them down her body. "Does this mean you'll actually buy a dance?" She pauses for a moment. "Or perhaps a VIP where we can speak more privately?"

Suddenly that confidence slips as my palms begin to dampen, doing everything I can to remain stoic and not show my sudden nervousness. But as a Succubus, she can probably smell it off of me.

And as her grin deepens on her face, I don't have to wonder for long if she can or not.

I internally smack myself in the face at my idiocy. Silently cursing the secrets of my past that threaten to plague me to a fear that I want nothing to do with.

But no matter how much you work through your trauma, convincing yourself that what happened wasn't your fault, it never fully goes away. Rearing its head at the most inconvenient moments.

"That's okay, sweetheart." She says, pulling me from my thoughts as she stands herself up onto her feet. "Since you've already paid generously, you can just stay for the show."

She gives me a wink before she slowly walks away, leaving me to stand there staring after her like a statue cemented into the ground. Against my own rigid self-control, my curiosity has my gaze lowering down to her perfectly round ass.

Look away you perv.

I manage to move my feet and step back from the stage, lowering myself back down into my seat and leaning back as my hands lay on the armrests. I debate for a moment on ordering another bourbon but quickly realize that's probably not a good idea. I'm not a heavy drinker as it is, and there's a chance I may loosen my tongue *too* much and possibly do something embarrassing.

So for the last ten minutes of her stage performance, I'll sit quietly and watch her work.

Slipping back into the comfort of the shadows once again.

CHAPTER 4

Cynthia

"Oh, gods—"

My finger rubs my clit at a faster pace as my orgasm builds hotly through me. My legs spread wide open with my tripod in front of me, the image of me fingering myself reflected back to me as my phone records it.

After I got off work I still felt sexually worked up over Dex finally talking to me. The way his eyes were trying so hard not to lower themselves down to my bare breasts. The smell of some pine and citrus cologne wafting from him.

I had wanted to record a short video tonight for my subscribers when I got off work anyway. So, I'm killing two birds with one stone.

"*Yes,*" I hissed as the veiny dildo pumps in and out of me, the machine it's connected to situated on my burgundy sheets between my legs.

I cry out as my orgasm pushes me over the edge, sending wave after wave of pleasure spasming through my body. After I catch my breath I turn the machine off, slowly releasing the dildo from me as cum drips down to my soft sheets. I run my finger through it, bringing it up to my lips and plopping my finger into my mouth. A grin curves up my lips as I taste myself.

I make a low humming noise as I release my finger, making a popping noise as I lay there exposed for a moment longer before leaning up and ending the video.

After I get my toy cleaned up, as well as myself by running through a hot shower, I edit my video as the moonlight filters through my bedroom windows. My property nestled within the woods that outskirt Lilitu City.

Sure, I could've easily just gotten a house closer to the club, but I like being away from people. I guess I'm an introvert in that way.

My finger hovers over the keyboard on my phone as I think of what to write as a caption. I take another bite of my leftover pepperoni pizza as the idea comes to me.

Sweet ;)

I hit upload and set my phone onto my bed, waiting until the loading bar turns green. A few moments later when it does, I log out and lean up against my plush pillows and finish my pizza.

I'd normally stay logged in for a few more minutes to get caught up on my ever-growing inbox of subscribers requesting special content from me, but it's nearing three o'clock in the morning and I'm beat.

As I finish off my pizza I dip myself beneath the covers, turning onto my side and fall fast asleep.

I woke up the next morning to a quiet thud tapping against glass. I try to ignore it when after a few minutes, he does it again.

I peel one eye open, looking at the large glass terrarium at the other end of my bedroom. I watch as Boe flicks his forked tongue out, nudging himself closer to the side of the terrarium as he taps the end of his tail onto the glass again. Impatiently telling me he wants to say hello, and wants to say hello *now*.

Why get an alarm clock when you have a needy pet to wake you?

I peel my other eye open, lifting myself up onto my elbows and squinting against the sunlight filtering into my bedroom. "I heard you the first time, Boe." I lift the thick covers from me and step down from my four poster bed. Fake green vines wrap around the dark chestnut canopy rails, making me feel like a whimsical fairy every time I lay in my bed.

I sleepily walk over to his terrarium and watch him slither up against the glass, my bare feet padding along my accent rug until meeting the hardwood floor again. For an impatient little thing, he sure is affectionate.

I lift the top of his enclosure, lowering my hand inside as the albino ball python inches closer to me. His forked tongue flicking out as he sniffs me.

I grin at him, tilting my head. "It's been a week, which means you get dinner tonight."

He nudges my fingers before I carefully rub the top of his scaled head. He lowers his yellow and white body back down into the cage as I place the cover back on top.

I throw a black silk robe over then head into my conjoined bathroom to take care of my personal needs. When I'm finished, I walk out into the hallway lined with antique artwork and little oddities. Golden framed art ranging from moody floral paintings to bones encased behind glass. Soft light filters in from the floor to ceiling beveled glass window at the end of the hallway, painting my ferns and lush monstera plants against the ink black walls a vivid evergreen.

I descend down the wooden staircase until I reach the bottom landing, turning the corner and stepping into my kitchen. The polished white and black tiles cool against my bare feet.

I head to my coffee pot and fix a cup of coffee before grabbing the irish-cream creamer from my stainless steel fridge. I take a sip of my dark roast coffee, sighing my content as I set the white ceramic mug onto the black counter. I lift my hand to the awning window above my kitchen sink, unlocking it and opening it up.

I'm so relieved that winter has finally passed us and spring has come to pay us her welcome visit. I cannot stand the cold weather.

I take my mug and make my way back up to my bedroom, setting it on my mahogany dresser before walking back over to Boe's terrarium. I lift the cover up as he slithers slowly towards me.

"Time for a snuggle puddle."

I lift him out of his enclosure as he slithers along my arm, his length now reaching four feet. I walk us over to my dresser as I pick up my phone, guiding us to the bed.

The time in the top right corner of my phone reads twelve-forty. Since I have nothing to do before my shift tonight, I plan to spend most of my day in bed.

I unlock my phone as I lower Boe to the burgundy sheets, allowing him to roam within my sight. Yet he remains close to me.

I unlock my phone and go to my cam site to see if anyone has tipped me on the video I posted last night. To my unwelcomed surprise, I notice a notification in my messages center first. I tap on it, internally reading it as it expands across my screen.

ALERT: user BigJohnny *has screen recorded your recent video, violating our site's confidentiality and privacy rights. This user has been notified that this is prohibited, and has been removed from our site completely. If you have any questions, please contact our customer support hotline. Thank you.*

I hold my phone in my hands for several seconds until my fingers get moving again.

I go to try and see if I can still pull up his existing account and grow frustrated that it has indeed been wiped from the site. "I bet the little punk still has my video on his phone."

I swipe to the bottom of the toggle menu, tapping on *Contact Us* and calling the phone number listed. I gently move Boe to the side as I get up from my bed, needing to walk off my frustration. I step over to my dresser and pick up my coffee, taking a generous sip as I try to wash the sudden irritation away but it still clings to my insides like a hot brand.

It only takes a few moments for me to be patched through to someone. "Good afternoon, thank you for calling our support line. How may I help you today?"

"Yes, I just got a notification that someone screen recorded my content without my permission. And I'd like to find out who it was." My foot begins tapping on the hardwood floor.

"Yes ma'am, I'd be happy to help however I can. Can I verify your account please?"

"It's Virtual Vixen. Account number 6668369."

"Perfect, I do see your account here with the automated message that was sent to you. Let me see what I can do for you, just give me a few moments."

She places me on a brief hold as I turn around to check on Boe, making sure he's still on the bed and hasn't plunged to his death. He lifts his head, sniffing the air as he watches me slightly lose my shit.

A few moments later she gets back on the phone. "Thank you for your patience. So unfortunately, as part of our policy, we are unable to give you any information as to who exactly it was that screen recorded your video because we have disabled the account permanently. So therefore, we no longer have access to their personal information."

I roll my eyes at the stupid mortal woman who cannot give me a lick of information on this man. I get it, being in the sex industry means that you unfortunately *have* to have some acceptance of the fact that there's a very real possibility your content will be leaked at one point or another, or that people will try their luck with you. The sensible person in this situation would want his information to sue him for copyright infringement. But I don't want to sue this man.

I want to end him.

"However, aside from his username the only information I do have access to is the email he used with his account. I can give that to you if you'd like?"

I pull the phone away from my ear, placing her on speaker so I can open my notes app on my phone. "Fine. What is it?"

"The email address is Big D Johnny at Gmail dot com."

Again, I roll my eyes. Of course the man is some testosterone-engulfed loser. "Great, thanks."

"Is there anything else—"

Her voice cuts off as I hang up on her, not trying to be rude but now I have this to take care of—

Okay, yeah that was rude as fuck. Oh well, she'll live.

He won't.

I look over at Boe again, shaking my head. "You are so lucky you don't have to deal with men. You get to be just a spoiled baby and live in a nice big home."

His tongue flicks out as he sniffs the air, slithering towards the edge of the bed when I meet him halfway.

I lower my hand as I gently boop the top of his head. "But this man is not taking my content without paying for it." A wide grin curves up my face. "And unlucky for him, he took it from someone who *thoroughly* enjoys serving vengeance."

I place Boe back into his enclosure, fitting the cover back on top. I open my text logs up, tapping on one thread and typing away. *So when you said Levi does the kind of work that can't be discussed in public, what kind of work exactly? And...can he help me deal with someone?*

I hit send, walking over to my vanity and looking at myself in the mirror. I had planned on spending the day in bed, but now it looks like that will have to wait.

Men, always ruining things for women.

I sit down on my antique bench crafted with faux leather, tucking my short hair back behind my ears. I take two black pins and use them to pull my bangs back on each side.

I hear my phone buzz as Amelia replies back to me. I grab it, looking down at her reply.

Who exactly do you need dealt with?

My fingers hover above the keyboard for a moment before responding. *That's the thing...I don't know him. The motherfucker took my content without my permission but customer support won't give me a name.*

We can see what we can do. But you're probably asking the wrong person for this then. I could point you to who would be better able to help you actually find him.

I take another sip of my coffee before responding. *And who would that be?*

I then realize her use of *we* instead of him.

Oh, what a sneaky bitch. What has she not been telling me?

But before I get to ponder long over it, she responds back and it's like I instantly feel that piercing gaze settled over my entire body again. *You already know who he is ;)*

CHAPTER 5

Dexter

"Pull around back." Sawyer's impassive gaze remains focused ahead as I turn down the alleyway. "This won't take long."

I drive down the worn pavement, pulling up to a red exit door that leads inside to a well-known barbershop in The Pleasure District. The bold, white painted letters on the door that reads *Exit Only* are beginning to look like the faded white paint on the exterior walls.

I put my car in park as Sawyer steps out, turning my car off before doing the same.

I pull out my phone from my pocket, checking the hacked security footage that displays the inside of Al's Parlour. Knowing he doesn't open for another twenty minutes yet, but still making sure he's alone anyhow.

"No strays." I confirm to the Don, putting my phone back into my pocket as we approach the exit door.

"Good." He says, fixing his black suit jacket before pulling the door open.

The early afternoon sunlight briefly glints against his silver earring cuff hung at his cartilage. His jet-black, shoulder length hair tucked behind his ears reveals the tattoo on his neck. His hair pushed back from his face exposes his sharp, chiseled jaw while a few loose strands hang above his brow.

Anyone that didn't know Sawyer would—upon meeting him, know right away that he's not a man to be fucked with. His demeanor may be calm and collected, but he carries an aura of immense power.

As the Don of The Deimari Mafia would.

Immediately we step inside to a dimly lit storage room where Al keeps his extra grooming supplies, clean towels, and other miscellaneous items on wooden shelves propped up against bare beige walls. We walk beneath the arched doorway and exit the room, the soft click of Sawyer's black dress shoes enough to alert his presence.

We walk down a narrow hallway lined with deep emerald green walls. Jazz music softly plays from speakers mounted into the corners of the walls as the sound of humming draws closer to us.

We follow the herringbone-styled hardwood floor to the front of the shop as Al looks up at us through deep brown eyes. His humming falters as he steps to the barber station to his right, his hand reaching for the light switch as round vanity lights above the wood-framed mirror turn on. "I appreciate the visit before business hours gentlemen." He sprays a cream rag with a bottle of isopropyl alcohol and begins wiping down the black leather parlour seat.

"I find I can be quite generous when I want to be." Sawyer casually strides across the shop floor, standing now in front of the beveled glass front entrance door. He lifts his hand behind his back, letting a beat of silence pass. "Rumor has it now that this is the most sought out parlour in all of Lilitu City." He lowers his hand back down.

I glance over at Al as he steps into a small conjoined room, tossing the rag into a hamper. "The rumors are true. Business sales have increased by about forty percent in the past month." He wipes his hands onto his black waistcoat, the linen material cinched snugly over his white button-down shirt. I find myself wondering if he's trying to wipe the sudden nervousness from his palms.

Because even through his calm exterior, I see the trickle of fear lingering beneath his gaze.

"What an interesting development." Sawyer says calmly, too calmly.

I watch as Al's chest sinks suddenly before righting himself neutral again. "Therefore, I have already made the necessary adjustments to your share. It was just deposited this morning."

Well, he just saved himself from getting whacked.

Sawyer spends several moments staring out of the glass door, making no immediate effort to respond. His silence causes Al to shift from one foot to the other, shooting a glance over at me before fixing his gaze back onto Sawyer's back.

I made the connection a week ago that there had been a significant rise in sales with Al's Parlour. With the intel I gathered, I'd brought it to Sawyer's attention. He insisted we met with Al to make sure we're all still on the same page with our business arrangement.

To give Al a chance to be honest first before killing him is a generosity that is not in Sawyer's nature, and was a suggestion on my part. But when I suggested we pay Al a visit today, the parlour's three year anniversary, he seemed pleased with the compromise and message it'd display.

That it'd be a shame if the owner lied about the parlour's profit gain and wouldn't be able to make it to his own anniversary party.

Sawyer finally peels himself away from the door, turning around to give Al a grin that is far from warm and welcoming. "Excellent." He takes a step towards us. "And the operations down below?"

Al nods his head curtly, his wavy cropped hair staying close to his head. "All is good. Your shipment should be ready."

"Should?" Sawyer purrs as a hint of calm irritation lances his words.

Al clears his throat. "It *is* ready. They've been working all morning."

Sawyer lets out an emphasised sigh, grinning. "That's better." He walks over to Al and lifts a hand, resting it on his shoulder. He pats his hand down and I watch as Al fights to keep himself from trembling beneath him. "Same time next week?"

Al forces a thin close-lipped grin, nodding curtly.

Sawyer gives another pat on his shoulder, moving to turn away from him when he halts. "Oh," he flicks his cold gaze to Al. "I do believe congratulations are in order. Three years and many more to come, I hope."

Al fights the dread from reaching his face as he catches me watching him. I give him a parting nod before following Sawyer back down the hallway to a door at the end of it.

Sawyer turns the bronze knob as we walk down the concrete steps. A light haze of cigarette smoke greets us as we descend further down into the basement, the sound of printers going off in the distance. It's at this moment that I'm thankful the smell of cigarettes no longer triggers me.

The metal-shade hanging lamps reflect a golden hue onto the long-white tables and the concrete floor below them. The fans doing very little to cool the damp room.

Sawyer and I walk into the other part of our business arrangement with the parlour owner upstairs. Keep your parlour and gain protection from The Deimari Mafia, while keeping your mouth shut about the money laundering in the basement. On top of our operations, Sawyer gets a thirty percent share of the parlour's income. An extra five percent if Al brings in more revenue at any given month.

Men garbed in loose T-shirts and denim jeans hover over the long tables with printers as they spew out the laundered money, the origin of the smoke coming from the cigarettes hanging limply from some of their mouths. At a nearby table two guys in black caps run the money through a currency detector, making sure we don't fall into accuracy issues.

Some of them look up at us, giving a vague nod before they get right back to work. These guys are like scavengers; they'll get their hands dirty as long as they get a fair cut, so working for us is the least of the illegal activities they've participated in.

I walk over to a black duffel bag set on one of the tables, pulling the zipper open to inspect the contents inside. I pull a few of the stacks out, pulling a hundred dollar bill out of each and walking them over to a currency detector. I run them through, waiting until the light turns green for each. "All greens." I say over my shoulder.

Sawyer approaches me from behind, giving a nod over my shoulder. "Good. Let's go before I have to get rid of this suit because it reeks like a fucking ashtray."

I chuckle as I put the money back into the duffel back, zippering it up before I haul the strap over my shoulder as we leave Al's Parlour.

CHAPTER 6

I grab an ivory towel from the brass towel bar, wrapping it around my waist as droplets of water glide down my chest. I close the glass shower door behind me as I step in front of the vanity, running my hands through my damp hair and pushing it back.

I glance down at my phone and tap the screen, the time in the right hand corner displaying eight-thirty. Two and a half hours until she goes on for her first stage performance.

I do my usual skincare routine before running a pomade through my hair, slicking most of it back aside from leaving a few strands loose against my forehead. I ditch the towel and walk out of the bathroom. My feet padding across the rug set beneath the foot of my bed as I walk over to my dresser. Pulling on a pair of black dress pants and a black button-down shirt.

The usual.

I hear my phone buzzing from the bathroom and go to retrieve it, seeing Levi's name popping up on my phone. I accept the incoming call and press the phone up to my ear. "What's up?"

"Are you getting ready for your usual Friday night rendezvous?" Levi's chuckle glides through the phone like cool whiskey.

I roll my eyes. "Did you call to discuss anything actually important or just to talk shit?"

"Mostly just to talk shit," he begins as I hear him inhale slowly, pausing before exhaling a long breath. I can practically smell the marijuana from here. "But I actually do have something to discuss that might fancy your interest."

I look over at the small glass dish on my nightstand, walking over to it and picking up the pre-rolled joint I left out for myself. "I doubt it's anything that'll actually pique my interest, but go on."

I light the joint, inhaling a hit as I open my balcony door. I step out onto the wooden platform, the quiet night surrounding me.

"Not even if she's a cute blue-haired dancer?"

My movements cease entirely from advancing closer to the balcony railing, my heart feeling as if it's frozen inside of my chest. For a split moment, I forget to breathe. "What happened?" My words are gruff as the amusement is wiped from my tone.

"Amelia called me and said that Sapphire—*Cynthia*, is looking for help on locating someone. Told her that some subscriber of hers stole her content without her consent. I guess now she wants him dealt with."

My hand grips the phone tighter as I inhale another hit. Ever since I first laid eyes on Cynthia, and did my intel on her, I've known that outside of being a dancer she also operates a spicy content page. I know her username is *Virtual Vixen*, and that she makes a substantial amount of money from doing it. I also know from her bank statements that she spends a lot of her money clothes shopping at some boutique called Jamelia's, and that lately she's been buying lots of new plants from a local—

Gods, I *am* a fucking stalker. A damn obsessive lunatic for a woman I can barely speak to unless I have some liquid courage in me.

Okay, maybe it's really not that bad. I mean, hacking into people's shit and getting personal intel on anything and everyone is what I do so...I'm essentially just doing my job.

Whatever.

Even with the knowledge of her online platform, I never felt enticed to become a subscriber. It wasn't the annoying seedling of shame that tried to convince me I'd be invading her privacy, even though she consentingly posts that kind of content. It wasn't even the small voice in my head that threatened to bring up the words of my parents when I was a small boy. Brainwashing me to believe that women are meant to be proper and submissive to men, and that to show their bodies in such a way to anyone other than their husband is a sin that grants them a one-way ticket to Hell.

They'd lose their shit if they knew I'm irrevocably attracted to a Succubus.

But the real reason I never hit subscribe was because I don't want to know her in that way. Not just for her body, but for her mind. Her quirks, and her fears. Even if the thought of actually being close to her unravels the intimacy wound settled deep within me.

"Does she have at least a name? Anything?" I take another hit, blowing the smoke out as I step back into my bedroom. I close the balcony door as I walk over to my nightstand and put the blunt out into my glass dish.

"All she has is an email. Customer support said they couldn't give her anything because they automatically deactivated his account."

"Of course they did." Annoyance biting my tone as I grab my work laptop, opening it up. "They'll say it's due to privacy policy but really they just don't want to get their hands dirty with any legal lawsuits or having the millions they make annually be tampered with."

The screen lights up as I go into my hacking software, pulling a new search bar up. "What's the email?"

Levi gives me the email and I roll my eyes. If men protest that they aren't as overly-concerned with exerting their dominance like women say they do, then they sure have a weird fetish with putting the word *big* in front of their names.

"Alright, I'll see what I can find on him." I start typing away, inserting hacking codes and trying to first identify his IP address. I get access to the location his email has been accessed to recently. "He probably will be easy to—"

An alert comes up on my screen, showing me his IP address automatically reroutes itself to a different remote server. "Interesting."

"What?" Levi asks.

I pinch the bridge of my nose, sighing. "He's covering his tracks by rerouting all of his internet usage through a VPN. It's a service that encrypts your internet traffic, masking your real IP address." I try to bypass it by getting around it.

"Is that unusual?"

"No, but it's a service not many people think to install." I get another alert when I try going around it. "This guy knows what he's doing and has been doing it for a long time. I can get his information, it'll just take a bit."

"Well, Amelia said she told Cynthia that you'd help. That you'll talk more with her tonight about what the next steps are."

I shut down the software, closing my laptop as I stand up from my bed. A lump forming in my throat as my breath hitches in my chest. I force myself to swallow and continue breathing. "Okay."

"Are you nervous?" I can practically feel his smug grin widening through the phone.

"No." I say quickly, trying to sound confident and definitely not affected at the fact that I have no other choice but to talk to Cynthia tonight.

Of course, I want to. Who wouldn't want to be sharing the same air as her? I'm—

Fuck, I need to get it together.

I release a long sigh, forcing myself to ease the sudden, scattered nerves that have nothing to do with tracking this guy and everything to do with being in close proximity to her. "Fine. Maybe a little."

Levi lightly chuckles, and at this moment I'd kill for his composed demeanor. "Looks like your opportunity to finally make your move just got delivered to you on a silver fucking platter."

CHAPTER 7

Cynthia

If this guy continues barking at me I think I might actually fucking lose it.

It's Friday night and the club is packed, unsurprisingly. I got on stage five minutes ago for my first stage performance and the money is already flowing in. I'm wearing my favorite cropped long-sleeved shirt, the sheer material leaving little to the imagination. Gem rhinestones dot the underneath of my breasts along the trim of the thin fabric. A matching thong and garter set sit high on each thigh.

I tuck the back of my ankle above my hand as I push my body away from the pole, my other leg sticking straight out as I come into an extended butterfly. The pole spins me around at a slow pace as I stay in this pose for a few moments before transitioning into a different move.

I bring my extended leg close to the pole, forming a V shape as my legs widen on each side of the pole. I spin like this for a few moments before angling my body, lowering my right foot down before my left foot follows. I keep my left hand connected to the pole as I slowly walk around the pole.

A series of howls comes from the man in the navy baseball hat. His thumb and index finger connect in his mouth as he whistles at me. "Come here, girl." He yells out, a twenty dollar bill tucked between his fingers and a bottle of draft beer.

I internally roll my eyes. Please spare me the idiocy.

I turn my back on him as I begin doing some floor work, trying to make the most of my last ten minutes on stage until I'm back up here again in a few hours. And I'd be lying if I said I wasn't a little disappointed to not see Dex sitting in his usual seat tonight.

In the months he's been coming to see me he hasn't missed a stage performance yet. But tonight, he's nowhere to be found.

Which is mostly annoying because I'm supposed to talk to him tonight. After Amelia told me everything—from who Levi and Dex work for, what they do, and the things that Amelia and Levi have done together, I was intrigued to say the least.

I knew there was something mysterious about him. Very rarely do I actually find myself attracted to a mortal man, but when I am, I'm always drawn to the ones whose lives brew of mystery and secrets—

That insufferable barking noise continues again.

"Come and get it girl." The man repeats.

Is this mortal man asking for a death sentence by talking to me like I'm a damn dog? Or is it just his first time interacting with a woman?

I turn myself around, locking eyes with him before I raise myself onto my black pleaser heels. I walk over towards him, watching his gaze lower from my breasts down to what's hidden beneath my thong. As I near the edge of the reflective stage, I lower myself down. Bending at the knees as I rest a hand on the center of his chest.

"Come closer." I say huskily.

He steps closer to me, away from the sea of men hungrily watching me. I will my Succubus energy to the surface, keeping his focus on me as I ask, "Do you enjoy treating women like mongrels? Be honest."

His face smoothes out as my power of compulsion forces him to do as I say. "Yes. I do." He says in a voice hardly above a whisper.

I grin at him. "And why is that?"

The compulsion spills the truth out of his lips like running water from a faucet. "Because even though I like watching the dancers, I know I'll never get a woman as beautiful as them. Not because I think I'm ugly, but because I'm broke and can hardly afford to take care of myself. But instead of doing something to rectify that, my ego pushes me to mask my lazy and stubborn nature by being overly-domineering."

I hum my approval as I glance down at his shoes, smirking. "Very well, then." I lift my gaze back up to him. "For the remainder of my stage performance you can watch on all fours, and you will not get up from that position until I have walked off the stage."

He blinks at me as he nods slowly. "Yes, Sapphire."

I lift my hand from his chest as I step back and away from him. I watch as he lowers himself down to the carpet and kneels onto all fours, his head lifted to meet my gaze.

His friends shoot wild glances over to him and start laughing, one of them coming up to smack a hand on his upper back. "Bro, what the fuck are you doing?"

I giggle to myself, satisfied with his public humiliation as I turn around and finish my dance.

I take a fresh wet wipe and rub it beneath my armpits, the sweet rose scent wafting up to my nose. I toss it in the garbage and take a new one out, wiping it between my breasts and anywhere that I was beginning to sweat while on stage.

I grab my deodorant from my amethyst dance bag, applying a fresh coat under each arm before tossing it back into my bag. I continue freshening up by lathering on some jasmine scented lotion and spritzing a matching perfume. I lock my things up into my locker and head back out onto the main floor.

I walk out to rhythmic music blasting all around the club. The moving headlights above highlight the sea of men occupying the sections near the stage. Club patrons crowd around the bar counter as Ace pours clear liquor into a line of shot glasses.

Before I can head over to merge myself between them to get a drink, I feel someone grab my arm.

Bad move on their part.

I whip my gaze towards them and find that the same man from earlier is touching me.

This man *really* must have a death sentence.

"Hey girlie, have time for a lapdance?" He gives me a wink.

I roll my eyes at him. I'd rather drink battery acid than let this man talk to me any longer. "I'll pass."

I go to remove my arm from his grasp when he remains hanging on, digging his fingers into my skin. I don't need to look over to the far left corner of the club to know that Maverick is standing guard at the door, watching the interaction. I see him from my peripheral vision as he begins to walk towards us.

Irritation bubbles to the surface as I lose my patience. "Let go of me before I flay the skin from your bones." I warn.

"Is there a problem here?"

I lift my hard gaze as Dex inserts himself between us, clasping the man's hand and removing his grip from my arm. The hard lines in his sharp jaw stand out, as does the sternness in his glacial eyes that promises violence. My stomach does a little flip at the sight.

The man clutches his hand with his other, glaring up at Dex. He goes to open his mouth.

"I would advise against whatever it is you think to say right now." His words carry a calm, yet imminent warning as he begins rolling his black sleeves up to his elbows. I notice the tattoos peeking through his sleeves, my gaze lifting to the center of his chest, exposed from the undone top buttons. An interesting tattoo revealing itself.

The man's gaze must've followed where mine landed because he goes completely silent, stepping back from us entirely and walking away without ushering another word.

Only when the man has left does Dex turn his gaze to me. His hard, penetrating stare holds mine as a subtle softness blooms beneath. "Are you alright?"

I nod. Looking over my shoulder to Maverick, I wave him off as he halts from advancing further over to us. He gives me an affirming nod before returning back to his post at the door. "Yes," I turn my attention back to Dex. "Thank you."

"You're welcome." A moment of silence passes between us. "I hope you can forgive me for missing your first performance for tonight."

I chuckle, his gaze momentarily lowering to my lips. "It would surely be a first."

A smile widens up his perfectly chiseled jaw, a dimple forming in his left cheek. "I assure you it was not intentional. I'd like to make it up to you."

He lowers a hand into his pocket, pulling out a wallet and handing me a stack of hundred dollar bills.

"I would like to buy a VIP room with you, if that is alright." He leans in ever so slightly as he lowers his wallet back into his pocket. "It would also give us the needed privacy to discuss some important matters, of course."

I hold the money in my hand. Two thousand dollars this guy is paying me to take him back into a VIP room. If only all men were like this.

I fold the money and nod, grinning sweetly. "Of course. Follow me."

I take us through the club, Dex following close behind me as if he's bodyguarding me from any man who tries getting handsy with me again. I normally would be annoyed at a man standing so close to me, but his presence is oddly comforting.

Not to mention the pine and citrus smell of his cologne is more than appeasing my senses.

I walk us beneath the large awning that leads to the VIP rooms and playrooms. Rooms essentially for those who are looking to get a quickie in, or where the dancers get paid to enact some strange fetish for high-paying customers.

Surrounded by elegant walls with red filigree detailing, I take us down the dimly lit hallway to an unoccupied VIP room. I push the frosted glass door open, a credenza cart with a bottle of champagne stationed next to a leather couch inside. The crystal chandelier hung in the center of the room gives off a warm ambient glow.

Dex steps in after me, the soft fabric of his shirt brushing against my arm and sending goosebumps pimpling down my skin. He takes a seat on the leather couch as I close the door behind us.

Feeling not only my pulse thrumming a little faster, but his as well.

CHAPTER 8

I bring the glass flute to my lips, the crisp liquor bubbling on my tongue. I'd offered Dex if he wanted some and he'd politely denied.

More champagne for me then.

"Have you found your content being distributed onto other platforms since then?" His soft gaze remains focused on my face.

I shake my head, setting the glass down onto the low table. "Not that I've seen, no. But it wouldn't surprise me if it were."

His brows furrow slightly. "Does that not upset you?"

"Of course it does." I sigh as I lean against the back of the sofa. "But when you decide to get into sexwork, you have to be able to accept that there *may* come a chance that your content will get leaked. If you can't handle that being a possibility, then you shouldn't be in the industry."

Dex watches me curiously before he vaguely nods his head. "I guess you would make a valid point."

I lean my head up against the palm of my hand, my elbow digging into the leather as I shrug my shoulders. "I don't mind as much about my content getting stolen as I do about finding out *who* is behind stealing it. Once I find out who, I'll take care of the rest."

A slight grin curves up the side of his face as a chuckle gets trapped beneath his lips. "Well, I've already done a little digging and he seems to know how to hide his tracks. It'll take a little time but I'll agree to help you."

I tilt my head further into my palm. "But..."

His grin slips as he furrows his brows. "But?"

"But," I lower my elbow and lean away from the couch, reaching for the glass flute as my feet press against the carpet. Relieved that I was able to take my heels off even if just for a little while. "You want something in return for your good deed, I presume." I take a sip, noticing his gaze lowering quickly to my feet before training it back onto my face again. "So, what is it you want?" My voice lowered a notch as I set the flute back onto the table.

He chuckles as he leans back into the couch. "I see you get right to the point."

"I don't see the point in wasting time." I inch closer to him.

I watch his chest rise as he inhales deeply, his gaze remaining steady on me. And as I sit myself right next to him, my body angled to face him as my bare legs brush up against his thighs, I watch his chest still entirely.

"Your time is all I want in return." He says after a long moment, his chest moving in steady tandem with his breaths again.

I stare at him for a moment before I laugh at his response. He can't be serious. My time? That's all he wants for helping me to track down this pervy man?

But as his face remains serious, with no hint of amusement threatening to rise to the surface, my laughing dwindles as my lips smooth out into a frown. "You're being serious?"

He looks at me as if I just spoke French to him. "I thought I made myself pretty clear." He glances down at the nearly-emptied glass flute. "Maybe that champagne has begun to impair your ability to comprehend me."

I roll my eyes as a wide grin curves up his lips. I hook a bare leg over the other, resting the glass flute on my knee. "No, seriously. All you want in exchange for helping me track this guy down is just to spend time with me?"

He passes a brief glance down at my leg, quickly trailing his gaze up and nodding his head. "Yes."

He raises his arm, propping it on the back of the couch. His finger begins tapping idly against the leather a few inches away from my face. "And what does spending time entail exactly?" I ask.

I watch him work on a swallow as a beat of nervousness beneath his calm exterior passes between us. "I understand you work weekends, so all I ask is that you set time aside for me during the week. I can pick you up and take you for breakfast, lunch, dinner, or all three." A soft smile curves up one side of his lips. "We can do stuff at my place, yours, go shopping. Whatever it is you desire—"

"Do stuff?" I cut him off, raising a brow at him as I tilt my head curiously.

The movement brings my head closer to his hand, my hair dusting his knuckles. His hand stills as he shakes his head, clearing his throat. "What I mean is we can hang out. Aside from me taking you on dates."

His hand resumes its movement. When he glances down and realizes how close it is to my hair, he tentatively, then slowly, lifts a finger. His eyes soften into luminous pools of cerulean as he sifts through the ends of my hair, his fingertips lightly gliding along my shoulder.

"Does this mean we have a deal?" He asks, a hint of sultry smoke in his tone as he peels his gaze away from his hand.

I lean my head closer to his hand, his finger now lightly tracing the curve of my jaw. I watch his chest still for a moment but he doesn't falter his exploration. A breath gets lodged in my throat as that finger idly brushes down my neck, a chill skittering down my spine. His gaze wholly on his finger and how I lean into his touch. A few moments later his chest suddenly rises and he pulls his hand away, lowering it to his lap.

I narrow my gaze. "Do I make you feel nervous?"

He gestures for my glass, and I lift it from my knee and hand it to him. His hand clasps around mine as he says, "You make me feel a lot of things, little jewel."

The way his words rumbled with a sensual snare has me reeling for more. He leans down and sets the flute onto the low-lying table. His black pants hugging his lean, muscular legs in all the right ways. The slight bulge in his veins on his hands draws me in like a magnet.

When he leans back he catches another glance at my legs. "So, do we have a deal?" He repeats.

A faint smirk curves up my lips as I angle my hooked leg closer to him, brushing my toes along the side of his knee. "Yes."

His hand clasps around my ankle in an instant, halting my movement. His thumb slowly caresses along the top of my foot, a wicked curiosity lingering in his gaze before it smooths over. "Excellent."

He lowers my foot to the ground, his hand slowly snaking up my calf for a split moment before his touch evades me once more. "I'm looking forward to it."

Loose strands of his hair fall over his forehead as he looks down, pulling his phone out of his pocket. The screen lights up as he begins tapping it. "I'll pick you up Monday at noon. We will have lunch and I'll inform you of any developments I've made." The warmth from where he sat immediately chills as he stands up from the couch.

My eyebrows knit together as I scoot to the edge of the couch. "You haven't even asked for my phone—"

Suddenly my phone vibrates on the table, my gaze lowering to the lit screen. I snatch the phone, glancing down at the text message displayed there.

I look up at Dex who's tucked his phone back into his pocket, a grin curving his handsome face as he makes his way over to the frosted door. "Have a good night, Cyn."

He exits the VIP room, his steps drowned out as the club music filters into the private space. I look down at my phone again, re-reading his text message. A satisfied grin of my own forms as a light laugh slips out of my lips.

His death might come by your hands, but your legs will be my undoing.

CHAPTER 9

Dexter

I press the graphite pencil against the large canvas, keeping my strokes light against the stretched cotton as I sketch thin lines that curve upward from a horizontal oval.

The lamp atop my laminate art table illuminating the sweating glass of bourbon, and what I've been working on in my spare time.

As soon as I got home from the club I ran myself through an ice cold shower to stifle the heat that was coursing through my body. The need that was elicited from just the touch of her silky hair, her soft skin—

My cock grows hard again just thinking about it.

I shake my head, attempting to dislodge the sudden need festering inside of me. An urge to touch her, to feel more than just her skin beneath my fingers—

I'm not that guy, I tell myself.

I meant what I told her. I just want to spend time with her, I assure myself internally. So why do I feel guilty for feeling so intensely aroused by her?

A knot centers itself in the pit of my stomach as I refocus my attention on the canvas. I'm glad I arrived when I did though. After spending fifteen minutes in my car having a *pep talk*—where my objective to help her couldn't get on board with my jumbled emotions and faltering confidence, when I finally did make it into the club I completely missed her performance. Which further engulfed my already disarrayed emotions.

It was easy to spot her once I got in the club, and I noticed the look of agitation on her face immediately. The way that man was clutching onto her soft skin had me reeling with a cold rage I've never felt before. That fucking bastard putting his hands on her—

He's lucky I didn't do worse to him.

But here we are now. I've finally talked to her, and made my deal. My help in exchange for her time. Except I see that want in her eyes when she looks at me. It's the same hunger I've felt in my bones since the second I laid eyes on her.

And I'm afraid that my rigid self-discipline won't stand a chance, challenging the very confinements I've kept myself in.

How would she feel to learn I'm still a virgin? Would she laugh? Have no visceral reaction at all? What I do know is that if she ever let me do more than just touch her calf, if she'd let me touch her pussy, I'm absolutely positive I'd reveal my secret in a heartbeat. She'd no doubt have me coming in my pants in a matter of seconds to know I could please her in that way. To hear her say my name as she comes around my finger—

I set the graphite pencil down, running my hand through my hair as I exhale my frustration out. Resentment tempts me with its promising well of bottomless misery, whispering all the ways my thoughts don't belong. I've never thought this way—this *vulgar*, about another woman.

I stand up straight, eyeing what I've done to my canvas before putting my pencils away and shutting the table lamp off. I make my way up the basement steps, closing the door behind me as I wander into my kitchen. I open the stainless steel fridge, grabbing the pitcher of purified water and pouring myself a glass. I put the pitcher back into the fridge, letting the cold water slide down my throat to ease the rising thoughts from digging their claws into me.

We are safe. There is nothing wrong with feeling attraction, I internally remind myself.

I feel my phone buzz in my pocket, pulling it out as I walk up the mahogany staircase, rounding the corner to my bedroom. I flip the lightswitch on, chuckling to myself as I read the text on my lit screen.

Noon is the time I wake up. Pick me up at four instead.

I respond back to Cyn, wondering why I didn't think working a late night shift would probably make a lunch date unfeasible. *You need four hours to get ready?*

Is that a serious question?

I chuckle to myself, those previous feelings of unease slipping away like leaves sifting through a gentle breeze. *I'll be there at four, then.*

And you know where I live because…?

Is that a serious question? I toss my phone onto my bed as I lift up my shirt and toss it into the hamper. I unbutton my pants, sliding them down my legs and tossing those, too.

I walk over to my bed, laying down on top of the covers as I read her response back. *If you knew where I lived this whole time, why are you only exposing it now?* She sends an emoji with his thumb up to his chin, insinuating a curiosity.

I'm a hacker, not a creep. Not technically a lie.

Coming from the man who has been silently watching me dance for months?

Well, she has a point. *That doesn't make me a creep. It makes me motivated.*

I prop a pillow up behind my head, chuckling at her response. *You're obsessed with me.*

Is that a serious question?

I watch the typing bubbles appear before disappearing a moment later. My wide grin remains as if I'm some high-school boy again, talking to his long-time crush for the first time.

Hell, who am I kidding. I'm over here damn near giggling and kicking my feet because she *is* my crush.

Where are you taking me to eat? I need to know how to dress.

I had planned to take you for brunch, but now that we're meeting later, I will make reservations for the Gilded Flame.

Perfect. Don't be late.

I am never late.

You were for my stage performance.

A pang of sorrow stings my chest but it quickly vanishes. *I'll never be late for you again.*

I set my phone on my bed, turning onto my side as I slip myself beneath my cinnamon brown sheets. As I try to settle myself, I find my mind reeling with giddiness for Monday. Overriding that overwhelming nervousness of being around her.

Before I can close my eyes, I feel my phone buzz again. Picking it up, I grin at her text.

Pink peonies and white and red roses are my favorite flowers. In case you were wondering, since you're obsessed with me and everything. K, goodnight.

I press my thumb down over her text, selecting the heart response before I set my phone down again.

Her request remains at the forefront of my mind until I finally drift off to sleep.

CHAPTER 10

Cynthia

Pinching the gummy bear I hold it up close to my phone, making sure it gets into focus. I turn the green candy from side to side before pulling away. "Such a puny little thing you are."

I plop the gummy bear into my mouth, chewing slowly before I swallow. I hum as I look at the camera lens. "Now, you're all gone." I make a pouty face.

When I got the request from a subscriber to eat a gummy bear, pretending it to be him and degrading him for how small he is, it was the easiest yes. Compared to some of the things men ask me to do, when I get a client that doesn't even ask to see me naked? It's always an automatic yes.

Well, in most cases. I once had a guy ask me to shove a golf ball into my ass and vlog my whole day with it stuck in there. I'm up for a lot of things, but that was definitely a hard no.

I stop the recording, lifting my phone out of the tripod holster and watching the short video over. I edit out the very beginning and end of the three minute video before saving it to my photo library.

I log into my account, tapping the notifications button. I see an alert that David's payment of forty dollars successfully went through, so I send him the video.

Enjoy. Xoxo

I hit send on the message then close the app, setting my phone down onto my bed.

Saturday came and went within the blink of an eye. Work was jam-packed busy, and I ended up walking out last night with three thousand dollars. I hadn't heard from Dex at all, not since the night prior.

I make my way downstairs, stepping outside through my patio door. The late afternoon breeze softly brushes my blue strands across my face, the sweet smell of lilacs wafting towards me. My bare feet sink into the lush green grass as I check on my tropical and ornamental plants scattered along the perimeter of my yard.

I check the soil of each one, watering the ones who could use a little TLC. I do this for about a half hour before returning back inside, watering my indoor plants.

By the time I'm done I'm sitting at my vanity and getting ready for work. I groan in displeasure.

Working Sundays are usually the worst.

The one night where all the stingy college guys over from The Academia District come in and watch the dancers without paying much for their time. And since the semester is just about over, there will be a fuck ton of them in the club tonight.

Great.

I lift my phone, typing into a text thread. *What are you wearing tonight?*

I set my phone down and pull my makeup bag out from the side drawer, setting it on the black vanity counter. My gaze glances at my phone as Amelia replies back.

I'm considering going fully clothed. The more money they fork out, the more I take off. Maybe then they won't be so greedy.

I laugh at her response. *I'm afraid Vivienne would not be so thrilled.*

Vivienne—our house mama, and the sweetest lady I've ever known. Most nights she stays cooped up in her office in the locker room, but once in a while I see her walking the floor. Making sure her girls are okay and are taken care of.

She's the one who the dancers go to when they need sanitary items, or when they need to take a night off. Or when they just want to complain about how the men are being foul or handsy. Vivienne's the one who oversees the dancers, while Janice oversees the club and everyone within it.

I respond back. *I'm thinking I'll wear my purple and black plaid skirt with some fishnets. Match with me? Xoxo*

I'll wear my red one ;) See you later, boo. Xoxo

I press my finger down, heart reacting to her text before I finish getting ready.

I've been on stage for ten minutes and only three dollars have been thrown on stage. After I noticed their beady little eyes gawking at me, with no intention of throwing me any more money, I took it upon myself to sit down onto the stage. Legs crossed out in front of me with my back leaned up against the dance pole.

To my surprise, it caused one man to start throwing me more money. I was expecting a full blown hissy fit from these frat guys, but at least one man got the message. He throws me a few twenties on stage, the harsh creases in his face making him appear older than these young guys. Definitely not a man in college.

I finish my stage performance by dancing for the only man tipping me, keeping my gaze on him while some of the college guys get pissed off that I'm not making eye contact with them.

You snooze the cash, you get the sass.

After I collect my money and walk down the stage, I feel my phone buzz in my pocket. I look down expecting to see a text message, when instead I see a deposit being made into my bank account.

I stop in my tracks, furrowing my brows together at the random one thousand dollar deposit. Before I have long to ponder over who sent it, *he* sends me a text message.

To make up for their stupidity.

A grin forms my lips as I respond back to Dex. *How did you know?*

Did you really think I, as a hacker, wouldn't tap into your work's security camera feed to keep an eye on you?

I should be concerned that this man has access to my bank account, that even when he's not at the club he's still keeping a close eye on me. That knowledge *should* bother me.

But because I've always been drawn to the dark and depraved things of life, that understanding only stimulates an ache to creep into the pit of my belly. Enflaming that newly churning desire.

I force my feet to continue their steady stride as I discreetly look up at the camera mounted high above, facing the main stage. My phone buzzes again, drawing my attention back to the lit screen.

Purely for safety measures, of course.

I laugh as I make my way to the locker room. *Did you at least enjoy the show?*

A smirk curves my lips at his response. *I always enjoy watching you.*

When I make it to the locker room I secure my money into my amethyst dance bag before pulling my pack of wet wipes out. My curiosity for where else he keeps a watchful eye on me piqued as I freshen up. *What else do you like watching me do?*

If he has access to so much of my life already, then it begs the question on whether or not he's a subscriber to my page. But before I am able to sift through that curiosity, he says what I didn't expect. *I only have interest in watching you work here. Nowhere else.*

I lift my brows at the screen, mildly shocked. *And why is that?* I toss my pack of wipes back into my bag before fetching my deodorant.

Because I don't need to watch you play with yourself to feel entranced by you. You do that enough by merely existing.

I stare at my phone for a moment, pondering over what to say next. A small part of me was expecting a response like *because I'm waiting for my free trial* or something corny like that. Most men have this weird fetish for thinking that because you're a cam girl you automatically *owe* them your time. Most men don't know how to conceptualize the fact that women don't do sexwork *for* men, they do it because that's how they choose to make money, and it just so happens to be in a way where *we* finesse men of their money.

We're not doing it because we're starving for their attention, we're monetizing off of their easy nature and—in return, making a substantial income off of it. But most of them aren't ready to have that conversation.

Even through my surprise at his response, a large part of me hadn't expected Dex to be like that. Through our brief interactions, I knew he wasn't a man who watched me, talked to me just because of what I do. I can smell a man's vile intentions before I even make contact.

A *gift* that has come in handy one too many times.

Still, I guess I just didn't know what to expect from him. Rarely does a man not find any excuse to objectify me because of what I do for a living.

"Sapphire."

I look up at the sound of Amelia's voice, her fire red pleaser heels clicking against the linoleum floor as she walks deeper into the locker room. "Two-wheeler Rick is out front." She stands in front of me as she tosses her long red-wine hair back over her shoulder. "Says he wants to buy a dance from you."

I all but nearly squeal my excitement as I clap my hands together. "This night might not be so bad after all." I spritz some jasmine-scented perfume over my body. "I'll be out in a bit."

She gives me a quick smirk before heading back out onto the main floor.

I lower my gaze back down to my phone, heart reacting to his message. I finish freshening up, exiting the locker room a few minutes later to walk out and see one of my favorite regulars. "Rick." I purr.

He looks up at me through soft hazel eyes, his cropped blonde hair turning a shade of grey. He wheels himself closer to me as I lean down and give him a warm hug. "I thought maybe you had run off on me since I haven't seen you in a few weeks." I pull back from him, grinning as I tilt my head to the side. "You look good."

A throaty laugh bellows from his lips. "Where would I go?" He jokes as he glances down at himself. A lighter laugh slips from his lips. "But you? Never would I do such a thing.

Are the young ones treatin' you right tonight?"

I give him a knowing look, narrowing my chin.

A soft grin curves his lips, creasing the subtle wrinkles under his eyes. "Yeah, I figured as much. I was a stingy bastard when I was their age, too." He sighs. "They learn in time."

I raise a brow at him. "I'm not so sure they *all* do, Rick."

He chuckles as I come around behind him, clasping my hands onto the cool handles of his wheelchair. "Come on girl, spend some time with an old bastard and I'll tell ya all about it."

CHAPTER 11

Dexter

I watched as she wheeled the man into a private section, closing the curtain behind them for a short while until they reemerged back out onto the main floor. For the past thirty minutes, they've been laughing and chatting in a seated section close to the stage. A leather chair pulled away to make space for him to be wheeled up next to her.

The man seems to light up in her presence, and I think to myself, who wouldn't?

I can't help myself from thinking how kind it is of her to give him the time of day and be so warm towards him. He seems to also be very respectful of her space, opting to keep his hands to himself unless she's reaching to hold his hand.

It's a really sweet interaction to witness.

After some time they make their way to the main entrance, Cynthia wheeling him to the double-doors before a man waiting for him wheels him outside. Escorting him to a handicap accessible van parked at the curb.

Shortly after I watched her retreat to the locker room again before getting back on stage. She starts her second and final stage performance for the night, and I watch as young college frat guys crowd the stage. This time throwing more than just three fucking dollars.

Thank fuck, because what an insult that is? The audacity of men.

I watch the effortless way she glides the pole, looking far less like a demon and much more of a goddess. I wonder what she looks like in her real form.

Though Levi made it abundantly clear to me that they aren't terrifying, and that he was actually turned on when Amelia shapeshifted for the first time in front of him. Normally I would shake my head at him and ask him if he was insane, but for some reason, I believe him.

Cyn's wearing this cute little black and purple plaid skirt tonight. It barely reaches her thighs, and every now and then on the pole, the skirt flips up and exposes her perfectly round ass.

Fuck, the things I would do to her. It makes me hard just thinking about it. I don't even have to touch her to get off. Just watching her, *looking* at her has me hotter than fucking Hell.

I cast the screen from my phone to my bedroom TV, setting my phone down on my bed. I look over at my nightstand drawer, opening it up and grabbing my silicone toy from inside. I cup the stretchy, clear jelly material in one hand as I lower my sweatpants down with the other.

I lean over and grab my bottle of lube, squeezing some onto my cock as I palm myself. I seat myself at the edge of my bed as I watch Cyn lower herself down from the pole, her hands gliding up her thighs as she teases the crowd.

Teases me.

She goes to put her hands behind her back, slowly removing her matching halter top from her chest. I slide my toy down my shaft as she cups her breasts, groaning my satisfaction. I jerk into my touch as I exhale a heavy breath.

I work the toy up and down my cock, a wet suctioning sound filling my room as pre-cum drips out of the tip. "So beautiful."

You're just like the rest.

My hand movement stops, two different kinds of frustration hotly riding the surface while shame tries to rear its head into the mix. The thoughts are right, I'm just like the rest of her subscribers if I masturbate to her dancing. Guilt threatens to sink its claws into—

She lowers her hands from her breasts as she looks up at the camera above the stage, a grin curving her lips as she kneels onto all fours. She winks at the camera.

She knows I'm watching.

The unwanted guilt quickly subsides as I resume movement and work myself a little faster. She crawls the stage with a tauntingly slow pace, keeping her gaze lifted to the camera as if no one else is in attendance but me.

Fuck, that's so hot.

She lowers herself down, doing some floorwork on the stage. She moves her hips, touching her breasts every now and then. Working me into a damn frenzy as she teases her nipples. My cock rock hard now as I pump myself faster, my orgasm riding the surface.

As I'm about to bust, she lowers herself to her back. Arching herself into the reflective surface as she opens her legs open, bending at the knees as her fingers trail down her thighs. Before I can fixate on how flexible she is, she lowers a hand to her pussy. Trailing a finger along the center of the thong beneath that tiny little skirt of hers, and I instantly wonder what it would feel like to be buried deep inside of her.

I lose it and cum instantly, moaning my release as I spill myself out of the opening at the other end of my toy. Cum shoots out before falling back down onto my thigh, my toes curling as wet sounds intensify and spasms rock my body.

I slow my pace down, my hips jerking up as I lift the jelly sleeve from me. I take long, steady breaths in and out as I sit there for a few moments longer. I lift my gaze to my TV as I watch Cyn collect her money from the stage, a smirk on her face as she traverses down the steps and wanders off the main floor.

A deep satisfaction stays with me long after my release to know that she wasn't dancing for those men just now. She was putting on a show for *me*.

I clean myself and my toy off in my bathroom before getting under the soft brown covers, turning off the security footage of The Playground as I settle in for bed.

But before I close my eyes, I send her one final text for the night. *Get home safely and I'll see you tomorrow.*

CHAPTER 12

Cynthia

Concentric circles ripple in the narrow puddles on my freshly-mowed lawn, reflecting the overcast sky through the water. I fixate on the raindrops hugging the glass, pimpling into tiny circles until some of them break free and slide down the smooth surface. I idly wave the bamboo stick, sandalwood-scented smoke trailing behind me as I step away from my porch door.

I insert the stick into the incense holder. The round, muted green ceramic dish set beside a glass vase of red roses above a silver decorative tray. The hanging crystal chandelier dimly illuminates the dark olive green ottoman beneath.

I fix the golden brown throw blanket, laying it along the edge of the wide ottoman before fluffing the pillows on my matching sofa.

We're literally going on *one* date to a public restaurant, but with how much I've been tidying up my house, I'm acting like I'm insistent on bringing him back home with me afterwards.

Who knows, maybe I will.

I walk out of my living room and make my way upstairs to my bedroom, heading straight into my walk-in closet. I pull the velvet hanger off the bronzed rod, a grin creeping up my red lips as I admire the satin dress.

I pull the black dress over me, fixing the thin straps on my shoulders. I grab a pair of black high heels and step up to the terrarium. Boe slithers out of his hiding spot and closer to me. I lean down, making myself eye level with him. "I'll be back later."

I press a finger to the glass, giving him an air-kiss before turning around to my vanity. I spritz some perfume over my body before grabbing my purse and head downstairs.

The moment my bare feet hit the bottom landing I hear my phone buzz from the living room. I walk over to the fireplace mantel and anticipation thrums beneath my skin as I read his text.

I'll be there in a few minutes.

I heart react his message before tucking my phone into my purse. Leaning up onto my toes I blow out the taper candles, snuffing out their golden glow and ceasing the ivory wax from further dripping onto the mahogany wood. I turn around, slipping my french-tipped toes into my five-inch strappy high heels, then wait near the door for his arrival.

I free my hair from beneath the collar of my leather coat as a set of bright headlights crests over the top of my driveway. They penetrate through my stained glass sidelights before curving away as he parks in front of my garage.

A garage that hasn't—and probably will never, store a vehicle inside of it.

Sure, I could learn to drive. It doesn't seem that challenging, I mean...men do it. But where I'm from, we don't drive vehicles to get to our destinations. We fly, or just portal ourselves to appear where we want. But that's in Hell.

In Lilitu City, I can't exactly do either of those things without drawing the attention from a mortal. And yeah, I could then just compel them to forget that they just witnessed a Succubus magically appear in their vicinity. But to have to do that over and over again? Just seems like a lot of unnecessary work.

And a lot of headaches I don't particularly want to deal with.

Through the patter of rain I hear a car door close shut. I look through the sidelight to see Dex walking towards my front door, holding a black umbrella above him. I open the front door as he walks up the steps.

From his hair to his suit he resembles a starless midnight sky, swallowing every glint of light within his vicinity as if he is darkness incarnate. But when he looks up at me, I am reminded that with darkness there must also be light. For one cannot exist without the other.

And in his glacial blue gaze, it's apparent where the balance of the two come together.

He approaches the door, staring at me as his piercing gaze roams over my face. "You look incredible."

"Thank you." I say through a smile as I take in the sharp angles of his jaw, the collar of his black button-down shirt as it hugs gently around his neck.

A grin curves one side of his lips, that dimple making an appearance. "I'd be flattered if you wanted to compliment me back. Unless there's another reason why you're staring at me."

I refocus my gaze, rolling my eyes at him as I chuckle lightly. "You look nice." I step out of my house, closing the door behind me.

"Just nice?" Dex asks as he steps closer to me. Shielding me with the umbrella in his hand. "I was hoping for exceptionally handsome, but I'll take it."

I turn around as we both walk down to his car, unable to fight the grin that's forming on my face from his charm.

Damnit, I *am* actually charmed by this mortal.

I look up to see an all black vehicle with tinted windows. I laugh softly as we step up to the passenger door, Dex leaning down to open the door for me while keeping me shielded beneath the umbrella. I glance briefly at his hand and notice the silver rings on his fingers. "Can you even see out of these windows?"

"Not at all."

I jerk my gaze back up to him. He flashes me a handsome grin as that damn toothpick hangs loosely from his lips. I sigh, rolling my eyes again. "Sarcastic bastard." I say as I seat myself into the passenger seat.

I hear a low chuckle escape from his lips before he closes the door, walking around to the driver's side door. The rich sound sends the hairs along my arms to perk up.

Upon my nosiness I immediately look around inside but find nothing other than his cell phone. No leftover to-go food bags laying around, no garbage, not even ring lines rim his cup holders. To know that he's not a slob is a definite turn on.

Yet, I see he didn't take my suggestion for flowers seriously. So he loses points for that—

Points? Girl, get it together. We're spending time with him because he's doing me a service by helping me locate someone. That's it.

He opens the door, seating himself inside before angling the umbrella out of the door, then closing it. He shuts the door as he sets the umbrella in the backseat. "Have you ever been to the Gilded Flame?" He puts the car in reverse, backing out before driving down my long pavement.

"I have." I lower a leg over my knee, trying to stifle the raised bumps forming on my skin. I cross my arms over my chest.

"Are you cold?" He looks over at me, his hand leaning down to turn a dial on the dashboard. Heat begins circulating inside the vehicle within moments.

"Thank you." I internally tell myself that my skin is only chilled due to the cool weather outside, and has absolutely nothing to do with the enticing smell of his pine and spice cologne. "So, what have you found so far about this man?"

I look out the tinted window as we drive through the quiet road that leads to my house, pitch-dark out aside from his headlights guiding us through the tall, douglas fir trees that snake up each side of the pavement. We reach the end of my private drive as he turns onto a backroad, leaving my little sanctuary and emerging us with the rest of the world.

"He unfortunately knows how to cover his tracks, but that doesn't make him impossible to find."

I turn my gaze away from the window and look at him. "How does one make themselves hard to find on the internet?"

"They use a VPN. An anonymous network that encrypts your real IP address, so others can't trace your identity or the location from which you use internet services from."

"VPN?" I repeat.

"Virtual Private Network." He looks over at me, and when I stare at him confusedly, he explains. "When you use the internet, you are most likely using an IP address, or Internet Protocol address. Think of this like a digital address for the device—your phone or laptop, to send and receive information from. But for people like me, this can be exploited to trace your physical location or gain access to your device and everything on it." He keeps one hand on the steering wheel as he turns down the street, the kaleidoscope of lights of downtown Lilitu creeping closer to us. "So when you don't want to be traced, you use a VPN to hide yourself. But even with this, you're never truly untraceable. No matter how many decoys you put into place."

Yeah, I am not tech savvy for all of this but I think I get the jist of what he's saying. "And how do you get a VPN?"

"You go through a third-party that offers them. Usually you buy a subscription to be able to use their software that provides it."

Dex stops at the intersection of Olara Boulevard and Main Street. The blaring red stop light beams through his windshield, illuminating us and the dark corners within the vehicle.

I watch as a couple runs across the sidewalk in front of us, both of them laughing as they get ambushed from the steady rainfall. "Is that what you use to hack people?" I turn my gaze to him, smirking. "How you learned everything about me."

He chuckles as the red glow turns to a vibrant green, driving forward. "No, I do not use a VPN service."

"Why not?"

He rolls down his window a crack, takes the toothpick out of his mouth and flicks it out of the window. Raindrops splatter the grey door panel before he rolls the window up, leaning back in his seat. "Because even though VPN's protect your browsing history and your real IP address, they are not foolproof and can be easily exploited with the right money and resources."

I nod my head slowly. "So, what do you use then?"

He looks over at me, grinning. "I use a variety of things, and take a lot of precautions." He turns his gaze back to the road.

We ride in silence for a short while as I file that information away. When we pull up to an upscale building with walnut front doors, I notice a smiling male greeter waiting at the front entrance dressed in a tailcoat and matching top hat.

Dex turns the car off and steps out, umbrella expanded above his head as he walks over to my side. He opens my door, reaching his hand out as I place my hand in his. "Thank you."

His eyes reach mine, warming at my words. Something passes over his gaze too quickly for me to read. "You are very polite."

I raise a brow at him. "Did you expect me to be rude?"

He chuckles as I step to his side beneath the umbrella. The scent of pine and citrus envelopes me as he takes my hand, lowering it to his bent elbow as we step away from his car. His hand remained atop mine. "Not at all."

A gentleman dressed in similar attire to the male greeter at the door comes rushing towards us. A wide smile lighting his young face. "Good evening, sir. Valet is twenty dollars."

Dex releases his hand from mine to reach into his pants pocket, and I swear there was a hint of hesitation as he did.

He pulls out his wallet and shuffles out a fifty dollar bill, tucking it into the man's breast pocket of his sleek black vest. He hands him the keys to his car.

"Thank you, sir." The man hands him a valet ticket before he rushes to Dex's vehicle.

Dex guides us forward up the small set of steps, the greeter at the entrance opening the door for us and bowing generously. "Welcome to the Gilded Flame."

CHAPTER 13

From the doorman to the hostess, I watched as Dex slipped each of them a fifty dollar bill. Hell, he even slipped a staff member twenty dollars just because he came over to collect our coats. I know what he does for a living, I know he's the right hand man for the Don of The Deimari Mafia. But still, I was in awe at his utter lack of selfishness.

It inevitably made me more attracted to him. And I'd be lying if I said it didn't make me more convinced I might actually take this man home with me tonight.

Our hostess guides us through the restaurant as Dex keeps his hand on the small of my back. The moment his hands were freed and slipped his wallet back into his pocket, he immediately returned to touching me.

She guides us past sections with oval-shaped tables illuminated by vintage lights hanging from above. Ivory table cloths lay over the polished wood surfaces as crimson red chairs accompany them. Floor to ceiling decorative columns accentuate the sophisticated atmosphere with a touch of sensual ambiance.

The hostess guides us over to a section that is more private from the rest of the establishment, and my gaze snags on one table in particular and what is situated on top of it.

We approach the table as Dex pulls my chair out for me and I seat myself down. As Dex seats himself and says something to the hostess, I remain fixated on the vase of pink peonies, with white and red roses before me.

"Do you like them?"

I finally managed to lift my gaze to meet his. The amber-hued lights above us casting a warm glow across his sharp features. Softening the intensity in his gaze.

I nod. "They're perfect."

Okay, he definitely wins those points back.

I watch as a glimmer of satisfaction graces his face, intertwining with the generous curve of his smile. "I'm really glad to hear that."

A man with short copper hair approaches our table. "Good evening, and welcome to the Gilded Flame. My name is Yanis and I will be taking care of you both tonight." He raises a hand to his chest before lowering it. "Can I get you both started off with something to drink?" Yanis looks over to me first.

"I'll take a glass of Merlot." I pick up the menu in front of me, browsing their dinner options.

"Absolutely." Yanis turns to Dex. "And for you, sir?"

"I'll take a bourbon. Neat."

"Right away." The waiter nods his enthusiasm before walking away from our table. He returns a few minutes later with a tray of our drinks, as well as two glasses of water.

"Here you are," Yanis begins, setting my drink down first before setting down Dex's. He sets my water down. "I'll give you both a few moments to look over the menu—"

His words cut off as the glass of water he sets down for Dex spills onto the table. His eyes widen in horror as he scrambles for a napkin. "I am so terribly sorry."

The waiter panics as he wipes up the *trickle* of water on the table. Dex helps him blot it up with another cloth napkin. "It's okay." He assures him.

"I could understand if you'd like me to switch tables—"

Dex rests his hand on Yanis', drawing the waiter's wild gaze to him as he smiles. "We're perfectly fine here. Don't worry about it."

A palpable wave of relief washes over the waiter at Dex's empathy, as if worrying was exactly what he was about to do for the rest of the night. Dex pats his hand before lowering his hand back down to his lap.

The waiter gives a grateful smile before turning away from our table.

This whole *spending time with him* would be a lot easier if he was a fugly prick. It would be easy for me then to not look at him as more than someone just doing a service for me. But of course, on top of his good looks he's exceptionally kind. Only heightening the attraction I already feel towards him.

"So how do you plan to find this man?" I raise the glass of Merlot to my lips, taking a sip.

His eyes linger on my mouth for a moment before lifting his gaze. "With my charm and wit, of course."

I sigh audibly as I roll my eyes, setting my wine down onto the table. "No, seriously."

He leans into his seat, reaching for his bourbon. "Once I find out which VPN provider he uses, I can go to them directly and...incentivize them to leak his real IP address to me."

I raise a brow. "And you think they'll willingly do that just because of who you work for?"

"So you *are* aware of what I do." He takes a drink before setting the amber liquid back down onto the table.

"Just like you're aware of what *I* actually am." I say, crossing my arms over in front of me.

His gaze remains wholly on my face, not even once lingering downwards at the swell of my breasts pushed up. "I am." He says, his words both calm and impassive.

So he *does* know I'm a Succubus. My brows knit together at his impassive reaction to that knowledge. But before I can ask, Yanis comes back to our table to take our dinner orders. Once he finishes, he leaves our table with our menus in his hand.

I tilt my head. "Yet, you're not afraid. Why?"

He vaguely shrugs his shoulders, as if I've just asked him the most rhetorical question. "Should I be afraid of you?"

A mortal discovering my kind would normally be met with fear, terror even. But instead, admiration and calmness is prevalent in his gaze.

It makes me want to both jump him, and wrangle his neck.

The confusion of both feelings suddenly spikes an irritation within me. I lean forward in my seat, resting my elbows onto the table. "Not as long as you act accordingly."

He blinks at me before he chuckles long and deeply, completely unaffected by my threat. His reaction—and the words spoken next, stir a spark of irritation. "That was really cute."

My calm demeanor slips as I fume at his words. *Cute?* "You may be good looking but do not mistake my generosity to spend time with you for being easily swayed by a mortal man's charm."

"So you *do* think I'm handsome?" He tilts his head as he grins at me.

My brows smooth out as I lift my elbows from the table, leaning away and closer to my seat. Shit. "Well, I surely wouldn't have agreed to go out with you otherwise." I lift my wine to my lips. "But if you think this guarantees you getting laid tonight then you'll find yourself disappointed when that doesn't happen."

Even though moments ago I was literally just thinking of whether I would take this man home with me or not. But I can't let him know that. I have to allude to the mystery, or whatever.

I watch as his grin falters a little, but not with a look of disappointment but of nervousness. It happens so fast that

I second-guess if I saw it at all. But why would he be nervous that I said that?

"I promise that was not my intention for tonight. Just dinner. Though I had wondered if I could come inside for a bit when I dropped you off."

Yanis comes back to our table carrying a tray of food. He leans down, setting a plate of baked salmon and greens in front of me before placing a plate of steak and asparagus in front of Dex. "Why?" I ask.

"Thank you, sir." He says to Yanis before starting to cut his steak up. His gaze lifts up to mine. "I want to set up a security system in your home."

"So you can spy on me at the club *and* at home?" I fork a piece of salmon into my mouth. Taking my annoyance at his severe kindness out on my food.

He watches me with eerie stillness, not a lick of shame hindering his gaze. "I watch to make sure you're safe. There's a difference." He takes a bite of his steak, swallowing. "But no, I would not spy on you in your home unless something was wrong. But I think it's a good idea to have a security system in place."

"So just in the club you creep on me?" I lift my leg up and cross it over my knee.

His index finger begins to tap idly against his glass of bourbon as his voice lowers a notch. "I prefer the term watch."

A breathy laugh gets trapped in my wine glass before I take a sip. I set my wine back down. "And if I said no?"

He gives me a faint grin. "I fear I would install it regardless."

I sigh as I jab some greens onto my fork. "Fine. You can install your little security system."

"Wonderful." he says before continuing to eat his steak.

I want to be annoyed by his demand, but as I meet his gaze a softness settles in my chest for his request. Even though I know he'll set it up so he has access to my security camera feeds, and has access to what I do in the privacy of my own home, it doesn't make me feel disturbed.

Not even in the slightest.

CHAPTER 14

Dexter

I find myself unable to stray my gaze away from her for more than a few seconds. Gods, she looks like the epitome of what utter bliss is. So incredible to look at, just as enjoyable to talk to.

After we both finished our dinner I ordered a dessert for us to share. Which turned into Cyn hogging most of it. But I didn't mind.

I'm just happy to spend time with her.

She goes to lift her wine glass when I reach my hand out, stopping her. "You have some tiramisu on your lip."

I wipe my thumb beneath her bottom lip, careful not to smudge her red lipstick as I wipe the dessert from the corner of her mouth. She sits there watching me with a subtle hunger in her gaze that I know has nothing to do with food.

Please don't look at me like that. I want to do devious things to you when you look at me like that. Things that I have zero experience in.

I lift my hand from her and plop my thumb into my mouth, tasting the rich dessert on my tongue. Wishing it were her instead—

Focus, you sick bastard.

"Thank you." She manages to say sweetly, her gaze trained steadily on mine.

I grab my drink and lift it to my lips, swallowing down what's left as I try to stifle the arousal that threatens to press against my pants. "So, what are you going to do when we find him?"

Without hesitation, she says, "Kill him, of course."

I have to fight back my laugh at her dispassionate response. Though I knew from the very beginning that that's what he'd face for what he did.

Whether his death came by my hands or hers. His fate was always going to be the same.

Before I can open my mouth Yanis comes back over to our table. He sets the checkbook down in front of me. "You both have been wonderful guests tonight. Thank you for dining with us and have a great rest of your evening." He bows with a wide grin on his face before leaving us.

I pull out my wallet, slipping three hundred dollars into the checkbook before placing it in the middle of the table.

"How much was dinner tonight?" Cyn asks, her curiosity adorable.

"One-eighty."

Her brows lift only slightly. "That's one hell of a tip."

I push my seat out as I stand up from the crimson chair. "He was one hell of a server."

I step around behind her chair, pulling it out for her as she stands up next to me. The scent of her jasmine perfume like a siren's song, magnetizing me to her like she's the very source of the air I breathe.

"I should have known you were generous." She steps closer into me, resting a hand on my arm as her voice lowers. "You sure have been with me."

It takes everything in me not to pull her flush against my body and kiss her. But I can't, it's not right.

Not right now.

She begins walking away from the table when I lightly place my hand on her waist. "You're forgetting something."

She turns around as I pick the vase up from the table. "You can't take the vase, too." She remarks.

"Sure I can." I grin at her as she gives me a quizzical look. "I'm kidding. I'll have them wrapped in the back."

She rolls her eyes at me but quickly graces me with a wide grin of her own. I think she's rolled her eyes at me a total of twenty times tonight. Call me disturbed, but it turns me on.

We walk to the front to collect our coats and for the staff to wrap her flowers into a bouquet. After the valet attendant brings my car around, we both step outside to the chilled air. Pleased to see the rain has finally settled.

Cyn lowers herself into the passenger seat before looking up at me. "Thank you."

I nod my head before closing her door, walking around to the other side of my car.

Her politeness being the other thing that strangely turns me on.

We step inside Cyn's house, her hand reaching over to a light switch on the wall to illuminate the entryway.

"Shoes off when you're in my house." She slips her heels off onto a patterned rug.

I huff out a lazy chuckle. "Yes, ma'am." I slip my shoes off and follow her down her hallway.

We step into her kitchen as she flips on the light. I move over to the kitchen island and begin opening up the box in my hands. "I'll need to download an app onto your phone. This will make it so you can see inside your home at any given time, and be alerted to trespassers."

She lifts her phone out of her purse, handing it to me. "I'm going to go upstairs and change while you...do all of this."

I grin softly. "Sounds good."

She turns on her heels and walks out of the room.

As I get the equipment out of the package I take note of the room around me. A light breeze pulls my attention over to my left, originating from a cracked window above her kitchen sink. I find myself walking over towards it.

I close the window, locking it as I hear Cyn walk back into the room. She stops abruptly. "What are you doing?"

I turn to face her. "Your window was open. Anybody could get in when you're not—"

As soon as I turn around and look at her, I lose all ability to form words. She's changed out of that stunning black dress into a pair of fuzzy pajamas. The plaid shorts barely reaching mid-thigh, and that cropped tank top—

Is it possible I could cum just by looking at her? Fuck, I hope not. That would possibly be embarrassing.

She nudges her head as she places a hand on her hip. A hip that I can see because her tank top barely reaches her pierced belly button. "Have you suddenly gone deaf?"

I clear my throat as I fix my gaze back onto her face. Yes, let's keep our eyes there. "Do you always keep your window open when you leave the house?"

She walks further into the kitchen. "Not always, but sometimes."

A sudden rigidness solidifies inside of me, more constricting than my self-imposed abstinence. "You should really lock them when you're gone. You never know—"

"Who could break in?" She finishes for me as she stands next to me. Looking up at me through those wispy blue bangs. "They would be very stupid to try."

"That they would be." I turn my gaze back to the counter, to all of the cameras I bought to place inside her home.

As I go ahead and install all of the cameras, Cyn stands behind me and *observes*. Every now and then critiquing the way that I've hung them, or suggesting that I place one at a different angle. In which case, I argue my defense that they are perfectly fine as they are. But once I get the app installed on her phone and get it connected to her cameras,

I end up having to fix one of them because the angle was indeed slightly off.

She sure got a kick out of being right as she smugly rubbed it in my face. I told her how cute she was and she quickly reminded me that cute must not be her favorite word.

After installing the last of her new home security system, I step away from the alarm box. "Okay, now type it in and try."

She leans over the alarm box, her back facing me as she types in the code I programmed for her. "One zero two six." She repeats out loud as she presses the numbers into the keypad. When the light turns green, she turns around. "Why those numbers?"

"No reason." I say as a smirk plays up one side of my face. I lean my hand over her head to close the lid to the alarm box. "Now you are fully set up with a security system."

My hand brushes along hers when I lower it back down to my side, eliciting a warmth in my chest. Our chests only inches apart. "Well, thank you. I think it was a little unnecessary but I appreciate it."

I find myself lifting my thumb to caress it along her hand, stealing another moment of her touch before I pull away. "Measures to ensure your safety are always necessary."

She steps closer into me until I can almost feel her clothing touching me. My breathing threatens to ramp up but I keep it neutral somehow. "Would you like to stay for a drink?"

YES. Yes, I would love that. To sit on your couch and talk all night while I feel those soft legs—

"Thank you, but I'm afraid I have to take a rain check for another night." I say, hating every word that comes out of my mouth. But knowing that if I don't create a little distance between us, I'm afraid I'll expose my virginity and well—

I want to relish in what we have going on before she finds out. Because I don't know how she'll react when she does and...that kind of scares me.

Thankfully, the look in her face shows me she's not terribly disappointed in my response. "Of course. Another night." She gives me a smile as she opens the door.

A pang of guilt threatens to swarm my insides at turning down the opportunity to spend more time with her, but no matter how much I look forward to seeing her, I'm still swimming in unfamiliar territory.

Both in matters of intimacy and...well, just experiencing closeness with another in general.

I lean down, pressing a kiss to her forehead. Feeling the rush of her warm skin beneath my lips, the closeness of her body to mine. I pull away slowly as I meet her gaze. "Goodnight, Cynthia."

Her eyes shine like twin spheres of jewels. "Goodnight."

I force myself to step outside and walk to my car, seating myself inside before I drive away from her house. Missing her touch every second of my drive back home.

CHAPTER 15

I am the biggest idiot.

Those five words have been circulating themselves through my mind since the moment I woke up. The only short reprieve that I'm allowed in even remotely dulling those thoughts is when I have to pay attention during this monotonous meeting.

"As long as my team stays on deadline, the site will be completed mid-summer."

"Which means we can begin opening applications to prospect tenants within the month."

"Correct." Mateo says, his thumbs idly tapping against one another as his bronzed hands remain folded on the table. He glances over to me before training his gaze back onto the real estate investor to his left.

He lifts his gaze up from the paperwork in front of him, upturned hazel eyes meeting mine. "This project has been underway for twelve months. All the costs have already been taken care of. So forgive me if I ask what exactly you are interested in investing in here?"

Smart bastard to ask the right questions.

I stand up from my seat, slowly striding over to the floor-to-ceiling windows. The afternoon sunlight gleaming through the plexi-glass of this mid-rise commercial building. "Correction, all *hard* costs have been taken care of."

The realtor remains silent as I turn around, fixing my black suit coat. "You took out a construction loan for eleven million dollars, with a down payment of almost three million. A forty-unit apartment complex, each unit totalling three-hundred and fifty thousand dollars in total costs to build and furnish each unit with appliances. Totaling fourteen million."

He gives me a look as he nods his head. "Yes, that is correct."

"And what about legal expenses or repairs? Each of these things that inevitably happen should a tenant refuse to pay their rent, or you need to have the plumping replaced."

Victor keeps his gaze on me but I watch his shoulders lock into place, his body going utterly still. He notices my attention to his change in body language and forces himself to relax.

I approach the long table again as Sawyer begins to slowly drum his index finger on the arm rest. A tell-tale sign that he's either becoming annoyed, or he's stifling the calm rage brewing beneath.

I'd say it's the former this time.

"Sure, you may be left with maybe two million at the end of each month after you use rent payments to pay off your mortgage. But I'd bet with that million dollar home of yours that you really aren't left with much afterwards."

He stands up from his seat abruptly, fists clenching inwards. "You son of a—"

Mateo quickly rests a hand on his arm, drawing his angered gaze to him. "I'd advise you to be careful how you proceed from here, Victor." He glances over to Sawyer who has remained silent the entire meeting. Observing and listening in on our proposal. Mateo turns his attention back to Victor as he says slowly, "These are not men that lose, so I would advise you to take their help."

He stares at him for a long moment before forcing himself to sit back down. His face quickly smoothing out as he takes one look at Sawyer's stern gaze. Whether it's the fact he remembers he's talking to the Don of The Deimari Mafia, or that he quickly learned some common sense, he shuts his mouth from whatever was about to spew out of it.

I take my seat as well as I lean my arms onto the table. "We are not here to be enemies, Mr. Hillson." I assure him.

"But in exchange for your help, you want to become the new owners of my building." He remarks.

I nod my head slowly. "Correct."

I lean away from the table, lowering my hand down to the duffel bag next to my feet. I pull the zipper back, grabbing a stack of hundreds and placing it onto the table. I place another next to it, and watch as Victor's eyes go wide.

"There's three hundred thousand there. That should be more than enough to keep in savings for repairs, and other related costs." I push the money towards him as he eyes it up. "You'll have full control over the apartment complex, over who resides in it, and will remain the property manager and landlord. We each own the building and take ten percent of the property's earnings each month."

He lifts his gaze up to mine, then trails it over to Sawyer who has taken to bringing his index finger to his chin now. He remains silent for a moment, pondering over our offer before he says, "Alright. We have a deal. But I also want protection."

I look over to Sawyer for confirmation. He stares at the realtor for a moment before he nods. "You'll be taken care of."

I watch him inhale deeply, his chest sinking as he exhales and nods. He picks the pen up from the table, hovering it over the blank line before signing his name. He lowers the pen down, pushing the papers over to me as Sawyer and I sign our names as the new owners of Riverside Residence. The first apartment complex to be built along the river that stretches out to the Cimeteria Sea.

We hand the paperwork over to our lawyer as he files it into his briefcase, concluding the meeting.

Victor is the first one to exit along with our lawyer. Leaving Sawyer and I alone with Mateo.

Sawyer shakes the contractor's hand, his skin deathly pale in comparison to Mateo's golden tan. "Pleasure doing business with you, as always."

Mateo chuckles. "You're going to make working with that man for the remaining few months hell for me."

Sawyer twirls a silver banded ring on his middle finger. "He'll get over it." He looks out the window next to him, the view overlooking our new soon-to-be property. "Besides, he should be flattered. I only make deals with the best."

A statement I would have to agree with.

Mateo is the leading contractor in all of Lilitu City. Working primarily with building commercial properties and luxury homes, he's made a substantial name for himself.

And a great business partner for Sawyer.

Ten years ago when Sawyer was looking for contractors to build his mansion, he didn't want just anyone building it. Leaving the location of his personal residence up for just anyone to have access to. Upon doing my own intel we met with Mateo, who I learned had a fascinatingly long criminal record prior to becoming a contractor. Turns out he paid some officer on the inside to clear his record prior to going into construction.

And when Sawyer mentioned how inconvenient it would be to have this suddenly exposed, threatening his credibility and trust with future investors, he was more than willing to comply with us as a long-term partner.

His silence, in exchange for ours.

The three of us leave the office room, Mateo parting ways and heading towards the main entrance as the elevator lands. Sawyer and I walk in the opposite direction, heading down a long hallway towards an exit door.

We step outside to a light breeze, the smell of burgers and barbeque carrying down the narrow alleyway from a nearby food truck. Sawyer pulls his phone out of his pocket, pressing it up to his ear. "I promise I did not forget. I got held up with some business."

We both slide into my car, fitting my key into the ignition as I turn it over. I can hear his sister's voice through the phone, chuckling softly to myself at her bickering.

"Just tell Priscilla to be ready within the hour. I have to stop home first then I'll be on my way." He waits for her to say something before hanging up the phone, tucking it back into his pants pocket.

"Another business meeting?" I glance over at him, smirking. I turn right as we exit the alley.

Sawyer sighs audibly as he leans back into his seat. "Hopefully the dean won't dick around and get right to the point."

"Something tells me he won't have such strong opinions about her choice of clothing once you talk to him."

Sawyer scoffs at my statement. "I don't understand what the problem is. She wears a shirt that says something she likes and he reacts like she just killed a hundred children." He shakes his head as he presses the sides of his temple with his thumb and index finger. "He told her it was a *political interference* with the university's inclusivity policy. Give me a fucking break." He pulls his hand away from his head.

"Something tells me when he finds you at this meeting with her, he'll have a change of heart." He'd be a real stupid man not to.

I don't understand it either. She wore a shirt that says *I approve a man's right to shut the fuck up* and the dean is up in arms about it. I, as a man, don't find it offensive at all.

In fact, I think more men should shut the fuck up. Because what usually comes out of their mouths is not even remotely worth saying.

"He'll have a change of heart alright." Sawyer says as he cracks the window open, glaring out the front windshield as if the dean is standing right outside.

If there is one thing about Sawyer it's that he may be a broody bastard, but he is a family man first and foremost. And there is no mountain he wouldn't move, no sacrifice he wouldn't make for his family, especially for his niece Priscilla.

I find myself inspired by that selflessness in him, and am sometimes even jealous of the closeness he and his family share. I've never been close with my family, my parents having disowned me when I was fresh out of high school. They were extremists in their religious beliefs, and anyone that didn't follow the same set of beliefs as them got the cold shoulder.

But what started as the cold shoulder turned into years of zero communication. No reaching out to wish me happy birthday, no checking in on holidays. Completely shunning me out because of my resistance to conform to their ideals.

My hand flexes on the steering wheel, gripping the leather momentarily as I try to stifle the rise of hurt feelings that no matter how much therapy I attend, there will always be a small fractile of sorrow that feels I deserved better.

My gaze threatens to lower to the memory of our relationship embedded on the back of my hand, but I keep it trained forward.

By spending so much time alone that's where I got into learning how to hack into data systems. It became a little escape for me, but I found myself so obsessed with it that it became a genuine hobby—and later, a career. Now, I'm the right-hand man to the most powerful man in Lilitu City, and I make more money than I even know what to do with.

So, I'd say I'm doing alright.

I look down at my phone, knowing I should text Cynthia at some point. I haven't been able to do more digging on finding this guy yet today, but plan to as soon as I drop Sawyer off and return home.

I may be a disappointment to my family, something that took me a very long time to understand I have no control over. But I will prove my capability to Cynthia. I'll find this guy for her, and give her the justice she rightfully deserves.

It's the very least I can do for her.

CHAPTER 16

My fingers type away on my work computer, entering in this douchebag's email address and cross referencing it with the VPN he's using to have his IP address rerouted from. When my search comes up blank, I try a different alternative.

I pull up the dark web, entering the same information in there and seeing if I have better luck. If I can get a match on something that leads me to his activity in any of these chatrooms, then maybe I can—

A box pops up, alerting me to a message exchanged between him and another person in a secured chatroom.

JoNN4: A sneak peek.

AnonTi: You always deliver.

My skin feels tight as rage surges within me. I hover the cursor over the link, hoping that this is just a coincidence and that I won't find Cyn on the other end of it. A large part of me doesn't even want to open it, but I have to check to make sure it's actually her.

I click it, the picture blowing up on the screen as I see Cyn's vivid blue hair. Her face contorted into pleasure as her breasts are exposed to the camera. I catch a quick glance of a dildo connected to a machine between her legs before I quickly close out the link. Turning my gaze away from seeing anything further between her legs.

That son of a bitch is *leaking* her content to other pervs on the dark web.

I shoot out of my seat, pacing my living room floor as I run my hand through my hair. I pace for a moment longer before sitting back down onto my couch. Scooting to the edge of the seat cushion as I start trying to encrypt anything I can from their usernames. Addresses, real names, locations. Anything.

It takes me several minutes until I'm able to crack something. Even though I can't find the VPN provider that Johnny uses, I do find a leak with the other user. Using it to backdoor my way into his network.

Most VPN providers eliminate breach of safety with their clients by having a no-log policy, which basically just means that they don't keep record of which user is browsing which websites. But this one—

This company *does* keep a search log. And seeing that this user has been logged for visiting the same porn website every single week for the past six months, I'd say he set himself up for that one. Fucking dumbass.

I manage to get through by hacking into his real IP address, sneaking my way into his database. I start sniffing out everything on his computer, including his work email and personal files and learn his name is Antonio Weyer, CEO of some life insurance company. I dig a little deeper and find the address to his personal residence, his work schedule, bank statements, and that he has a wife and two children. Perfect.

I send a copy of everything to my phone, keeping all of his information there so I can easily access it when I go to pay this guy a visit.

I shut down all of my windows, erasing my history and running it through my nodes and bug detections. I power down my work laptop and stand up from the couch.

It's four o'clock, which means Antonio will be off work in the next hour. I think when I see him I'll wring his neck, or tell his wife the things he watches on the internet.

Perhaps both.

I pick up my phone, hitting the call button before setting the phone to my ear. It rings for a few seconds before she picks up. "Miss me already?"

If it weren't for my blood boiling I probably would've laughed at her remark. But all I can think about is enacting great violence on this man. "Where are you? We need to talk. I found something."

Cyn chuckles lightly over the phone and it instantly simmers some of that brewing anger. "Come find me."

She hangs up as I pull my phone away from my ear, staring at the screen.

I actually chuckle at that and bring up the tracker I have on her phone. When I see that she's not at home, I zoom in on where she is. Reading the building name out loud. "Pauline's Pet Shop."

I scrunch my brows together. She has a pet? *Pets,* maybe? How did I not know this through everything that I dug up about her?

I send her a text before I grab my keys and head out the door. A damn cat willingly playing chase to a mouse.

I'm on my way.

CHAPTER 17

Cynthia

I slip my hand through the cage's bars, petting behind the orange cat's fluffy ears. "I wish I could take you home with me. But I'm afraid you and Boe would not get along." I pout my lips at the adorably furry kitten.

"You have no idea how many times a day I hear that." The owner says as she restocks a basket of cat toys nearby.

I turn around to face her. "Okay, that's not fair."

Pauline gives me a half smirk, her dark brown eyes glancing over at me through her round glasses. "But if you did know anyone that was looking to adopt a new pet, you know where to send them." She sets the basket down as she walks to the next one. She begins filling it with colored wands that have little blue and yellow fish attached to them by a piece of red string.

She looks over at me as she says honestly, "I'll do anything to make sure these guys go to good homes instead of spending their lives trapped in a store."

I glance over at the far wall, the clear glass showcasing the available cats and dogs inside. My chest squeezes at the thought of these babies spending their whole lives stuck in a cage.

I walk over to Pauline, wrapping my arms around her as I lean my head on her shoulder. "And suddenly, my house is not big enough." I pull away from her, sighing. "I'd take them all if I could."

She gives me a warm smile, scarce strands of grey hair peek through her thick blonde braid. "I know you would, dear." She pats me on the shoulder before she walks further down the store to the back room.

She comes back out a few moments later with a bag of frozen mice. She hands it to me. "One bag of dinner for Boe."

I chuckle as we both make our way over to the register. She rings me up as I pull out my wallet, paying for the mice before she puts it into a brown paper bag. I feel someone approach me from behind, a familiar pine and spice scent alluding me to who it could be. "Perfect timing."

I turn around and come face to face with Dex, except his expression doesn't carry any humor in it. Even when he tries to force a grin that doesn't reach his eyes.

"I'll see you later, Pauline." I say over my shoulder.

"Come anytime, dear. Even just to chat." She says warmly. Gods, what a sweet older woman.

I grab my bag and walk out of the pet store with Dex beside me. "I assume your lack of enthusiasm has nothing to do with being in my presence."

"I am always enthusiastic to be in your presence." He says as we walk across the parking lot.

I reach the passenger side door of his car, Dex opening it up for me as I slide inside. When he comes around and slides into the driver's seat, I ask, "What did you find?"

He hesitates for a split moment before he turns towards me. "I found someone that may have some intel on that guy."

A wicked, wide grin curves my lips. "Good." I say slowly. "And what of the other guy?"

"Nothing yet. I'm still working on getting past his protective barriers."

I set the bag on the floor by my feet. "Okay."

At his silence I turn to look at him. Tilting my head at the look on his face. "What else are you not saying?"

He sighs. "I found him because the guy who stole your content was exchanging it with him. On the dark web."

A calm fury blows hotly through me. And because I have no one—and nothing to unleash it onto at this particular moment, I laugh.

And there is nothing humorous about it.

After a few moments, I find it in me to formulate words again. "Well, this just got more interesting." I turn to look at him. "When do we kill him?"

Dex stares at me with a mix of worry and...intrigue. "I think you mean question him, and *then* kill him."

"Whatever, same thing."

He starts his car up. "He works at an insurance company downtown and gets off at five. But I noticed he frequents a bar near his home every Tuesday night."

I tilt my head. What the fuck does that have to do with me?

Dex grins—and this time, it does reach his eyes. "How do you feel about going to grab that drink now?"

"Do you think there will be dancing?" I ask as I round the corner, entering my kitchen and dumping my purse onto the counter.

Dex stops through the moulded archway, crossing his arms as he leans himself up against the wood frame. "It's a dive bar so I highly doubt it. But I'm sure you can create your own dance floor."

A mix between a scoff and a chuckle escapes my lips as I open up my fridge. "So a bunch of creepy old fucks can gather around and prey on me like starved coyotes? I'll pass." I pull out a glass tupperware of leftover lasagna, setting it into the microwave to heat it up.

I glance at him over my shoulder as I grab a glass from a cupboard. "You can come closer. I won't bite." I turn around, setting it on the island as I smirk up at him. "Unless you're into that."

He chuckles but I sense that nervousness slither out with his words. He finally steps away from the archway and seats himself into a black stool. I expect him to say something snarky—to say *anything* flirty, really. Instead, he changes the subject. "When we get there I want to question him for information on this guy. And since we'll most likely be around other people, it would probably be wise for you to use that compulsion ability of yours. To keep him calm and cooperative."

The microwave goes off as I grab the tupperware, setting it on the island. "As long as I get to kill him afterwards." I fork some lasagna into my mouth, flashing a grin.

"I would normally agree with you, but I think we should keep him alive."

I raise a disapproving eyebrow at Dex as I take another bite.

"We might be able to use him to draw Johnny out if he actually knows him. He could be useful in that regard."

I sigh as I take a drink of water. "Fine. You have a point." I set it down, gesturing down to the lasagna. "You want some?"

He shakes his head. "That's okay, I—"

"Come on, try some." I smirk as I add on, "I made it."

I turn around, grabbing another fork from a drawer before jabbing some lasagna onto it. I hover the fork in front of his mouth, watching his glacial gaze narrow as he reaches for it. He pinches the silver fork, his warm fingers pressed up against mine.

He hesitates for a split second before taking the fork out of my hands, and takes a bite. I watch as he chews, tilting my head to the side. "Well?"

He swallows as he looks up at me. "It's good."

"Good?" I query.

"I mean," he quickly adds, then pauses. "It's remarkably exquisite. Best lasagna I've ever had."

I nod slowly in appreciation. "That's what I thought."

"But it could use a bit more seasoning."

Now I am the one hovering my fork in front of my mouth, lowering it back down. "You lie."

He remains silent as a grin curves his lush lips. I swat him on the arm as he deeply chuckles, but instead of annoyance the sound sends my pulse skittering. "Careful. I may feed you to Boe if you don't behave."

He tries to fork another piece of lasagna when I push his fork away with mine. That handsome smile of his remains on his smooth and sharp face as that dimple in his left cheek appears. "Do I even want to know who Boe is?"

"He's my baby."

Dex looks up at me so fast it's a surprise he didn't twist his neck. "*Baby*?" He all but nearly exclaims.

I fight back the laugh at the sudden widening of his eyes, the splash of shock on his face. "Yeah. Do you want to see him?"

Gods, he totally thinks I mean a literal baby. He's so fun to mess around with.

He slowly lowers the fork down to the tupperware, blinking once at me in complete silence.

"What? You didn't gather that in all of your research about me?" I take the now empty tupperware and silverware to the sink.

"That's impossible. I would've known by all of my—" He stops himself, continuing again. "I am very thorough when I get intel on someone."

"What else are you thorough with?" I ask huskily as I lean against the counter next to him. I watch his gaze lower from my face down to my hand touching his. He stares for a moment until I break away.

"Come. I'll show you him." I walk out of the kitchen, hearing the soft scrape of the black stool as Dex follows behind me upstairs.

I feel his steps falter as we reach the top of the steps, turning around to see him admiring a piece of artwork on the wall. "Do you like art?"

He says nothing for a moment before he nods his head, a soft smile curving his lips. "I like to draw in my spare time." He turns away from the gold-framed art, striding closer to me.

"What do you like to draw?" I ask.

He lightly shrugs his shoulders. "Abstract, flowers, nature, anything really." He pauses as he stops in front of me, narrowing his gaze. "But portraits are what I mainly find myself gravitating towards."

I look at him, gaze trailing from his eyes down to his chest. "I could see that."

We round the doorway to my bedroom. Approaching the terrarium I lift the cover up, leaning my hands in to reach for Boe. "This is my baby."

I lift him out, turning around and holding him up to Dex. He stares down at the albino ball python for a moment before lifting his gaze back up. A chuckle escapes from his lips. "Ah, I see now."

"You want to hold him?"

The humor from his face instantly vanishes as a subtle fear replaces it. "No—I'm uh...I'm fine."

I laugh as Boe begins to slither up my arm. "He's very friendly, I promise."

Dex hesitantly steps closer to me, leaning his head closer to Boe as he suspiciously observes him. He lifts his hand up, bringing it closer to him before rubbing a finger along the top of his scaled head. When Boe turns his head to look at him, he instantly jerks his hand away.

I burst out laughing as I put Boe back into his tank. He works for the mafia and he's scared of a sweet little snake? How adorable. "So what time do you think we should leave?"

"From what I saw on his bank statements, he seems to order his first shot around seven. So..." He pulls his phone out of his pocket, looking down at the screen. "In about an hour and a half."

I hum my response, stepping in closer to him. "So, what should we do until then?"

I notice the way his chest stills momentarily at my question, how he forces himself to release that trapped breath when I take another step closer to him.

The featherlight touch of his fingers brush against mine, sweeping his thumb over my knuckles. He places my hand into his, and I feel a patch of raised skin beneath my fingers.

I narrow my gaze to our joined hands, lifting them as I observe a small round scar. "What did you get that from?"

He continues sweeping his thumb over my skin, his voice lowered when he answers. "I was a very adventurous child growing up." He brings our hands up to his chest.

Before I can think about how vague of an answer that is he steps closer to me, bringing my chest flush with our hands. I lift my gaze and see the startling intensity in his eyes, a shallow breath leaving me as he leans his head down. His lips hover inches above mine and I drink in the warmth of his skin, the way his gaze locks onto my lips—

"Tour." He blurts out as he steps back. I watch him work on a swallow as he slowly lowers his hand from mine. "I would like a tour of your house. Please."

CHAPTER 18

Dexter

I am once again, the biggest idiot in all of eternity.

A tour? A fucking *tour*? That's what I thought of in that split moment?

I really am going to be a virgin for the rest of my life if I don't get it together. But gods, aside from being giddy she just makes me so fucking nervous. I can usually hide it but sometimes, I just fold up like a damn lawn chair.

So far she's shown me her bedroom, bathrooms, her kitchen—again, her backyard and now we're sitting in her living room.

"I really love the moody aesthetic, so I wanted all of my walls—aside from the kitchen, to have a darker hue to them." She fans her hand over to large windows on the other side of the spacious room. "But I need a lot of natural light, so this house was perfect for that."

I nod. "You have a very beautiful home."

She truly does. Aside from the luxurious furniture and rich color schemes, what really brings each room together are the finer details. The accent pillows and rugs, the artwork, even the obscene amount of plants. When I asked her how many she has, she told me somewhere around thirty.

That's a lot of damn plants. Not to mention she has more out in her yard.

Everything in here just screams Cyn. I would've pictured nothing different—

Holy fuck I'm *inside* of her house. *On* her couch.

Am I...freaking out a little bit right now?

"Dex."

I turned my gaze to her, realizing that it drifted to a random corner at the other side of the room. "Sorry, just taking the space in. You were saying?"

She rolls her eyes before she repeats herself.

I really must be a deranged individual because I *thoroughly* like it when she rolls her eyes at me. Fuck, it gets my dick hard.

"I was saying that we should probably get going soon." She stands up from the couch, an emptiness left where her warmth just occupied. "I'm gonna change and freshen up."

"Okay, I'll wait here." I say as she walks out of the living room.

Did she say something important to me? Her tone wasn't indicative of disappointment in the slightest, but I can't help but wonder if me dodging making a move has truly fucked everything up.

I sit forward as I run my hand through my hair, pushing down the building thoughts. Maybe I'm just overthinking it. Or maybe I need to just realize that I have exactly what I've been pining over right in front of me and not waste the blessing of the opportunity I have to get to know her.

Twenty minutes later Cyn comes back downstairs wearing a pair of black leggings, a grey cropped T-shirt, and a pair of low-top white and black sneakers.

She hauls her purse over her shoulder as she looks up at me. "Ready?"

A grin curves my lips. "You look beautiful."

She smiles as she says, "Thank you."

I would give my life away to the devil himself to see that smile every single day. Gods, she's so gorgeous. Even when she's dressed casually she makes me feel giddy.

As she searches for her keys in the kitchen, I feel the light breeze of fresh air hit my cheek. Turning around, I spot the window above her kitchen sink cracked open. I close it, locking it before we exit the kitchen and leave for the bar.

I take a seat at an empty bar stool, the metal hoisting the seat cushion up creaking beneath my weight. The bartender approaches me, his age showing through the wrinkles and exhaustion in his face. "What can I get ya?"

"Bourbon, please." I go to lean my arms onto the counter when I notice a trail of sticky residue. I lower them down at my sides, quickly changing my mind. The bartender pours me a shot, sliding it over to me. "Thanks."

I hand him a twenty and slam the liquor back. I set the empty shot glass onto the counter, pushing it towards him.

"Yeah, I'll be home in a bit—oh, just give me a fucking break, Kim." The man seated beside me says to the phone held up to his ear. "I'm hanging up now."

What a dick.

He hangs up the call, shoving his phone back into his denim pants with an exaggerated sigh. "Women." He scoffs before he takes a sip of his draft beer. "I work, I pay the bills, and can't even get one hour of peace to my damn self."

I shake my head, chuckling. "I hear ya. Never good enough for them."

He laughs deeply as he looks over at me, holding his hand out. His thick fingers reminding me of tiny little sausages. Gross. "Antonio."

I lower my hand into his. "Dexter." He shakes my hand before I release my grip from his.

"Not often we get a youngin' in here. Most guys your age come to the East Side for those hipster bars."

I shrug my shoulders as I look up at the baseball game playing on the flat screen TV hanging above us. "Maybe I'm looking for a bit of quiet myself."

He laughs again, slapping a hand on my back and patting me. "Boy, do I ever get it."

Making a mental note for myself to wash this shirt when I get home.

Antonio reaches into the breast pocket of his wool-knit flannel, digging around until he pulls a cigarette out. A gruff curse gets muffled under his breath as he searches his pockets for a lighter, coming up empty.

"If you bum me a smoke, I've got you on a lighter."

Antonio looks over at me, his teeth showing through his grin as he says, "Deal, kid."

He hands me a cigarette as I pull a lighter out of my pocket, both of us standing up from our seats and heading outside through a side door. A heavy weight settles in my hand as I hold the cigarette, and I try not to focus on the feelings that accompany it.

"So, you got a miss's?" He asks before he lights his cigarette, the other end dangling between his lips. He hands it back over to me.

I shrug my shoulders, grinning. "Something like that."

I drop the cigarette he gave me as the sound of someone approaches us from behind. The flickering street lamp above dimly illuminates a head of short blue hair as she approaches Antonio.

Cyn tilts her head up at him as she smiles sweetly, the edge to her voice carrying anything but warmth in it. "Hi."

Antonio's eyes widen as the cigarette trembles between his lips. He quickly takes it, clearing his throat as I watch him try desperately to keep it together. But when he recognizes her, a smug grin curves his lips. His expression oddly smoothing over. "I didn't know we were doing house calls now."

His choice of words causes me to furrow my brows. Is he insinuating that she's a...prostitute?

But before I can enact great violence onto him for assuming such a thing, she draws on that Succubus power of hers and reaches out for him. It completely wipes the smirk off his face, the cigarette between his fingers falling to the concrete. I watch as he stands there, completely ensnared under her control.

"You will answer our questions honestly." She says through the compulsion. "Understood?"

Antonio nods his head slowly. "I will answer honestly."

"Good, now who is the man who sent you that screenshot of me?" She asks.

"His name is Johnny. That is all I know about him." Antonio blinks once before continuing. "He is known by many on the dark web but no one has actually ever met him in person."

"Is there something that would entice him to meet someone in person?" I ask as I step closer to Cyn, keeping my gaze on him.

"No. He likes to remain a middle man, keeping his identity private other than his username—which, some say Johnny may not even be his real name." Antonio continues staring blankly at Cyn. "I'm closest with him out of everyone he's interacted with, so there is one thing I do have knowledge about."

"And that is, what?" Cyn asks, hearing the annoyance in her tone.

"He uses a VPN to reroute his activity—we all do. But he has connections with one man in particular who specifically runs a tech company for people like us."

"What's it called?" I ask.

"OnioNone." Antonio says slowly.

My brows knit together.

Cyn looks up at me. "Do you know it?"

I nod my head. "It's not just any VPN provider. OnioNone uses a specific network that doesn't just reroute your online browsing through one provider, but several. Therefore, your real IP address is nearly impossible to trace."

She shakes her head, confusion clouding her gaze. "I don't get it."

I turn to face her. "Okay, let's use sending mail for example. If you want to send an anonymous letter to someone named Beth without them knowing it was you, you'd probably give it to a trusted friend, right?"

She nods her head. "Yes."

"That in a nutshell is how a VPN works. The only person that knows it's you sending the letter is your friend—or in this case, only the VPN provider has access to what sites you're browsing. But now think of the same scenario, except you don't want anyone to know it was you who sent the letter. So, you find let's say three strangers who use an anonymous network and will volunteer to deliver it for you. In this case, you'd write the letter to Beth but put it in an envelope addressed to one of those three strangers."

I can practically see the wheels turning inside of her head. "But the first person you hand the envelope to would still know it's you."

"Not in this case. Think of it like a domino effect. I take that letter for Beth, addressing it to stranger number three. Placing *that* envelope into another one addressed to stranger number two, and finally another one addressed to stranger number one. Stranger number one opens the first envelope, only seeing they have to deliver an envelope to stranger number two, and so on and so forth. So by the time Beth gets her letter, it's from stranger number three, and that person has no idea who the letter was written by."

I watch her internally process the analogy. "Okay, I'm getting it now."

"*That* is what OnioNone is. So not even the company has access to what you're browsing because it's immediately rerouted to several different locations."

She stares at me a moment longer before turning her gaze back onto Antonio. "Is there anything else you can tell us about how to find him?"

"That is all I know."

"Perfect." That's all she says before placing her hands on his neck and twisting, an audible crack following. His body falls limp to the ground as I feel her power dissipate rapidly.

I look at her, raising an eyebrow.

She turns her gaze to me, holding a hand up. "What? He was annoying me and there was nothing left to gain from him." She leans her weight onto one hip as she asks, "Is there a problem?"

My brows flatten as I shake my head, fighting the smirk from showing up on my lips. "Nope."

"What are we going to do with him?" She leans over him, looking at him as if he's nothing more than a speck of dirt on the ground.

"I know a place." I begin lifting him up by his shoulders, dragging him back the few feet to my car. "Open the trunk for me."

Without hesitation Cyn opens the trunk and helps me haul his body in. "Shouldn't we be worried about fingerprints?"

That smirk on my face actually does make an appearance as I chuckle. "It won't matter where he's going." I lift his legs and set them inside before shutting the trunk door.

I walk around to the passenger side door when she grabs my arm, gently pulling me back.

When I turn around she has this mischievous grin on her face, those blue eyes displaying an unrestrained wildness in them. Nothing that I would've expected from any other girl who just witnessed me hauling a dead man's body into the trunk of my car. But Cyn...she's not just some girl.

She's something else entirely.

She steps closer to me as she states plainly, as if she didn't just break a man's neck right in front of me, "You still haven't bought me that drink."

CHAPTER 19

Cynthia

I bring the straw to my lips as I take a long sip, tequila and lime sliding down my tongue. I smile widely as I hum my appreciation and set my drink down onto a small wooden table.

When I'd asked the bartender for a lime margarita, he said that he didn't have any margarita mix to make me one. But I saw the lie in his words, so I compelled him to make me one anyway.

Soon enough, he was excusing himself to the kitchen and coming back out with an unopened bottle of lime margarita mix. He even cut me up some fresh limes and served it to me with a cute pink straw.

What a lazy brute. It took him a total of five minutes to make it and the bar has a total of five people in it—Dex and I, included.

I hold the billiard cue in my hand as Dex hovers over the pool table. Strands of his dark hair fall over his forehead, barely touching his brow as he concentrates on setting the rack. "You're staring."

I balance the other end of the billiard cue onto the floor, tilting my head. "You're nice to look at. Is that a problem?"

I watch as faint blotches of pink dot his cheeks as a smirk curves up his lips. "Not at all."

He stands up straight as he lifts the rack from the table, stepping away. "Do you have a preference?"

I step over to the head of the pool table, lowering myself down. "I get stripes."

I bend down, bringing my torso close to the table and leaning the top of the billiard cue across the back of my hand. Lifting my thumb, I keep it snug against my index finger as I line the billiard up with the cue ball. A sharp click sounds as I strike the triangle formation, object balls scattering across the table.

I watch as two striped ones sink into pockets.

I reposition myself down the table, angling my body as I try to strike another but end up missing entirely. I laugh at myself as I turn around, handing Dex the billiard. "Your turn."

He chuckles as he takes it, moving himself further down the table to where the cue ball is. He angles his body over the table, striking it to hit a solid that shoots itself—along with another, into a pocket. He manages to do this again until he misses the next shot.

"So how exactly does that work?" He asks as he walks over to me, handing me the billiard.

I take it from his hand. "The compulsion?" When he nods his head I continue. "It's just something that I will to happen." I shrug my shoulders. "It's kind of like digging my claws into someone's mind, taking control of it as I tell them what I want. Or rather what I want them to do."

I lean over the table, angling the billiard to the cue ball as I strike it. Missing again as the billiard goes flying to the side of the table.

"Your hand is too far away. Here." He says as he fixes my hand holding the billiard, repositioning it so that it's a little higher up. Creating a ninety degree angle with my elbow to the billiard. "Now try."

I try it, missing again.

He chuckles. "Let me show you."

In the next moment I feel his lean body hover over my backside, caging me to the pool table. His right hand reaches over mine, keeping my hand firm on the billiard as he rests his left hand over my waist.

His face leans down next to mine, the soft touch of his breath sending a chill down my spine as he speaks. "You don't have to strike it so hard, that's what's getting you to become off balance and miss. You just have to—" His hand over mine pushes the billiard forward with a fluid grace, striking the cue ball with ease. "Loosen up a little."

His hand on my waist remains there as I feel a hardness press against my backside. He moves his hand up an inch, his fingers pressing into my lower belly exposed from my cropped top. I feel him shudder a breath before he stands upright, removing himself from me entirely.

I stand up and hand him the billiard, my gaze glancing down to his pants before raising it back up. "Thanks for the demonstration." I say huskily before walking over to the table, picking up my drink as I feel his heated stare on my back.

"Mind if I join y'all in the next game?" A sly voice asks.

I turn around to see some bearded man having interjected himself into our space. A wide grin exposing his stained teeth.

"Yes, I do." I say bluntly as I sip my drink.

The man looks at me as if that was not the response he was expecting. As if he thought I'd respond in a meek and polite manner, despite the true intentions I see lurking beneath his fake sincerity.

He goes to take a step towards me. "Awe, don't be rude girlie—"

Dex has his hand up to his chest in a flash, shoving the man back until he's stumbling three feet backwards. "The lady said no." The calm anger in his tone is like a quiet night before a heavy storm.

The man turns his gaze to Dex, irritation flashing hotly. "Watch it, punk. I was just trying to ask the bitch—"

He doesn't get the chance to mutter another word before Dex punches him straight in the nose. The man's head flings backwards before he jerks his hand up to cover his mouth.

I watch as blood trickles down his lips, his enraged gaze set on Dex.

"Hey, take that shit outside! Not in my bar." The bartender yells out.

"Let's go." Dex says as he grabs my arm, guiding us out of the bar. The force of his grasp steady on my skin, but not rough.

I follow him as the bearded man follows behind us, but instead of further picking a fight with him, Dex ignores the man's further advancement.

The blood running down the man's nose should set off warning bells inside me, the quickness of Dex's brutality should be a cause for concern. If I were anyone else, I should probably be revolted by his display of violence.

But all I feel is satisfied and aroused. *Highly* aroused.

Dex pushes the door open as we step outside to the chilled night air. The scent of trash from a nearby dumpster wafts towards me before the smell of metallic replaces it as the man steps outside with us. "What? You start a fight you can't finish?" The man yells out before spitting blood onto the concrete.

Dex halts abruptly, closing his eyes and taking a long inhale. I sense the building tsunami raging inside of him as he exhales a rough breath.

He turns around, stepping towards the man. "I'm trying to spare your life. So I suggest that you take the opportunity wisely."

The man laughs as he wipes his bloodied hand onto his jeans, stepping closer to us. "Fine, so be it. But when your bitch is tired of—"

Dex rushes the man and wraps his arms around his neck, putting him in a headlock and immediately stifling his words. I watch as terror flashes violently in the bearded man's eyes before dulling into a sudden lifelessness as Dex cages his limp body to his chest. Siphoning the breath from his lungs and rendering him dead.

I stand there, blinking in silence as he hauls his arm under the man's limp arms. My gaze follows him the few feet to his car, and without another word, he opens his trunk and dumps the man next to Antonio.

He strides slowly over to me, placing a steady warm hand on my cheek. The storm raging beneath his glacial gaze finally settling as he looks upon me. His eyes roam over my face, as if mapping every crease and dimple to memory. When he finally speaks, his voice carries an ember of palpable sternness with it. "I will not tolerate men disrespecting you."

His thumb caresses my cheek as he lifts my head higher up, bringing my face closer to his. The warmth of his breath dancing on my lips mimics the welcomed, pleasant heat furrowing beneath my skin. "Have I made myself clear on that?"

His hand moves down to my neck, his grip loosening as he rests it there. Loosening my breath, I nod. "Yes." My voice barely above a whisper.

His eyes narrow down to my lips before lifting back up again. "Good." His hand slips away from my neck as he leans down to open the passenger door. Stepping to the side.

I blink once at him before I remember how to move my legs again. I take one last look at him, noticing the seriousness in his gaze. The lack of humor that encased his words. The way he just killed that man with no remorse. For *me*.

I finally peel my gaze away and seat myself in his car, Dex closing the door once I've settled in.

Our lips were so close to one another that I thought he was going to actually close the distance and kiss me. I can practically still taste the mint that slipped from his breath, further chilling the bumps pimpling along my skin.

And I would've allowed it, if he had.

Dex seats himself into the driver seat, starting the car and turning the heat dial up a notch. He doesn't speak another word as we drive away from the crime scene.

Both of them.

CHAPTER 20

Twenty minutes later we're pulling into an empty parking lot. I look out my window and read the entrance sign set beside low-lying shrubs.

Harmony Funeral Home.

I look at Dex. "So, we're going to bury them?"

A faint grin curves one side of his lips, that dimple making its appearance. "Not quite."

He drives us around to the back of the building, pulling up next to an exit door. I look out my window, noticing that the premises is otherwise surrounded by a terrain of headstones and walkways that filter in and out of them.

He pops the trunk before we both step out of the car. He walks over to the back door as I follow behind him, watching as he slides a key inside of the lock. He turns the knob and I follow him inside to the darkened space.

He lifts an arm, moving it to the wall next to us and flipping a light switch on. The room is suddenly illuminated, revealing ivory walls and an archway leading down a long hallway. I take a step towards it when he whistles.

"Down here." He opens a door, flipping another light on. He begins descending the stairs as I follow closely behind him.

We reach the bottom and I feel like I've just entered a hospital room. We walk across the polished linoleum floors until we reach the back half of the expansive basement, approaching a wall with a metal sliding door built into it.

Understanding dawns me. "Correction, we're *cremating* them."

He nods his head as he moves around to the side, flipping some switch. "Correct."

"So—wait, you own this place? How else do you have access to this?"

He chuckles. "I have access to a lot of properties, little jewel." He finds a metal cart and wheels it over to me. "I am good friends with the owner who allows us to use the crematorium in exchange for protection." He pushes it past me as he walks back towards the staircase. "It's my preferred method of getting rid of a body. But Levi would tell you he prefers dumping them into the Cimeteria Sea."

I follow him back up the steps and back out to his car. "That's..."

"Fucked up?" He says, glancing over at me.

"I was gonna say interesting, but sure."

He gently nudges me with his shoulder, chuckling at my response before we begin hauling both bodies down to the basement. Loading one up onto the metal cart, he wheels him over to the cremation chamber before doing the same with the second.

It's hard not to notice the sudden lightness in his demeanor—and, again, instead of being disturbed it thoroughly arouses me.

I watch as Dex hauls each one into the giant furnace, pulling the metal door down before hitting a button on the side. Through a tiny window I watch as flames roar to life inside as it begins disintegrating their bodies.

Dex leans against a table propped against the far wall, subtly flexing his hand at his side.

I approach him, taking his hand in mine.

"I'm fine." He assures me, gently pulling his hand away. "He deserved it."

I raise a brow at him. "I didn't say he didn't." I pause, bringing his hand up again. Feeling the swollen knuckles beneath my touch. "But you should still ice this."

He stares at me for a long moment, as if we're stuck in this infinite pocket of time. Just when I think he's going to pull away from me again, he nudges his chin to the right. "There's a freezer around the corner. Sabine keeps ice in it."

I go to the freezer, opening it up and pulling out a small bag of ice. I walk back over, inserting myself in front of his legs as I place it on top of his knuckles. I feel his arm tense beneath me but he immediately relaxes as I hold his hand in mine.

"Better?" I ask.

When I look up, I find him already staring at me. He gives me a faint smile as he answers softly. "Much better."

His soft gaze roams over my face again, the prior harshness no longer visible. He lifts his finger and trails it along the underside of my wrist, the simple contact causing my nerves to come alive. More aware than they ever have been before.

The look in his eyes draws me in like a magnet, and for once it feels strange to be on the receiving end of being pulled into someone's embrace.

"So," I begin, trying to distract myself from the sudden tension that has nothing to do with his swollen knuckles. "Should I expect this to be the consequence for customers at work, too?"

He laughs, the sound raising the hair on the back of my neck. It really is a nice laugh.

"I'm sure going around punching men who talk to you wrong would be bad for business." His smile falters. "That's why I would have the common decency to do it outside of your job."

I swat playfully at his arm. "Then I fear you'd have your hands full for the rest of your life."

A look of sorrow crosses his gaze. "Do you get a lot of creeps like that for customers?"

I shrug my shoulders. "Yes, and no. I have been lucky enough to meet some amazing regulars, but most men are not a treat to be around when you work in the sex industry." I lift the ice and move it an inch over. "Most men see sexworkers as these objects that they get to ogle or even grope at. They forget basic decencies like compassion, or respect, and assume that women working in the industry have morals lower than the floorboards beneath our feet."

The soft pass of his finger along my wrist continues, and I focus on the ice on his hand instead of the gaze that I know is locked onto me. "If you freely express your femininity and sexuality, you're a whore. But if you're modest or abstinent, it's because you're ugly and can't attract a man." I chuckle a harsh laugh. "As long as men continue to exist with the mentality that their ancestors have passed down onto them, with no incentive to change and recognize how their behavior is harmful, women will never win." I finally lift my gaze up to Dex. "So, if I can play men at their own misogyny but get rich in the process, then who really loses at the end of the day?"

His eyes search mine as he lifts his free hand up to my face. His calloused fingers push my hair back from my face, tucking the blue strands behind my ear as a ghost of a grin graces his face. "Very true."

The tips of his fingers trail themselves down my cheek, lower until he's brushing the strands dusting my collarbone back. My chest sinks at his touch as I exhale, my pulse skittering. "Is that why you call me little jewel?"

He lifts his gaze up to my face, and it's like he's searching for meaning behind my eyes. Probing into the innermost workings of my words, and letting them swallow him whole.

"Because of my hair?" I ask, stepping closer into him. To my surprise he widens his stance, giving me more room to step in between his legs.

"Yes, and no." He says hardly above a whisper.

Without another words his hand snakes back up my neck and he pulls my lips flush with his.

He frees his other hand from my grasp, dropping the bag of ice onto the table as I rake my hands up his chest. He kisses me like I am the oxygen to his breath, the answer to his final prayer. His hand cups my jaw as he tilts his head, prying my lips with his tongue.

And I answer his plea greedily.

The kiss deepens as my body is pulled flush with his, and he groans as my belly presses up against his hard length. He lowers a hand to my waist, his grip tightening as he urges me closer to him. I rake my hands down his chest, my tongue gliding along his as he twitches beneath my touch.

I grin at his reaction, lowering my hands further down until they're right above the waist of his pants. I lower them beneath his shirt, touching his lean abdomen. He groans as I go to pry the button of his pants free when he immediately stops kissing me. Jerking a hand to my wrist as he leans his forehead up against mine.

His breaths come out in ragged pulls as he releases my hand. A slight tremor to his words as he speaks. "Maybe doing it in a crematorium isn't ideal."

I step back, lifting my gaze up as I chuckle. "I guess not."

He presses a kiss to my forehead, his lips faintly trembling against my skin. Did I really just get him that worked up over a make-out session?

He tentatively steps around me, checking the cremation chamber before turning it off. "Good enough for now." He says, turning back around and grabbing my hand. "Sabine will finish cremating them in the morning."

And as we head back out to his car, he drives me home and doesn't let go of my hand for even a second.

CHAPTER 21

Dexter

"This is Rochelle O'Connell with Lilitu City News, reporting to you live with recent headlines that the CEO of Second Chance Insurance, Antonio Weyer, has been reported missing as of early this morning. Officials say there are no leads at this time, but if you have any information to help this investigation to please call—"

I shut the TV off, leaning over to set the remote on my coffee table before rising from my couch. The poor bastards will never find him.

I cross the room and hover over my dining room table, opening my laptop. I open a new search window into my software and type in *OnioNone.*

Right away I'm shown where the location of the office is, how much the company is worth, and most importantly, who owns it. After doing some digging, I know everything there is to know about him.

Halston Deveroe, owner and founder of OnioNone with a Bachelor's degree in Cybersecurity. Interestingly enough, he's also the account holder of a few off-shore bank accounts with monthly deposits ranging from five to ten thousand dollars. Other than that, his bank statements show little to no activity, which could only mean that he pays cash for most transactions.

A good way to not leave a paper trail. Smart for him, annoying for me. But a minor inconvenience I can always work around.

Upon further digging I find from his social media pages that he frequently poses with a blonde woman in his profile picture. I use the photo to do a reverse image search and find a match. Lilitu City's highly revered esthetician, Theresa Deveroe.

So now the question begs: how do I get myself alone with the guy? OnioNone doesn't accept appointments—for *security reasons*, I'm sure.

I feel a brief vibration in my pocket, pulling my phone out to see a motion alert from one of Cyn's security cameras.

I expand the screen, squinting my eyes as I focus in on a man and a woman standing outside of her front door. Both of them wearing casual clothing as they each hold a pamphlet in their hands.

After a minute of Cyn not answering the door, they ring it again.

I pull up the text thread between Cyn and I, typing a message to her. *Are you going to get that?*

She replies back moments later. *No.*

Before I can have the chance to reply back, she sends another text. *I thought you said you wouldn't creep on me? ;)*

My thumb hovers over the keypad. Shit, I definitely did say that. *I'm not creeping, I'm just checking in since there are two strangers standing outside your door.*

They're Jehovah's Witnesses. They'll leave eventually.

I chuckle, the grin on my face remaining. *I'm sure if you go out there and tell them what you are, they'll never bother you again.*

Not before they send a witch hunt to my house. Thank you for the suggestion, but I planned to live for at least another five hundred years.

My brows raise. *Wow, you are old as shit.*

She sends me a middle finger emoji.

I open up her camera feed again, looking to see the two at her door have finally decided to walk themselves back to their car. As they back out of her driveway and leave, I text her back. *It only took them four minutes to get the hint that you weren't interested in what they had to say.*

She heart reacts my message. *The first time they waited out there for fifteen. So I'd say that we're making progress.*

That has to be incredibly annoying. *How many times have they stood on your doorstep now?*

Five. The sixth time they won't find themselves leaving my property. :)

So very violent. It turns me on. *Or you could just compel them to forget about your residence altogether?*

I wait for her text back as if I'm hanging on by a thread, waiting for my next fix of whatever enchantment she's bespelled me with. *So if I followed through with it you wouldn't help me dispose of the bodies?*

A half grin curves my lips. *I'd help with any request you asked of me.*

Good boy, that's what I want to hear. Xoxo

A chill runs down my spine as my dick grows hard in my pants. Absolutely nothing gets me off more than being praised, and I would gladly shackle myself to my hands and knees just to hear it from her lips.

What do I even say back to that? Thank you, I am your good boy—

No, that's fucking lame.

My uncertainty causes me to set the phone down, turning my attention back to my laptop when I hear a chime sound go off. I look to see a notification alert to Theresa adding a picture to her story on her social media page. The background displaying what I presume to be her private office space. The caption pasted over it reading *Last minute opening available! DM or text me to book you in.*

A wicked grin curves my lips as I copy her phone number, pasting it into my phone as I send her a message. After I close my laptop up, I open the text thread again. Staring at her text for a few moments before I finally respond back.

What else do you want to hear?

CHAPTER 22

Cynthia

I set the timer on my phone to ten seconds, pressing start before I quickly get into position. I lean slightly to the right, hooking my left leg over my right knee as I hold myself up with my right hand. I trail my other hand over my upper thigh, leaving only my fingertips to touch my bare skin.

I hold still for a few seconds until the flash on my phone goes off. I straighten and unhook my leg, leaning over to grab my phone from the tripod. Feeling satisfied with the picture, I snap some more of myself before uploading them to my site.

My free hand digs through the bag of hot chips, tossing some into my mouth as I check for any custom requests. A crumb drops onto my chest and I nearly feel my soul leave my body.

I probably should've changed out of my lingerie before digging into the bag of chips.

I look down, exhaling a relieved sigh when I see my blush pink, sheer lace two-piece lingerie set hasn't been compromised by fire red crumbs.

I flick it off of my chest and continue snacking as I scroll on my phone.

I check my inbox and see that someone has already bought the photo I just uploaded. I open his message, reading it to myself.

You look so sexy. What are you doing right now? ;)

I shove some more chips into my mouth as I reply back. *Taking a shit. Xoxo*

At the sound of a thud coming from downstairs, I lean away from my headboard and freeze momentarily. Slowly removing my hand from the chip bag, I set my phone down as I quietly get up from my bed. Tip-toeing to the door, I lean my ear towards the hallway as I listen.

At the sound of the floorboard creaking beneath someone's foot, my hand at my side begins to shift. As I walk down the hallway and down the steps, no longer do my hands resemble that of my mortal form—

But of a Succubus.

Acrylic fingernails quickly turn into sharp long talons. Replacing my alabaster skin color with the ashen hue of my real form.

I round the corner, the doorway of my kitchen only five feet from me now. I flex my taloned hand as I ready myself for the fool who thought it was wise to break into my home.

I move faster than a viper, pushing a hard body back into my kitchen island as I raise my hand over him. The second I move to strike him I'm cemented in place, caught off guard by a familiar set of bright glacial eyes.

Dex.

"What the fuck are you doing?" I seethe as I step back, lowering my hand. My talons and ashen skin shrink away, replacing themselves to match the rest of my human form.

I saw his gaze lift to stare at my talons. I fully expected him to shrink away from me, to be so disturbed that he's left utterly speechless.

But when a wicked grin curves along that handsome face of his, I see not only the lack of fear in his gaze, but *intrigue*.

"Show me again."

I knit my brows together, taken aback by his question. "What?"

"Your hand? That was...interesting. Show me it again—" His gaze finally finds itself slipping from my face and lowering down to the rest of my body. The humor from his expression gone. "What is that?"

"This?" I say, posing with my hands on my waist. "This Dex, is what civilization calls lingerie. Women wear it for—"

"I know what the fuck lingerie is. I mean why are you wearing it?" His gaze remains wholly fixated on my chest before slowly lowering down past my navel. He takes a shuddering inhale as a small muscle in his jaw twitches, his jaw clenching tightly.

"I always put on a cute lingerie set on Wednesday and take pictures in it." I shrug my shoulders as I lower my arms at my sides. "It's part of my 'What am I wearing Wednesday' special for my subscribers. And actually—"

The breeze wafting towards me guides my attention to the window above my sink. I walk over to it, noticing it's completely wide open.

I whip my gaze back around to Dex. "Did you seriously just climb through my fucking window?"

Before I can be angry for long, I notice where his gaze has landed. The intensity of his fixation both sends a chill to slither down my spine, and warmth to brand my skin. His eyes remain on my thong as his voice lowers. "Turn around again."

A smirk plays up my face as I siphon the desire that's emanating off of Dex, using it to fuel that seductive energy. "Why?"

He exhales raggedly, the words that slip from his mouth sounding both like a desperate plea and a wicked command. "Just do it."

The breeze from the window lightly glides across my back, doing very little to chill my skin. But I use it to my advantage, to further inflame the desire that's nearly vibrating from his piercing gaze.

I slowly turn around, raising my hands up onto the window sill as I slowly lower the window frame down. Snuffing out the breeze completely as I lock it, feeling the weight of his gaze settling on my back. I move to turn back around.

Dex is on me in a flash, caging me in as his head lowers down to my neck. My breath hitches as he lightly caresses his lips against my skin, his hands lowering to the lip of the counter. "Can I touch you?" He releases a shaky breath as he adds, "Please."

I feel his hard length press into my lower back, wringing a soft gasp from me. I lower my gaze down to his big hands gripping the lip of the counter, the veins in his hands bulging out as he reels in whatever control he's trying desperately to maintain.

Without hesitation, I give him what he wants. What we both want. "Yes." I say, my voice hardly above a whisper.

I track the movement of his hands as they free themselves from clutching the counter. They tentatively, then slowly move to my waist as I stand there, waiting for him to touch me. To slip a hand down my thong and sink a finger deep into the wetness beneath. It feels like an eternity passes between us as his hands skim themselves over my skin—taunting *me*, and I can't help the soft moan that gets trapped behind my lips.

At the sound of it he presses his lips to my neck, exhaling a shuddering breath as he pushes himself harder into me. His hands caress down my waist, his fingers pressing into my soft skin before he moves them to my ass.

He sniffs my skin, tickling every nerve as his lips part against my flesh. "Jasmine." He whispers, pressing a kiss beneath my earlobe as his hands on my ass continue caressing me.

I rock my hips, wanting him to touch far more than that. I want him to turn me around and strip me bare, to put the

tension brewing between us to rest. I grind my ass onto the hard length of his cock, a heated satisfaction pimpling my skin as a rough, low groan emits from him.

His hands grip my waist, holding me in place as he moves with me. His breaths on my neck turn heavy and rapid, similar to my own.

Before I can lower my hand down to touch him he stills my movement completely by holding me in place. Taking a ragged breath in and out, he takes one last inhale of my skin before stepping back and away from me completely.

I turn around to see his palm resting on the marble, his back turned towards me now. "Get dressed. We have some place to be."

I furrow my brows together as I go to step in front of him. His gaze remains on the wall behind me. "For what?" I ask, annoyedly. Both at how he went to just grinding up on me to now he won't even look at me. Not to mention, I'm left sexually frustrated now because *he's* the one who got me worked up and for what then?

I watch his hand grip the edge of the counter, his fingers curling under the marble as the veins in his forearm bulge from his skin. "I have a lead on getting in touch with the owner of OnioNone, and I need you to accompany me." He says curtly.

Yeah, I'm not doing this shit.

I roll my eyes at him, shoving my hands up in the air before forcing them back down. "Fine, whatever. I'll change and go." I turn my back on him, making my way out of the kitchen. "But if you're going to do this weird hot and cold shit then don't—"

Before I can finish my sentence I feel his hand around my neck forcing me back, turning me to face him as his lips crash into mine. He cages me to the wall, pressing his body hard into mine as he grinds into me with feverish need.

I moan against his soft mouth as I wrap my hands around his neck, slipping my fingers through his jet-black strands as his hands shakily rake over my body. Our tongues glide along one another's as I meet his same hurried, feral pace.

He fits his knee in between my legs, pressing it against my pussy. I moan into his mouth as I grind my hips onto him, feeling that coil of tension expand within me.

His lips hover above mine as he tilts my head up, lifting my gaze to his. "I know this is what you want." He glances down at my hips churning against his thigh. "So take it."

I continue rocking my hips onto his thigh, feeling that coil of red-hot tension build and build before it bursts and unravels. Moaning through my orgasm as my body spasms against him.

"That's it." He says as he lifts his free hand to my breast, his shaken thumb rubbing over my hardened nipple. "Let me hear you."

I throw my head back as I rock my hips violently against his thigh, my moans filling the shared space between us. My hands in his hair lower down to his shoulders as I anchor myself to him. My thong bunches to the side as I find release on his thigh. And not for one second does he take his eyes off of me. Drinking his fill as he watches my face contort into pleasure.

When I finally settle he lifts his hand from my breast to my mouth, tracing his thumb over my lips. He tentatively lowers his thigh down as I can see words bubbling to the surface but struggling to formulate. His eyes roam over my face for what feels like a small eternity before he blurts out, "I'm a virgin."

I blink at him as my eyes slightly widen.

He takes a long breath in and out, steadying himself before he speaks again. "I am not hot and cold with you because I want to be, but because I am not experienced." He pauses, working on a swallow. "Because I am still a virgin."

He runs his hand through my hair, exhaling. "Even when my desire for you runs high, because—gods, look at you. And I don't just mean because of how you look." He shakes his head as a laugh bursts out. "I am still nervous in your presence. Yet I find myself incapable of keeping myself from touching you."

A virgin? I—

"You don't need to say anything." He steps back from me as I stand there leaning up against the wall, still speechless. "I just wanted to tell you the truth. As I do not wish to keep things from you." He narrows his gaze, a shyness sparking in his eyes. Or perhaps guilt, I can't be sure at the moment. "But I fear we really need to get going as we have a short window for this."

I finally regain movement in my body again as I nod my understanding, though I have no idea what *this* actually is. Did he find Johnny and we're going to track him down? Are we chasing a new lead?

My curious thoughts ricochet around the inner walls of my mind. But instead of bickering with him about his vagueness, instead of asking questions on exactly where we're going, I step back. "Just give me a few minutes to get freshened up and changed."

I turn to exit the kitchen and head upstairs to my bedroom, the reveal of his virginity pushing through all of those questions and taking center stage in my mind.

CHAPTER 23

He's still a virgin.

The disclosure of that personal detail about Dex circles through my mind the whole drive there. Aside from going over what the plan is, we mostly ride in silence together. It's not that I'm appalled at his lack of experience, I've just...it's been a very long time since I've met someone who is still a virgin.

But I know that when we leave here, I'll voice that to him. That my lack of discussing it further is not because I'm opposed to learning of that fact. Opposed to his inexperience.

No. If anything, it makes me attracted to him that much more.

To know that he hasn't been inside a single woman, to have gone this long without having sex?

Gods, that's...incredibly arousing.

"Remember, we're in a public building." Dex says as we both cross the polished linoleum floor of this commercial building. "So killing isn't an option this time."

I sigh as I say, "I didn't plan on killing him."

He looks over at me, raising a brow.

I sigh again. "I'm being serious this time."

A faint smirk curves up one side of his lips as we walk down the hallway, rounding the corner and approaching a suite door. Dex knocks on the frosted glass as a woman opens it. "Hello! Please, come in."

We both usher ourselves into the room. Theresa closes the door behind us as I get right to work.

The moment she turns around my Succubus energy reaches out for her, pulling her into my energetic snare. "You will not be afraid. And you will not tell anyone what has happened today when this is all over." My words riddled with compulsion.

Theresa nods slowly, repeating my words back to me.

"Good." I say sweetly. "You will call your husband, and tell him you have a surprise for him. To meet you at your office promptly."

Theresa nods her head, pulling her phone out of her muted coral scrub pants. "Yes, I will."

I guide her over to a chair as she dials for Halston, talking softly to him before hanging up. "He's on his way."

I smile down at her. "Great." I turn to look at Dex. "Now we wait."

He leans up against a table, lifting his gaze up to me as he nods his head. A stretch of silence passes between us, coating the air with a subtle tension.

"I get it." I go to stand directly in front of him. "Being a virgin at the age of...?"

He clenches his jaw. "Twenty-six."

"Twenty-six," I repeat. "Isn't normally heard of. I understand why you wouldn't have said anything at first."

A wave of disbelief weighs itself on my chest as I acknowledge what I've just said. The compassion behind my words and utter lack of judgement that carried them.

Am I...actually sympathising with a man right now?

He coughs out a harsh chuckle. "Yeah—well, it's not exactly always attractive to a woman either. But that never really mattered to me until—"

He stops himself but doesn't stray his gaze from me. As if he's debating on sharing whatever it is he was about to divulge.

Now it's my turn to laugh. "Unattractive? Are you—okay." I lean my weight onto one foot, resting my hand on my hip. "Being a virgin isn't something you should be ashamed of. It's, if anything, incredibly attractive."

His gaze widens slightly as his chest lowers with the breath he's kept trapped in his chest. "Really?"

I nod. "To know that a woman has never touched you in that way is..." A smirk plays up my face as I step closer to him. "Hot as fuck."

I watch as twin splotches of pink dot his cheeks as he turns his gaze away. A glimpse of that nervousness that he spoke about when he's around me revealing itself in real time again.

I notice the way his muscles have relaxed, as if this secret has been a burden that's been plaguing his thoughts and now that it's finally been set free, he can think clearly again. "If you're—you know, ever ready to learn."

That gets him to lift his gaze to mine right away, a heated glaze completely washing away that shyness.

"I can teach you a thing or two about pleasure. If you want, that is."

He releases a ragged breath as he shakes his head, placing his hands on my shoulders. "I don't want to be like the scumbags that you have to deal with on a day to day basis. Constantly pining over your body like ravaged animals." His hands gently rub up and down, a tenderness to his gaze and his touch. "I *never* want to be that to you, Cyn."

I tilt my head as I look up at him. "The difference is that I *want* you to touch me, Dex."

I watch his chest still as he goes rigid before me.

I put a hand to his chest, feeling the breath finally leave his lungs as his chest sinks beneath my touch. "If you want that, at least."

He grabs my hand, cupping his fingers over mine. "I have been a virgin my whole life. I never found a woman that I've been willing to end my virginity to. Someone that I want badly enough but you—"

He raises his hand to my cheek, his fingers splaying across my skin. "I have never wanted to lose myself so badly to someone then when I first laid eyes on you."

I stare up at him as the breath in my lungs goes nowhere. The intensity in his gaze cementing me in place.

"I have never wanted to feel what it's like to touch—to *worship* a woman, until I found you."

We both stand there for a small eternity as I soak in the oath in his words. The touch of his fingers leaves a warmth blossoming in my chest. But the sound of footsteps coming from outside the suite draws our attention to the frosted glass door, interrupting a moment that only belonged to us.

Dex grins as he removes his hand from my cheek, a chill left in its absence. I find myself oddly pining over wanting him to soothe that absence, no matter how little the contact.

He lowers his gaze as he asks, "You ready?"

I match his same smile as I nod. The click of a door opening forces me to turn around.

Halston Deveroe locks gazes with me as he enters the suite.

CHAPTER 24

Dexter

"Can I help you two?" Halston asks skeptically, brows knitted together as he slowly closes the door behind him.

He shifts his gaze over to his wife. Theresa sitting as still as a statue with her palms flat on her thighs, keeping her blank stare on the wall straight ahead.

He goes to slip his hand into his pocket to pull his phone out, but Cyn is far quicker.

She grips his wrist with her immortal strength, pulling his hand away from his pants. "I'd rethink that if I were you."

Her cerulean gaze flashes vividly, causing Halston's breath to hitch. He nods his head slowly. "Alright. What is it you want?"

Cyn releases her hold on his wrist but watches him closely. Taking two steps back as I step closer to him.

"Someone that we need information on appears to be a loyal customer of yours." I let a beat of silence pass between us. "Give us what we want, and we can all walk away as if nothing occurred here today."

He blinks at me, clearing his throat. "It would be a breach in our code of ethics to give you such information on any of our clients. Besides, if I walk in with you two at our headquarters it will raise—"

"I said nothing about going to your headquarters." I remark.

He looks at me with confusion in his hazel gaze. "Then how do you expect me to get you the information you need?"

I narrow my gaze. "From your home office."

He forces his expression to remain impassive, but I see the lie spun between his teeth. "I do not bring my work home with me."

I sigh as I stride past him and Cyn, looking out the window overlooking the city. "And yet six weeks ago you sent a work email to your assistant, stating that you would be working from home for the day due to maintenance needing to work on your plumbing." I turn around to face him again.

His impassivity falters as a chuckle slips out. A disingenuous smile curving his lips. "Should've known you were one of us." He passes a glance over to Cyn. "So what does she have to do with all of this?"

"Don't worry about it." I say, standing next to her. "I don't have all day so this is what we're going to do. You will drive us to your private residence—and as someone *like you,* I already know where you live. So I will know if you're leading us astray."

He laughs. "Okay. And what makes you think that the second I get into my vehicle I won't call the police?"

I smirk as Cyn advances on him quicker than a viper, her hands yanking his gaze to hers.

She smiles wickedly up at him as that power of hers reaches out to him, ensnaring him completely under her control. The sudden rigidness in his back and shoulders melts away like hot wax dripping from a candle.

With his slackened gaze on her, she compels him. "You will drive to your residence without making any stops, or any attempts to do anything otherwise."

She slips her hand down his pants, reaching down into a pocket and pulling out his phone.

"You will allow us entry into your home upon arrival, in which you will do exactly as we say with no hesitation or resistance."

Halston nods slowly, blinking at her words. "Yes. I will drive straight home and do as you say."

"Good." She releases her hands from his face but doesn't withdraw her power from him completely. "Now, let's go."

Halston turns on his heels and exits the suite with his hands loosely hanging at his sides. A tether of her power following him out.

Cyn turns around and kneels down, looking up at Theresa. "You will forget everything that happened here, and will not remember meeting us." She pushes a strand of wavy hair back from her face. "You will also not venture back home for at least another two hours."

Theresa nods her head as Cyn stands up, walking past me. "We're done here."

I follow her out of the room, walking close to her side down the hallway as I feel the energetic tether of her power dissipate from its claws on Theresa.

I look down at Cyn, a goofy smirk curving up my lips. "We make a good team."

She looks up at me, raising a brow as she tries to look annoyed at my statement. But as she fixates her gaze straight ahead again, I see her fighting to keep a smirk from hiking itself on her lips. "You mean that *I* am an exceptional asset to finding this fool." She looks up at me again, a glimmer of mischievousness in her gaze. "You need my help more than I need yours."

"Oh, is that so?" I laugh as I finally crack a laugh from her. The sound like a refreshing reward that I have done so little to earn.

She says nothing for a short eternity until she grins widely up at me. That side of mischief heightening in her gaze. "I bet I could make it to the car before you."

My mouth barely has time to part open to respond when she's already taken off into a sprint. She bypasses the elevator entirely and yanks the door open to the winding staircase that leads to the lower levels.

Oh, you're so on.

I chase after her, completely aware that a few people from other private offices have stopped to stare at us running like lunatics with our asses on fire.

But at this moment, none of that even matters.

I yank the door open and fly down the steps, following right on her tail as I yell out for her. "No cheating either."

She glances up at me, sticking out her tongue before racing down the last few flights of steps.

If I had asthma or were out of shape this would've absolutely ended me. But my determination to catch her in this game of cat and mouse has my adrenaline pumping like I'm a natural born athlete.

I jump the last few steps, landing next to her as I push my arm out against her chest. I use the other to yank the exit door open as she pushes against me. She quickly ducks down, dipping right out from underneath my arm and bolts outside.

"Ha! Nice try." She yells, racing for my car up ahead.

The sunlight above blinds me momentarily until my sight regains normalcy. Damn, she's fast as fuck.

I pump my arms at my sides as I round the corner of the alleyway, feet pounding on the sidewalk as I catch up to her. With her only five feet from my car, I watch her reach her hand out to touch the front passenger door. But before she can, I throw my arms around her waist and pull her backwards.

I use a little too much force and bring both of us down to the ground, my back taking the brunt of the fall. Which should've hurt like a motherfucker if it hadn't been for the bed of grass I landed on.

She pulls away from my hold on her, jackhammering up and reaching her hand out until she's touching my car. She raises both arms above her head, cheering. "I win!"

I pull her down next to me as we both start laughing, trying to catch our breaths as we lay underneath the towering tree above us. I sigh as a fleeting concern sparks in my mind.

"I really hope I did not just bring us down onto a pile of shit or something."

Cyn bursts out laughing even harder, the sound loud and infectious and—gods, there really could be no better of a sound to drown myself into. We both lay there howling our amusement as people walking on the street pass concerned glances towards us. One woman even stops to ask if we're okay.

The question—for whatever reason, causes Cyn and I to just laugh harder. The poor middle-aged woman scurries away as if she fears she'll catch whatever maniacal breakdown we're both having.

But little does she know I haven't laughed this hard—this genuine, in a very long time.

CHAPTER 25

We pull up to a two-story home with floor-to-ceiling glass walls that wrap around the exterior. Sleek, charcoal grey brick forms the base foundation and creates a unique geometrical layout.

Cyn and I walk up the concrete steps, approaching a gun-metal door. I knock twice, Halston appearing a short moment later as he opens the door.

He locks eyes with Cyn right away. His voice is mellow and calm as he greets us. "Please, come in."

We both step inside as Halston closes the door behind us. When he turns around, Cyn gets right to it.

"Take us to your home office."

Halston nods his head as he guides us through his home. We walk past his living room adorned with an expansive, antique rug set beneath plush white furniture.

We turn down the hallway and enter a room with floor-to-ceiling windows throughout. The office aside from the desk and computer on top of it is bare with no personal details to give it any life.

It truly feels like a fucking office in here.

He sits down behind his computer and pulls up OnioNone's database. He looks over his shoulder, waiting for his next instruction.

"You will find information on this man." Cyn hands him the piece of paper I gave to her with Johnny's username on it. Or rather the one he uses on the dark web, at least.

He takes it, turning back around as he gets to digging.

Cyn and I stand there for a total of four minutes until Halston finally finds him.

"Jerome Stiller. Seems he has been a client of OnioNone for six years now." His gaze roams over the text on the screen. I pull out my phone as I begin typing what he says next. "His real IP address is one-two-one, zero-five, zero, three."

I put that into the notes app on my phone, coming around to lean over him to make sure it matches. I pull the camera app up and snap a picture of his computer screen as well.

"Where does he live?" Cyn asks, noting the subtle urgency in her tone.

I look over the file they have for Jerome as I pull a flash drive out of my pocket. "He definitely isn't local."

Cyn hovers next to me, cursing under her breath. "Of course he lives on the other side of the city."

I connect the flash drive to Halston's computer, saving a copy of Jerome's file onto it. After a few seconds when the transfer is complete, I disconnect it. Slipping the flash drive back into my pocket. "I have what we need." I say to Cyn. "Make him forget while I hack into his security system feed and erase the past twenty minutes."

As I access Halston's wifi network, therefore hacking into his security system from my phone, Cyn compels the man to forget ever having met us and to forget everything that transpired in the last hour.

I cut all footage of Cyn and I being on his property, deleting the evidence frame by frame.

"I will forget everything that has transpired." Halston repeats, his voice hardly above a whisper.

"We should go. I'll have to resume his feed after we've left the premises." I look over my shoulder at Cyn.

She gives me a nod before stepping away from Halston, but not before we've both logged him out of his work system and cleared the browsing history from his computer. I take an extra step to even delete it from his work system's history.

I close the door behind us, opening the passenger door as we approach my car. She slides in as I walk around my vehicle, sliding into the driver's seat. "The Sixth Ward is at least a three hour drive from us."

I turn my car on, turning the heat dial up a notch as I notice tiny bumps forming on her arms. "I'll need to make arrangements for us to stay there overnight then. It'll be a day or two trip, depending on how messy this gets."

I drive down the pavement, heading in the opposite direction from her house.

She looks over at me when she realizes. "Where are you going?"

"I want to stop at my house quickly to make sure I can upload the file easily to my system." I pause. "I'll take you home afterwards."

"Well, I hope your house has a lot more character than his. I felt like I was in a damn hospital."

I chuckle as I turn down the street. Feeling a sudden anxiousness spark to life inside of me at one obvious fact that I hadn't even processed yet.

Cyn is coming over.

CHAPTER 26

Cynthia

I set my purse down onto his kitchen table as he flicks on a nearby light. By the time we made it over here the sun had already set, leaving in its wake a cool spring night.

"Make yourself at home. I'm just going to grab my laptop from upstairs real quick." Dex says before walking out of the room.

I eye the ivory-tiled backsplash between dark chestnut cabinets and the matching cupboards below. My gaze catches on a bowl full of fresh fruit tucked next to an espresso machine.

I walk over to his patio door, pulling it open as my jaw hangs open.

I step out onto an expansive wood deck surrounded by tall, lush trees. Grey patio chairs huddle around a square propane gas fire pit, my gaze falling on what lies near it.

I pad across the deck to a large inground hot tub. I nearly squeal with excitement as I rush over to it, finding the switch and turning it on. Judging by the clear water, it's safe to assume Dex actually keeps it clean.

Bubbles come to life as I lower myself down, pulling my leggings up to my knees as I lower my feet into the bubbling water. The water starts off cold but quickly heats up.

"I see you found the backyard."

I turn around to see Dex closing the patio door behind him, walking over to me. "This is the one thing I wish I would've opted for when I was looking to buy a home." I look down at the water, smiling widely. "I love soaking in a hot tub."

A soft chuckle brings my gaze back up to his. "Sorry. If I would've known that I would've told you to bring a swim suit."

He bends down to his knees next to me, loose strands of his midnight hair falling in front of his forehead before he pushes them away. I stare up at him for a few seconds before a wide grin curves my lips.

I stand up, water sloshing down my calves and onto the deck. "Or not."

I begin lifting my shirt off when Dex suddenly has his hands wrapped around my wrists, stifling any further movement. "What are you doing?" He forces out.

I shrug my shoulders. "Getting into the hot tub."

He blinks at me, and for a moment I think he's forgotten how to breathe. "In your bra and underwear?" He slowly releases his grip from my wrists.

"Nonsense." A heartbeat of a pause passes between us. "I'm going in naked."

This time, I don't have to guess. He's definitely stopped breathing. When his chest finally does move again I notice the way his gaze slowly lowers down to my chest.

I bring my hands back to my shirt, lifting it up my belly. "Is that going to be a problem?" I ask huskily as I slowly bring it over my head, tossing it far enough away where it won't get wet.

Dex has his gaze cemented on my black bra, to my breasts hidden beneath. I watch a tick feather in his sharp jaw as he shakes his head curtly. "No." The word sounding both like an omen and a plea.

"Good." I lower my leggings down my legs, taking my time with it. I feel the welcomed burn of his stare across my body as I lean over to release my feet. I straighten up again, tossing my leggings.

As I lift my hands behind my back, I swear Dex doesn't even risk a single blink. His attention to my every move thrumming the fire in my blood and fueling my want to tease him that much more.

As I unclasp my bra, I rake my fingers over my chest before slowly pulling it off. I watch his chest sink suddenly as I move my hands to my thong.

"Are you enjoying the show, Dex?"

"Yes." He mutters with zero hesitation.

I slip my fingers below the cotton fabric cinched at my hips, slowly pulling them down as I watch that hunger in his gaze turn into something feral.

I toss those as well before I let him get one last glimpse at my naked body, ravishing in the arousal that I can smell potently from him. I turn around as I slowly lower myself down into the hot tub, the warmth of the water nowhere near able to replace the warmth of his stare.

The water rises to my chest as I look up at him. "Am I going to enjoy the water by myself, or are you going to join me?"

That hunger in his gaze falters slightly as I begin to sense a different emotion from him.

Worry.

I decide at that moment to change my tactic, remembering that he's never done—well, anything with a woman before. I can't imagine that means he feels exactly confident being naked in front of one either.

I give him an affirming grin. "How about I turn around?" I put my hands over my eyes as I turn my back to face him. "See? I promise I won't peek."

As an entity that finds no shame and full confidence in sex and pleasure, I realize that it's been a while since I've met someone who may not share that same confidence. Someone who has never explored the depths of losing yourself so willingly to intimacy before. I start to wonder if he will get in at all. Maybe my invitation is too fast for him?

If he decided against it, I wouldn't be upset at all. Hell, I remember how I was the first time letting a man touch me. Confidence and all, I was mortified with nerves.

But before I can think longer on it, I hear the thud of clothing drop to the deck. Followed by the stir of water that has nothing to do with the bubbles fueled by the jets.

"You can turn around now." He says, his voice like smoke wrapped in velvet.

I lower my hands from my eyes, turning around to see a chest that looks like it's been chiseled by a god of steel. Water droplets cling to his fair skin, and I watch as one trickles down a tattoo above his right pec.

I move a step closer to him, glancing down to the water between us. The bubbles stirring the water enough to where I can't see what I know is beneath.

I change trajectory and decide to move further away from him, backing myself up into the other end of the hot tub. "So," I lean my head up against the edge, sighing at the pleasantness of the water. "Did the file upload to your computer successfully?"

He nods in a slow, predatory way. "Yes."

"Good." I say, closing my eyes and exhaling a relaxed breath. "I go back to work tomorrow night, so we'll have to postpone paying *Jerome* a visit until Monday."

I should've known he'd use a different name. What a dickhead.

"I think that actually works to our benefit. It gives us time to concoct a good plan so when we do find him, his execution can go quickly and smoothly without any hiccups." I feel the water stir in front of me.

"And how are we disposing of his body? I can't imagine riding with him in your trunk for three hours back into the city is a smart idea."

"I don't trust dumping his body in a part of the city I don't have as much control over like I do here." He pauses. "We'll be fine as long as we leave that night. I'll make sure

Carson keeps an ear out for any possible APB's from law enforcement should someone try to pull us over. But again, we'll be okay."

Curiosity finally draws my eyes open. I look up at him, noticing he's closed some of the distance between us. "Who's Carson?"

A chuckle escapes his perfect mouth. "He's the chief of police in Lilitu City."

"And I'm guessing he's an ally to The Deimari Mafia?"

He nods his head. "He keeps our business deals out of police hands and we bring crimes to his attention that do not involve us."

I hum. "Intersting. So, what exactly do you and Sawyer do?"

"That's kind of a loaded question." He chuckles as he steps closer. "We don't run illegal underground rings if that's what you're asking. Well, aside from making counterfeit money. Otherwise, we mainly make business deals."

"Wait," I lean away from the edge of the deck. "You mean to tell me that this whole time you've been throwing me counterfeit money?"

He laughs as he shakes his head. "No, little jewel. Any money you ever get from me will always be real." A soft promise to his words. "The counterfeit bills are mainly for investing in other properties so that we make straight profit from them."

"Oh, tell me more." I grin widely at him.

His gaze briefly narrows to my lips. "For instance, we just signed a contract for the new apartment complex being built by the river. I noticed through my intel that the owner Victor—*previous* owner now, had no money left over for repairs and things of the like. I used that to offer him a compromise: Sign over ownership to Sawyer and I, in return we invest a generous amount into the building's future repairs. He agreed, and now Sawyer and I are the new owners."

I raise a brow. "But Victor still gets to run everything?"

He nods again. "Correct."

Essentially, still making Victor do all the work that a property manager would do while they sit back and do nothing. "And I'm assuming you invested counterfeit money into the property. So…"

"So, that means the ten percent earnings Sawyer and I get back in return each month will be straight profit. And we just invested in a property that we technically didn't even invest in."

Huh, what a smart little bastard. I like the way he thinks.

A grin curves my lips. "Do you think he'll ever find out?"

He shakes his head, his eyes alight on mine. "The money has been made to be able to be withdrawn into banks without getting flagged."

"Interesting." I say.

Dex lowers his gaze to the water hovering above my chest. "It's just business." He pauses as he lifts his gaze back up. "I could name a hundred more interesting things."

"Like what?" I ask, edging on the tease in his words.

He steps closer to me, leaving only a few feet to stand between us. "You, of course."

I laugh as a cool breeze brushes past my cheek. But the heat of his body being so close to me now steals my attention. "What in particular interests you about me?"

His gaze turns into molten desire as he watches me. "Your laugh. Your smile."

I feel my heart flutter in my chest at his words. I fully expected him to mention how appealing my body is, but instead—

"The way pleasure lights your face as you come on my thigh."

That flutter is quickly melted into a hot desire that travels further down. I watch him like a hawk as he takes another step closer to me, feeling the full heat of his body now.

My gaze lowers to the water, to what's beneath. "Though pleasure didn't seek you in return."

"I don't need to touch myself to feel pleasure from you." He says lowly. "Watching you come undone did it enough for me."

I lift my gaze back up to his, my breath hitching at the stark need in his eyes. Something that I've only ever seen in the demons like myself that reside in Hell.

I tilt my head up at him. "And what if I want you to touch yourself?"

His chest stills.

I smirk as I stand up, the jet behind me beating on my back as water sloshes down my bare breasts. I bring my hands up my navel, tracking his gaze at my every movement. "I want you to find release, too."

He blows out a ragged breath as I bring my hands up higher, my fingers massaging my hardened nipples. He stares at me as I touch myself. As if it's the last thing he'll ever get the chance to see.

"Touch yourself." An invitation, and a plea.

He finally lifts his glacial gaze up to my face, silence stretching between us before he lowers a calloused hand beneath the water.

I watch the veins in his arms bulge as he palms himself, his movements starting off slow.

"Good boy." I whisper as I lower myself back into the water. I dip my hand beneath the water as well, rubbing my clit as I keep eye contact with Dex. "Does it feel good?"

His chest sinks suddenly as the speed of his movement remains the same. "Yes."

I hum my appreciation, letting a soft moan slip from my lips as I feel that delicious coil of tension blossom within. I back up into the jet, feeling the power of the water bursting out of it against my rear. I angle myself so that it's pulsating right beneath my pussy, wishing it were his cock touching me there instead.

He must catch what I'm doing because his pace quickens as a groan gets trapped behind his lips.

"Do you like watching me touch myself?"

"Yes. Fuck, do I ever." He groans as he steps closer to me. Feeling the movement of him working himself under the water closer now.

I rub my clit faster, feeling the tension build and build, my orgasm climbing with it.

"Tell me what you'd do to me." He manages to force out.

I smirk at him. "Such a dirty boy." I say huskily, watching the way his chest sinks and a fire comes to life in his eyes at my words. I lower my gaze to his arm pumping his cock. "You want to know what I'd do to you?" I repeat slowly. "I'd wrap my hands around your cock, my tongue would glide slowly, tortuously down your shaft while I work you just as fast as you're working yourself right now."

I smell his arousal intensify, a groan slipping from his lips.

"I wouldn't stop sucking you, tasting you until you were so overwhelmed with need, that you began to fuck my face. Dripping your cum down my—"

In an instant he's spinning me around, pushing me up against the edge of the hot tub and pressing his hard cock up against my ass.

He grinds into me and—gods, he really has nothing to be worried about. From what I feel rubbing against me, I'd say he's *huge*.

His breathing trembles as he presses his lips to my neck, lowering his hand beneath the water to lift my leg up. My eyes widen as a moan escapes my lips as he angles my pussy up against the pulsating jet, right over my clit.

I inhale a sharp breath as I writhe against it, the water beating powerfully against my clit while Dex grinds his cock against me. His voice trembles as he speaks, his hand holding up my thigh grips into my skin. "Gods, I want to fuck you so badly."

"Please," I pleaded with him, my orgasm riding the top. "I want you to. I want you to fuck me."

He releases a shaky breath as he grinds harder into me, his cock slipping lower as I feel him sliding along my pussy lips. The sensation of having him so close to slipping inside of me, yet not allowing himself to drives me wild with need.

He lets out a groan as his other hand grips my waist down, caging me in place. "Not yet. Because I don't deserve it yet. Not until you've teased me to the point of no return."

He humps me, moaning—

No, he's *whimpering* behind me.

"Not until you've made me beg for it. Made me *earn* it." He presses shaky kisses along my neck as I feel him go rigid behind me. He whimpers as he nips at my neck, wringing a soft cry from me. The tiny pinch of his teeth jolting my senses into overdrive. "Fuck, I'm going to cum."

I rock my hips against the jet as my orgasm spills over, his cock rubbing down between my ass, rubbing deliciously along my wet pussy.

I cry out my release as he rams into me, Dex whimpering against my neck as I feel his seed pulsate out of him. He trembles behind me as he nips at my neck to control his whimpering. Our orgasms go on and on for several moments until he finally releases his hold from my neck, along with his hands on my leg and hip.

He remains at my back for a short while, breathing in and out long after he's lowered my leg back down. It's been a while since I've allowed a man to get close to me like this, and normally I would run for the hills at the intimacy of it.

But right here, right now, I feel safe to enjoy it.

He pulls me away from the edge, turning me around to face him. "Did I hurt you?"

My brows furrow together as I look at him confused.

His hand touches my face, pushing my bangs back from my forehead as droplets of water trickle down my cheeks. "I didn't grip you too hard, did I?"

I shake my head. "No, not at all." A sated smile blooms on my face.

I watch as he forms his own before leaning down to kiss my forehead. "Good." I feel the comfort pull away from his kiss like the warmth leaving the chilled air.

He pulls me into his lap as he seats himself on a raised ledge, leaning back as he pulls my hand to rest itself on his chest. I feel the quick pace of his heartbeat beneath my fingertips as he wraps his hand around mine. I sink into his embrace and lean my head onto his chest.

And for a long while, we don't speak. We simply just sit in each other's company with nothing but the moonlight and our shared breaths to accompany us.

CHAPTER 27

Dexter

I press the graphite pencil down onto the canvas, using light strokes to shade a rounded edge. I'm not sure how much time has passed since I retreated down here, but I know that I won't be going to sleep anytime soon.

After I went inside to grab some towels for Cyn and I to dry ourselves off with, it was unfortunately time to take her back home. Which was the very last thing I wanted to do. I would've rather had her stay the night while I gawk at how beautiful she is all night.

Maybe she would've felt safe enough to fall asleep in my arms while I ran my fingers through her hair, or maybe we would've stayed up all night exchanging stories about our past. Nonetheless, I've never had my mind so jittered or my senses so heightened like this before.

It's safe to assume I should've expected nothing different considering I've never done that with a woman before.

My fingers pinching the pencil press harder into it as memories resurface in my mind. I force myself to exhale the excess energy out as I continue with my sketch.

Even beneath the water I could feel how soft her skin was, the way it melded to the grip of my hands. How wet her pussy was as I was gliding my dick against it.

Gods, it felt so fucking good I couldn't help the noises I was making. Though she didn't seem to mind. If anything, I think she even enjoyed them.

If she has me whimpering like that from just feeling her pussy rub against me, how the fuck would I ever last if I were to slip myself inside of her?

There's no fucking way I'd last more than five seconds. I'd probably get two pumps in and be completely done for. She'd have my body trembling like a damn leaf caught in a windstorm.

The thought makes my dick hard again and I have to stop myself from fantasizing any further, otherwise I'll end up pulling an all-nighter with how wired I am.

I force myself to think about how she turned around again so I could get out of the hot tub. It was just as sweet as the first time she did it. Though she didn't need to do that, it's not my manhood I'm nervous about.

It's getting intimate with *her* that makes me nervous.

But gods, after I got a taste of what it's like to please her, for her to please me beyond belief? I don't think I'll be able to focus on anything else for the rest of my life.

I might actually need to see a clinician about this. Is this normal to be so worked up like this?

She *is* a Succubus. Luring men in for her is as easy as breathing—I mean, who wouldn't be hypnotized by her? Maybe that has an added affect on me being—

Yep, I'm already spiraling. I am in deep shit.

I continue working on my project for another hour until I force myself to call it quits. When I finally do check my phone, and notice that the time in the top right corner of the screen reads two-thirty, I shut my table lamp off and make my way back upstairs.

After I change into a pair of grey sweatpants I climb into bed. Pulling my sheets up to my chest as I lean my head back, my bedroom pitch black aside from the moonlight filtering in through my window.

It takes me quite a while to actually fall asleep, but when I do, it's with the thought of how Cynthia looked in my oversized T-shirt. I'd given her one to change into, thinking that it might be warmer than a cropped shirt. When she put the damn thing on it did something to my chest, to my pounding heart beneath.

The thought leaves a grin on my face as I fall deeply asleep.

Don't be late.

I send back a thumbs up to Sawyer's text, slipping my phone back into my pocket. I refocus on the screen in front of me, scrolling through my search results on Jerome.

I was fully expecting with his advanced level of tactics to keep himself anonymous on the internet that he'd have a criminal record.

Guys that go to great lengths to keep themselves hidden usually do.

But when his record came up clean, I was a little shocked.

Disappointment was the second feeling I had. I'd really hoped I could find something on him that I could use to exploit him. I'm sure at which point he would've reconsidered distributing Cyn's content without her permission.

Aside from a lack of a criminal record, I also find out he recently got divorced—

Gee, I can't imagine why.

He's been employed as a cable installation technician for over four years, has no children, and lives in an apartment in the Sixth Ward. Which, from my further digging is because his ex-wife won ownership over their house during their court battle.

Good for her.

I continue digging through his life through his IP address, trying to find anything out of the ordinary. Particularly anything that can help us for when we pay the bastard a visit this week—

My brows knit together as I find a folder labeled *Lights*.

I click on it and several security cameras come up onto the screen. I count a total of seven of them, and notice a trend amongst each of them.

None of them are in the same home.

I click on one, the picture expanding across my screen. I first notice the wooden four-poster bed towards the far back wall, thick ivory and purple blankets sprawled on top of it. As my gaze narrows to the nightstand next to it, I watch as a woman walks into the frame.

She goes to sit on her bed, setting a bottle of lotion onto her nightstand as she hikes her pajama pants up. I close out of the live recording right away, anger swelling to the surface.

This fucking perv is *watching* women in their homes.

I have to stand up from my seat and pace my dining room for a few moments before I can sit back down again. I don't even have to ask how he was able to sneak cameras into their homes. These women probably thought nothing of it, too.

They trusted a service technician to install cable into their homes and were completely taken advantage of.

I have to find these women and tell them to remove these cameras. He doesn't get the luxury of spying on women in the safety of their own homes.

If I get each and every one of them taken down, he would realize something is wrong. In which case, he'd probably try to leave the city and completely wipe his computer clean. Leaving Cyn and I back to square one on trying to find him.

I run my hand through my hair, trying to shove the frustration away but it remains attached to me like a second layer of skin.

I open up the folder again, trying to see if I can figure out each woman's IP address through the files on the screen. I'm able to dig through and identify each of them, finding that frustration lessening only slightly.

I decide on the next best thing for now until I have Jerome taken care of.

It takes me a little over a half hour to hack into each of the seven cameras. I hack into the quality of each of them, rigging them all so that they have a slight blur to them.

That way when he tries to spy on them, the picture quality won't be as clear.

Not a permanent fix, but a temporary one for now until I can get into their homes and remove them completely.

But by then, he'll already be dead.

CHAPTER 28

Cynthia

I do another lap around the VIP room as I hold this man by his ankles, his ass cheeks scrunched up like shriveled up raisins beneath beige trousers. His palms lay flat on the carpet as he holds himself up, balancing his weight on the top half of his body. His nose only inches away from kissing the ground, his cheeks reddened from the blood pooling to his face. I asked him if he wanted me to slow down but he insisted I walk at this speed.

I'm all for being kink friendly, but I'm not sure how me walking this guy like a wheelbarrow is sexy or a turn on. Regardless of my curiosity though, I don't bother asking.

I know better than to ask.

I walk him around the room for another ten minutes until he tells me to stop. I lower his legs down to the carpet and step back. He rights himself back up onto his feet a few moments later.

He looks at me through a softened gaze, a sated smile curving his thin lips. His hand reaches into his pocket, pulling out a hundred dollar bill. "Thank you, Sapphire." He hands me the crisp bill.

"You're welcome." I smile, adding the cash to the four hundred he already paid me. "Stay for the show, if you'd like."

"I will." He says as he grabs his jacket from the couch, and we both walk out of the VIP room together.

The booming club music surrounds me as I step out onto the main floor, the moving headlights above shining down on the dancer currently on stage. In forty minutes I'll go on for my last stage performance for the night. Ready to take these heels off and soak in a hot bath once I get home.

The thought of hot water jogs my memory of Dex and I in his hot tub last night, sending a chill down my spine. It's almost as if I can still feel the tug of his teeth on my neck.

A sensation I would like to feel again.

I walk over to the bar, leaning my elbows onto the sleek counter as I feel the gaze of a customer on me. It takes him only a minute until I feel him approach me.

"Can I buy you a drink?"

I look over at him, grinning. "A shot of tequila, please."

He chuckles, turning his body to face towards me as he leans in closer. "Tequila before going on stage is a wild choice."

Maybe to the average mortal, but not to a Succubus. "How so?" I ask instead.

Ace comes over to us, nodding his head when the man orders for me. He turns his gaze back to me, chuckling again. "I've seen you on stage before. You do all of those cool tricks where you flip upside down, and spin around for what feels like a small eternity."

Ace comes back with my shot of tequila. Giving me a faint smirk before walking away to tend to a woman in a black low-cut top down the bar.

"To do all of that with liquor in your system? How do you not get nauseous?"

I take the shot to my lips, watching his gaze follow before training it back on my face. I shrug my shoulders as I say, "I guess I'm just lucky." I slam the shot back, setting it down onto the bar again.

He looks at me like I've just benchpressed five hundred pounds right in front of him. "Wow. And you didn't even chase it with a lime!"

Yeah, let's go ahead and wrap this up immediately.

I lean away from the counter, placing a hand on his shoulder. "Well, unless you're going to ask me for a dance, I think I might need to go get ready." I start to walk away when he stops me.

"Wait—yes, I'd love a dance." He smiles as he hands me fifty dollars. He goes to tuck it beneath my halter strap when I take it from his hands instead. Slipping it beneath my garter.

I'd rather you not touch me. "Let's go, then."

I lead us to an empty private section, my phone buzzing in my hand as I draw the heavy velvet curtain.

I open up the incoming text, grinning as I read it.

So, I was thinking instead of you getting an Uber home tonight like normal (not because I saw it on your bank statements but because you told me, of course), how about I pick you up and take you home?

As I go to reply back Dex sends another text.

It's also a safety concern for you to hitch rides with strangers, of course. Definitely not because I'm looking for an excuse to see you or anything.

I softly chuckle to myself. *Are you going to kiss me again if I say yes?*

I turn to face the man as he seats himself down. I sigh as I ask, "Have you ever had a lap dance before?"

He shakes his head.

"I have one rule. Keep your hands to yourself. If you break it, you get one warning before I boot you from the section. Understood?"

The man nods his head. "Yes, understood."

"Good." I say as I go to set my phone down.

But before I even get to lift my hand from the table, Dex replies back to me. His response stirring the nerves beneath my skin, leaving anticipation in their wake.

I could do more than just kiss you.

I send him a text back before I begin the dance.

I'll hold you to that. Xoxo

CHAPTER 29

This man has not stopped yapping since the moment I started dancing on his lap.

For the first few minutes I tried to drown out his insufferable blabbering, but once he started talking about his ex-girlfriend, I realized quickly that this wasn't just a lapdance for him.

It was a therapy session.

"She really broke me, you know? And I went through hell to make things right again but she said that it wasn't enough."

I would much rather be in Hell than listen to you yap about a situation you could've easily prevented.

"Like what was I supposed to do? Was I *really* supposed to fire my assistant over that? I told her that I was severely intoxicated and it meant nothing to me. It was *one* time."

Well, apparently it meant something to you if you've commented on your assistant's good looks at least three different times during this conversation. And for fucks sake, when will men finally stop using that line to justify their bad behavior?

It was one time and you know what else will happen only one time? Your existence. And I'm tempted to shorten it if you keep talking my ear off.

The song in the club finally dwindles as I silently thank the DJ for the impeccable timing.

I lift myself from his lap, leaning down to grab my halter top as I fit it to my chest.

"Wait, it's over already? I haven't even gotten to the part where—"

I turn around, holding my hand up to silence him. "I would rather drink battery acid than spare another minute being held hostage by your feelings."

He sits there with his mouth hanging open.

I grab my phone from the table. "Seek a *real* therapist."

I open the curtain and walk out onto the main floor, leaving him behind as I head to the bar. I definitely need a shot of tequila after that.

Ace catches me walking over and meets me by the bar counter. The soft glow of the chandelier above lightly illuminates the gleam of his smooth umber skin. "Do I want to know why you look so dissatisfied walking out of that section?"

I seat myself down onto a barstool, the velvet cushion comforting my chilled, bare legs. "I made my money from the dance. That's all that matters."

Ace slides me a shot of tequila, taking it and downing it. He gestures if I want another and I shake my head, declining his offer.

I look over my shoulder to see Starla dancing on the main stage, my cue to go in the back and change into a new outfit before I'm up next.

I glance at Ace as I get up from the chair. "Well, gotta go." I give him an air smooch. "Love ya."

He graces me with his handsome smile. "Show them who's the baddest."

His compliment follows me to the locker room as I change into the other outfit I packed for tonight. A black vinyl one-piece with a deep neckline that goes all the way down past my belly button.

I tie the halter strings around the back of my neck, fixing the vinyl material over my breasts. The one-piece leaves the sides of my breasts completely exposed, revealing lots of cleavage. The entirety of my ass on full display through the thong.

I slip my feet into my rhinestone pleaser heels, securing the matching cuff around my ankles. I begin spritzing my jasmine scented perfume on my body when my phone catches my attention.

I pick it up, reading the text that comes through.

I'm finding myself bored down here. I may make an appearance. Xoxo

I internally squeal as I reply back to Anastasia. *PLEASE do. I miss you so much! Xoxo*

Anastasia—another Succubus, is a good friend of Amelia and I's. But instead of keeping to the land of the living, she prefers to remain down below. Claiming that the demons that reside in Hell fuck a lot better than mortal men, and that there's no other reason for her to venture up here. But every now and then, she gets curious and finds herself paying a visit.

The last time she did was over one hundred years ago. She spent a total of four days up here before she went back home.

Anastasia is the most noncommittal person I have ever met, and the most ruthless. When she wants something, she takes it. No questions asked. The same goes for when she's finished with something, too.

She has absolutely no problem dropping a man after she gets what she needs from him. Which in most cases, is a one night stand to satiate her lust for a carefree life.

She reminds me a lot of Asmodeus in that way. Except he visits the land of the living far more frequently than her. As The Prince of Lust, I'd expect nothing less from him.

I go to set my phone in my locker when I pause, a smirk crawling up my red lips as I open the text thread between Dex and I.

I seat myself down onto the bench behind me, straddling each leg over the metal. I hold the phone above me, placing my other hand over my breast. I arch my back slightly and take the photo.

I glance the photo over, a smirk lifting my lips again. "I look so good."

I send it to Dex, followed by a text.

Do you like my stage outfit? ;)

He must've had his phone already in his hands because he texts me back almost immediately. *I think you'd look better straddling me instead of that bench.*

Heat creeps over every inch of my skin. It appears someone is getting bold.

That can be arranged. Xoxo

I set my phone down into my locker, but before I can close it, I see the text he sent pop up on my screen. Satisfaction blossoms within me as I read it, knowing I'm only riling him up.

And I have no intention of stopping anytime soon.

Your wet pussy will be rubbing up against me tonight. Remember that while you're up on stage.

CHAPTER 30

Dexter

It's two in the morning and I've been parked around back for thirty minutes now. I watch as Cyn exits out of the club's back door, her amethyst dance bag slung around one shoulder. I knew what time she got off work tonight but I still came early.

Her teasing got under my skin, sparking every nerve in my body and leaving me hot and bothered beyond belief. But most of all, I was just excited to see her.

She opens the passenger door and slides in, setting her dance bag down beside her feet. "How was work?" I ask, that sliver of giddiness rising once more.

She shrugs her shoulders. "It was pretty good for a Thursday." She looks over at me, her soft gaze ensnaring me for a moment. "How was your day?"

I pull out of the alley and drive away from The Playground. "I had some business things I needed to attend to. Otherwise, it was decent." I look over at her, knowing I need to tell her what I found out about Jerome, but for just this moment, I take in the sight of her.

She's wearing a dark beige zip-up sweater with a matching pair of flare leggings. A pair of memory foam slippers on her feet.

I chuckle as I ask, "Aren't slippers meant to be worn around the house?"

I catch the grin sneaking an appearance on her lips. "*These* slippers are for work. I have house slippers at home, if you must know." She glances out the window. "Besides, they're the most comfortable choice after wearing seven inch heels all night."

I turn down the street. "I would imagine so."

A few moments of silence pass between us before I hear her stomach growling. I look over at her. "Are you hungry?"

"Starving." She corrects. "But I have food at the house."

I nod to the road ahead of us. "Are you sure? There's a taco truck just down the street from us. I could get you something to eat."

She looks over at me, raising an eyebrow. "How do you know that?"

I chuckle. "I may or may not frequent it on the nights I watch you dance at the club."

She laughs, the sound blissful and attractive. How can just a laugh turn me on?

"Actually, I'd love some tacos."

I drive up the road and pull over to the curb, the bright lights from the taco truck nearly lighting the entire block.

I step around to her side, opening the door for her. "Thank you." She says as she steps out.

Her politeness stirs something inside of me, eliciting a desire to hear the word please on her lips, but for far more nefarious reasons.

I am definitely deranged. "You're welcome."

We step up to the window as I turn to see a few people walking over from a nearby bar. They must've had the same idea.

Cyn and I each order some chicken tacos and a lime soda. When our food is ready, I grab everything and we go to sit at a nearby table. Cyn chows down immediately once we sit down.

"So, I found something on Jerome." I say before taking a bite of my taco. Feeling as though now is as good of a time as any to reveal what I've learned.

She looks up at me with expanded cheeks, chewing a mouth full of food.

"I did some more digging on him to see what else I could find. And I found something on his computer." I take a drink of my soda, meeting her gaze as I lower my voice. "He has an entire folder dedicated to surveillance cameras he's hidden in women's homes. I counted a total of seven of them."

I watch the ire spark in Cyn's gaze, her chest sinking as she exhales her frustration. "I'm almost tempted to take off work for the weekend so I can kill him sooner." She finishes off her last taco.

"I've gone ahead and blurred the camera quality, at least for now. Once he's taken care of I'll go ahead and get rid of the surveillance feeds entirely."

She wipes her hands on a napkin before setting it into the paper container. "That's very kind of you to do that."

I catch a smudge of sour cream on the corner of her lip. "It's not a permanent solution, but the very least I could do for now." I lift my thumb to her lip, wiping it off. Careful not to smudge her lipstick that looks fucking incredible on her.

I plop my thumb into my mouth, noticing the way her gaze has cemented itself onto my lips. Gods, if she keeps looking at me like that I may just pull my car over to somewhere secluded instead of waiting until we get to her house.

I don't even want to have sex with her—not yet, at least. I just want to touch her. Touch her hair, her soft skin, her—

"Well, it's more than most men would do." She says, pulling me from my horny thoughts. Her gaze lifts to meet mine.

I sigh. "Unfortunately, I would have to agree with you."

I take our trash and toss it into a nearby metal garbage bin before escorting Cyn back to my car. I drive away from the taco truck, heading to her house.

Where I'm both filled with anticipation, and nerves for what's to come.

We both step through the front door of her home. She steps over to the side, pushing the code I programmed for her into the security system box before closing the door behind us.

"I'm just going to set my stuff upstairs. I'll meet you in the living room when I'm done."

I nod my head as Cyn sneaks upstairs, taking my shoes off and heading down the hall to her living room.

I look around and find a vintage floor lamp nearby. The soft glow of it greets me as I turn it on, though not bright enough to light up the entire room.

I walk over to a dark olive green couch, seating myself down as I notice the glass vase of red roses in front of me. I look over to the mantel above an unlit fireplace, a smile curving my lips as I see what's on top of it.

Another glass vase. This time filled with the white and red roses and pink peonies I bought for her.

"I still have them."

Cyn walks into the room and seats herself down next to me, having changed into a pair of black pajama shorts and a matching short-sleeved button-down shirt. "I'm happy to see that." I glance over to them again. "They still look very vibrant, too."

She gives me a soft grin. "Yes, they are." She gets up again, looking over her shoulder as she walks over to a corner bar cabinet. "Would you like something to drink?"

Actually yes, I would. But I promise what I want you can't get from that bar cabinet. What I want to drink is between those perfectly toned legs of yours.

As if she can hear my thoughts, she turns around to smirk at me. Shit, I forget that she can sense arousal.

I clear my throat. "Bourbon would be just fine if you have it." I say instead.

She grabs a glass and fills it halfway with the amber liquid, pouring herself a glass of wine before walking back over to the couch.

She hands me the drink. "Thank you." I say as I take a sip. Feeling the slight tremble of my hand but shoving down the jitters immediately.

She sits right next to me, her body angled to face me as she rests an elbow on the back of the couch. "You're welcome." She says as she lifts her legs up onto the couch, laying them over my lap as she leans into the back of the couch.

Okay, this is really happening. Does she want me to touch her legs? Is she expecting me to keep my hands right where they are? Fuck, what if she's testing me right now?

What is the fucking procedure here?

I lift my hands up, awkwardly hovering them over her legs before planting the hand holding my drink on the edge of the armrest, and my free hand flat on the couch cushion next to her legs.

I look like a fucking dweeb right now.

"It's okay." She says, breaking the ruminating thoughts stampeding in my head. "You can touch my legs."

I do as she says and lift my hand from the couch, laying it on her calf. My thumb caresses over her soft skin and it feels like running your fingers over a swatch of premium silk.

Okay, if I'm going to talk a big game in our text messages I've got to pull myself together. The last thing I want is for her to think that I don't mean what I say.

Nervousness and all, I meant every word.

She takes a drink as her heated gaze remains on mine. The next three words that come out of her mouth leave me bricked up with anticipation. "So, what now?"

CHAPTER 31

In this scenario, anybody else probably would've thought I'd have pounced on her the moment she asked me that. But instead, I decided that was the perfect opportunity to make small talk. Currently, she's telling me about her pet snake.

One would automatically think I was an idiot for that—and I'd partly agree with them. But there's always a reason behind any decision I make.

I'm a patient guy. And by the look in her eyes right now, she's getting off to the tension of us being so close to each other without actually touching as much as I am.

My hand on her calf glides up a little higher, my thumb tracing idle circles along her buttery soft skin. Without realizing it, she's managed to shift closer to me in the past ten minutes of us talking.

"I've thought about getting him a friend. But I don't know. We'll see." She takes the last sip of her wine before setting it down onto the ottoman.

I vaguely shrug my shoulders. "Maybe he's fine with just you two."

She leans up against the couch again. "Do you have any pets?"

I shake my head, drinking the last of my bourbon. "I thought about maybe getting a dog but I don't know if I have the lifestyle for a pet. I'm not sure it would be fair."

"How come?" She asks as she leans closer to me.

"I'm away from home a lot. Plus, I've never owned a dog before. I'd want to learn more about them before deciding to own one."

She nods slowly as she tilts her head. "Do you like to learn new things?"

Her hand on the back of the couch reaches up, sinking her fingers through my hair as a chill skates itself down my spine. It takes everything in me to remain steadily breathing, to not to nuzzle into her touch like a damn cat.

I lift my hand further up her leg, tracing my thumb along her inner thigh. The heat in her gaze thrums my blood, dizzying my thoughts. "Yes."

"What have you all done with a woman before?" She asks, getting straight to the point as tiny bumps form along her skin beneath my fingertips.

I forget to answer for a split moment, mentally hovering between a void that separates the present from the past. The gruesome truth of how far I've actually gone rides the surface of my thoughts, unyielding its grasp and beckoning me to succumb to its control. But I don't let it pull me under its suffocating embrace, not when I've worked through the trauma to understand that it doesn't define who I am.

Nor what intimacy has to mean for me.

I exhale a steady breath as I say, "Before you, I've only kissed women."

Her eyebrows raise slightly. "So, I'm the first woman you've ever touched?"

I nod my head because it's the truth. Cyn is the first woman I've ever touched, willingly. "Yes."

She hums her approval before lifting her left leg up, my hand along with it. "Move your hand lower."

My chest stills as I lower my gaze to what she's made far more accessible for me. I work on a swallow as what I've hinted at is right there in front of me, and suddenly my chest is squeezing shut. Threatening to siphon my breath.

Her expression smooths out as she quickly says, "I'm sorry. I'm moving way too fast, we don't need to do any of that tonight." She goes to lower her leg back down.

I grab her ankle, halting her movement. I lift my gaze from her ankle to her light blue eyes. I'm tired of waiting for the right moment. This is *my* moment, my choice.

And *I* want this.

I lift my hand up her calf, watching her chest jump as her breath hitches. My thumb glides up her inner thigh until it's brushing along the hem of her silk shorts.

A fire blazes in her gaze. "Further."

I exhale a ragged breath as I bring my hand further up, my thumb now rubbing against her pussy over her shorts.

"Do you feel how wet I am?"

I nod curtly as I touch the dampness through her shorts, feeling like I'm about to jump out of my skin. "Yes." I say gruffly.

A smirk curves her lips. "Slip your fingers beneath my shorts."

I follow her order as I lift my hand to her waistband, slipping down beneath the fabric. My fingers glide along her warm, soft skin before slipping further down.

My heart begins beating a mile a minute when the tips of my fingers touch what she was alluding to.

Fuck, she was not joking. She's already soaked.

I begin to explore with my fingers, touching her wet lips and running my thumb along her center. It's so fucking soft, so silky. I—

"Dex." She says softly.

I lift my gaze from my hand to her face, her eyes glued to me. "Put your finger inside of me."

I exhale a shaky breath as I work on a swallow. "Are you sure?"

She nods as she takes my hand, moving my thumb away from her pussy and bringing my middle finger to it instead. She presses it in between her lips. "I'm positive."

I waste no time laying her down on the couch, spreading her legs wider for me. I hover over her with the tip of my finger pressed to her entrance. I keep my eyes on her as I slowly sink myself inside of her, cursing under my breath when I feel her silken walls take me in like a blessed offering.

"That's it." She encourages, sparking my senses like fire to a flame. "Now move your finger in and out of me with your thumb on my clit. Like this."

She grabs my hand, moving it deeper inside of her and then pulling out again. She positions my thumb over her clit, then circles it around that tiny nub.

She lets out a breathy moan as she pulls her hand away and it sets a blaze to that fire within. I continue the movements as I watch pleasure contort her beautiful face.

I continue pumping my finger in and out of her slowly, lowering my gaze to watch myself pleasuring her. The sight of my hand between her legs—my finger pleasuring *her*, sends a dizzying need straight to my dick.

I lift my gaze and my dick grows brick hard beneath my pants as I see the look on her face. She lets out another breathy moan. "Curl your finger a little."

I do as she says and start working her a little faster, watching her expressions to see if I'm giving her what she needs. What she deserves.

"That's—yes, fuck yes." She moans again, this time louder.

The sound brings out a feralness in me that I've never known before.

I lean myself down and take her lips with mine, and she eagerly opens up for me as I slip my tongue between her lips. I tilt my head to deepen the kiss, and she greedily accepts it.

Her pussy is drenching my finger because *I'm* fingering her. *I'm* making her pussy wet.

She pulls her head back, moving my hand as she sits up. She forces me back as she climbs onto my lap, straddling me.

She grinds against me once and every self-imposed barrier breaks wide open. "Can I take these off?" She asks.

I nod quickly. Yes, *please* for the love of everything take them off. I want little to no fabric between us.

She lowers herself down, unbuttoning my pants and slowly lowering them down my legs. My cock twitches in my boxer briefs as I watch her from this angle. On her hands and knees before me. Gods, I never want to have it erased from my memory.

Her gaze shifts to my arousal, her eyes slowly lifting up to mine as she seats herself back down onto my lap. Pressing her wet pussy against my aching cock.

Her hands come to a button on her shirt, setting it free. She does this slowly as I watch her unbutton every single one until her shirt is hanging open. She brings her hands to her breasts, cupping them. "Touch them."

She removes them as I bring a hand to her breast. I feel pre-cum drip out from my dick, wondering if she can feel what she's doing to me.

I massage her breasts, rubbing my thumb over her hardened nipple as I watch her back arch into my touch. Her eyes fluttering closed as she moans at my touch.

But that's not all I want to do to her.

I bring my mouth close to her chest, pressing a kiss in between her breasts as I stare up at her. She brings her hands to my face, brushing my hair back as I slide over to the left. I rub my lips over her nipple, teasing her, causing her body to twitch but my hands quickly grab her waist. I keep her anchored right where she is as I continue exploring her body, relishing in every sound and jerk she makes.

I open my mouth, flicking my tongue out and lapping it around her nipple. Drowning myself in her little gasps as I please her.

I close my mouth over it, sucking on the hardened flesh as she begins rocking into me. My hands at her waist grip into her skin as her wet pussy rubs against me. The groan that escapes me gets trapped against her skin.

She lowers her head, looking down at me as she asks, "You like that?" She continues rocking into me.

I lift my gaze up to hers, her teasing further amplifying my dizzying need. I lift my head from her breast, moving to the other one as I nod. "Yes." My hands lower down, cupping her ass and helping her grind on me. "You have no fucking idea." My voice trembled with need.

I lower my mouth down as I rub my bottom lip on her nipple, wringing a cry from her as she quickens her pace. My hips begin rocking with hers as my need turns frenzied.

I close my mouth over her nipple as I lift her up, lowering her back to the couch. I grind my cock against her pussy, her legs wrapping around me as I begin humping the daylights out of her.

And there's nothing controlled or calm about it.

She urges my face up as my hands skim up to beneath her breasts. She brings my lips to hers and I drown in her entirely.

My orgasm builds hotly and wildly within me, spasms surging throughout my body. I grind my hips into her, my aching cock rubbing against her as I lift my mouth from hers. "Gods, I can't take it any longer. You feel so good I'm—"

My cock goes rigid as release finds me, spilling myself into my briefs as I tremble through my release. She moans loudly as release finds her at the same moment, feeling her pussy drench her shorts as she comes.

As we both ride out our orgasms, I can't find it in myself to stop humping her. I want to just keep feeling her wetness, her aching cunt. I want to taste it—

I reach my hand down, slipping it beneath her shorts. I glide a finger through her pussy, groaning as I slip through and feel that wetness for myself. She moans at my touch as she writhes against me.

I lower my finger inside of her, pumping quickly in and out of her and I don't stop until she's been sated. Until she's screaming her satisfaction.

I bring my finger to my lips and suck on my finger, tasting my sweet reward. Her sweet nectar a sustenance I could live off of for the rest of my life and never go hungry again.

I press a kiss to her collarbone as I exhale a breath. "Fuck."

She chuckles as she grabs my face, pressing a kiss to my lips. "That was just second base."

I lower my gaze to her lips, chuckling. "I don't know how I'd ever get through third or fourth. I can barely handle dry humping you."

She graces me with a soft grin. "We'll see."

I bring her up onto the couch with me, looking down at myself. Thankfully, I'm going straight home after this. "Where is your bathroom?"

"Down the hall." She points in the direction behind her.

I go to clean myself up when I grab another rag, walking back out to the living room with it. I sit back down next to her, motioning for her to open her legs.

She gives me a look when I say, "I figured you wanted to be cleaned up as well."

She looks at me for a moment as if those words were the last thing she thought I'd say, but quickly gives me a soft grin as she does what I ask, opening her legs up as I slip the rag beneath her shorts. Wiping her pussy and the cum that I brought out of her.

I fear I'm going to continue thinking about that for the foreseeable future. That I made her cum.

An internal smug grin lights me up at my accomplishment.

I set the rag into a hamper in the bathroom, seating myself down next to her after I've pulled my pants back on. She fits her arms through her shirt, buttoning it once again.

She frees her hair from beneath her collar, glancing over at the window. "I know it's getting kind of late. I understand if you have to get going."

I look at her as my brows scrunch together, wondering why she would think I'd just skip out right away like that. But as she lifts her gaze to mine again, I understand the silent invitation in her gaze.

That if I want to call it a night, after we just shared something so intimate together, she won't hold it against me. My chest aches at the thought of her being in situations that would've made something like that become so normalized for her. It makes me want to break any man's neck who has ever skipped out on her after being intimate with her, after having access to her body like that.

"I can get going if you'd like. But I had planned to stay for a little longer." I pause for a moment, giving her a shy smile. "If you'd like. I'd hate to overstay my welcome."

"No, not at all. That..." She smiles as she says, "That would be okay."

I feel my cheeks heat a little as I nod. "Cool."

She snuggles into me as I put my arm around her. And that warmth on my cheeks doesn't just stop there. It heats up the entirety of my body, and it has nothing to do with lust.

CHAPTER 32

Cynthia

The Uber driver pulls up to the curb, lifting his gaze to look at me through the rear view mirror. "Have a nice day, ma'am."

I scoot forward on the leather seat, keeping his gaze as the tethers of compulsion sink their claws onto his mind. "You will wait here until I return, then take me back home."

He blinks once before nodding slowly. "I will wait here."

I smile at him. "Good." I lower my hand into my purse, pulling out thirty dollars and tucking it into his breast pocket. "I'll be right back."

I step out of the navy blue town car, shutting the door behind me as a big yellow sign on the front entrance door catches my attention. I walk towards it, disbelief sending a knot to the pit of my stomach.

CLOSING OUT SALE! FIFTY PERCENT OFF ALL RETAIL MERCHANDISE! PET ADOPTION FEES ALSO WAIVED!

I shake my head as I swing the glass door open, rushing past the adoption center and scanning each aisle in search of Pauline.

I finally find her down an aisle stocked on each side with premium dog food. She reaches to place a red sale sticker on a price rack of canned food. "Pauline, why didn't you tell me?"

She places another sale sticker on the rack next to it. "Because you don't have a dog, dear. Unless you have switched Boe's diet—which, I would be slightly concerned with."

I sigh as I tilt my head, narrowing my gaze. "You know I'm not talking about dog food."

She lowers her hand back down to her side, a soft audible exhale sinking her chest and her shoulders forward. She turns to look at me with exhaustion in her eyes, defeat in her bones. "I tried to do everything I could. I really hoped that they would just give me one more month to try and find a solution, but they've had enough of my failure."

I step closer to her, resting a hand on her shoulder. "Pauline, you are not a failure."

She looks up at me as wetness pools in her eyes. My heart aches to see such defeat in her gaze. "But I have. I'm six months behind on my lease payments for the building." A tear slips free as she shakes her head, quickly wiping it away. "Business has become slower and slower for the past year, making it impossible to stay afloat."

She lifts a hand up. "The saddest part is...I've accepted that my store will be closing. But if I can't find homes for them by the end of the month? The city says I have to take them to the pound where they'll get euthanized." She shakes her head curtly as she lifts the hand to her lips, trying to stifle the tremble in her words. "I'd never forgive myself."

The frown on my face deepens as I go to hold her hand. I have to do something. "Let me see what I can do, okay?" I squeeze her hand, reassuring her that she's not alone in this.

I only know her through coming here every week to get stuff for Boe. But in the time that I've gotten to know her, she's always been sweet to me. I knew that she ran this small pet shop by herself, but I wish I knew sooner that she was struggling.

No one should have to see their dreams fall apart.

"I appreciate your kindness, dear. But I don't want you to—"

I stop her right there, narrowing my chin. "Let me help you." I reiterate gently.

She sighs heavily, staring at me for a moment before nodding her head. "Okay." She lifts her finger up at me. "But don't put yourself out just to help an older woman like myself."

I chuckle as I give her a nod. "Deal."

She releases her hands from mine, wiping the wetness from her wide eyes. "Well, enough with the heavy for now." She takes a deep breath in. "What are you in for today, dear?"

I only came in to get some more aspen snake bedding, but now my list just got a little longer. I spoil Boe enough as it is, why not spoil him a little more if it means I can help Pauline?

By the end of my mini shopping spree, my cart is filled with two large bags of aspen shavings, driftwood branches for him to climb on, artificial foliage, and another case of frozen mice. It might not be much cost wise, but hopefully it helps even a little.

She hands me my bags as I set them back into the cart. "Thank you. This means so much to me." She says kindly.

"You're very welcome. I'll keep in touch and come back sometime next week when I've come up with a plan." She pulls me in for a hug. "Stay hopeful."

"I will." Tears have rimmed her eyes again as I pull away.

I push my cart outside and load the navy town car up with my items, returning the cart back inside before sliding into the back seat. "Take me home."

The Uber driver nods his head, my power still latched onto his mind. "Yes, ma'am."

I reach into my purse, pulling my phone out as I send a text to Dex. *Will I be seeing you tonight?*

He responds back a few minutes later. *Is that a serious question?*

I smirk down at the screen because he's right, I don't even have to ask. It's his Friday night ritual to come see me.

I have something I want to talk to you about. A business proposition, if you will.

Dex told me the other day that he and his boss Sawyer invest in commercial properties. What if there's something he could do for Pauline?

You will have my full undivided attention, as you always do.

I send him a heart emoji before setting my phone back into my purse. Excitement sparks at the center of my chest, both at his response and the fact that I get to see him tonight. That sudden giddiness catches me a little off guard. It catches me *really* off guard, actually.

I'm a Succubus. It's in our nature to exude our sexuality with ease, to not feel shame in claiming what we desire in sex. But it's very rare that a Succubus actually grows feelings for another, something that many mortals become subjected to after being intimate.

Succubi *live* off of the chase, but not in the way that men do. We tease, we seduce. We pull men so far into our claws of seduction that they're the ones begging for us by the end of it. And that kind of power, that's what truly fuels a Succubus.

Having a man in our grips, rather than the other way around.

But while teasing and seducing Dex is enjoyable, it's the smaller moments with him that I've begun to find more pleasure in. Yes, we're both attracted to each other—that much has been obvious. But the deal was for him to help me find the one responsible for leaking my content, in exchange for spending time with him.

But what happens when we've dealt with Jerome? And the more glaringly important thing to consider: he's still a virgin.

I want him to continue exploring my body, learning how to please a woman—please *me*. But after this is all said and done, he'd have no obligation to continue seeing me.

But even as that coil of unease tries to burrow itself deep inside of me, I'm reminded by the other distinct characteristic of a Succubus.

That we're extremely territorial. And anybody would be damn fools to try and pry from our hands what we've claimed as ours.

CHAPTER 33

I lower myself down from the pole and land into a split. A man from the right side of the stage whistles at me, trying to gain my attention. But the only man who has my full attention is the one seated in front of me.

He leans back in his seat with his legs spread wide in front of him, as if taunting me to come take a seat on his lap. Reminding me of how feral he was just the other night, humping me until we both came on my couch.

A sensual, heated shiver runs down my spine as I keep myself from saying fuck it and leaping onto him right here, right now.

I watch his gaze fall to my bare breasts. Having slipped my arms free from my off-the-shoulder sleeves and lowered my bodysuit down to my waist. Fishnets plunge down the middle of my one-piece, stopping just above my navel. Rhinestones glittering the entire nylon bodysuit.

I bring my hands to my breasts, teasing him—and the crowd, I guess. Crisp and crinkled bills begin littering the stage as Dex pulls out his wallet. Standing up from his chair and meeting me at the edge of the stage.

But instead of throwing the money on the stage, he hands it to me.

A stack of hundred dollar bills.

"Thank you, sir." I say sweetly, taking the money.

I watch as something flashes in his eyes at that word, a heated glare branding itself on my body. He works on a swallow as he says, "You're welcome."

I chuckle as I lift myself onto my rhinestone heels and walk away. Making a mental note that Dex *really* likes to be called sir.

I finish up the rest of my stage performance and collect all of my money before I leave the stage. I walk all of my money back to my locker, putting it inside my dance bag before freshening up and walking back out onto the main floor.

Amelia perched on the armrest of a chair waves me down, Levi seated in it with his hand situated on her lower back.

I immediately notice that Dex has joined them. Perfect, I can talk to him about Pauline then.

I give Amelia a hug as I approach them, her long wine-red hair set into big loose curls tonight. I pull away as I admire the latex two-piece she's wearing tonight. It snatches her body in all the right ways. "Babe, you look good tonight."

She grins widely. "Thanks. Levi bought it for me."

I look over at him, nodding. "Nice to see you again."

He salutes his whiskey to me. "Good to see you, too." He takes a drink before resting it on his knee again.

"Hello, Sapphire."

I turn around to see a man in dark navy jeans and a beige and yellow striped T-shirt standing behind me. He looks at me with more than harmless interest in his gaze. "Can I buy lapdance?" A wide smile plays up his lips, allowing his bad breath to pass through his teeth.

Gross. Get a fucking mint before you try to approach me.

"Actually, she's already agreed to give me one."

I turn to see Dex standing up from his seat, his glacial eyes set on the man next to me. He watches him with a calm sternness, and it's apparent he sees what the man is badly hiding beneath his nice-guy façade. "I'm sure she'd be more than happy to afterwards, if she's available."

The man gives me a look before turning around and walking away.

Dex hands me five hundred dollars. "If that's alright with you."

I stand there for a moment, looking at the cash before I grin widely. "Of course, it is."

I walk him over to a private section, closing the curtain behind us as Dex takes a seat. I watch him wipe his hands onto his thighs, rubbing them along his black dress pants before resting them onto the armrests.

I tilt my head at him. "Have you ever had a lapdance before?"

He lifts his gaze up to me, hesitating on answering before finally shaking his head.

A smirk curves up my face. "Awe, I get to be your first."

"Shut up." He says, laughing. "You don't need to dance if you don't want to. I just figured you wanted to talk privately."

I take in the softness of his gaze, noticing the underlying nervousness beneath it. The way he's slightly clutching onto the edge of the armrests, as if to steady himself for what he's about to experience. He's trying so hard to remain calm and confident right now, but deep down—

He's a nervous wreck to get his first lapdance. And there's something really sexy about that. It makes me want to settle all of his nerves in a way I know best.

I nod as I lower the money and my phone down onto the small table, slipping my feet out of my heels. "I want your first time to be with me."

I watch him release a shaky exhale as I lower my hands to the back of the seat, bringing myself into his lap as I straddle him. I begin slowly moving my hips as he forces out, "Tell me of this business idea you had."

I smirk as I lower my lips below his ear. "How would you feel about becoming the owner of a small business? Particularly a pet shop?"

"The one I picked you up from that one day?" I feel his heartbeat begin to race.

"Yes." I say before blowing a soft breath on his ear. I grin in satisfaction when his breathing stills for a moment.

"Is the owner looking to sell it?" He asks.

I release my hands from the chair, standing up and repositioning myself so my back is facing his chest. I lean back. "Not exactly." I bring my ass down onto his lap.

I feel his hard length press into me, and it just makes me want to touch myself. But I let him set the pace, not wanting to rush his first experience.

I bring my hands to my breasts, caressing them. "She's being forced to close her shop because she's late on her payments. She doesn't deserve to go through that, and I want to help somehow."

"Well, I can't just—" His words end abruptly as I lower the body-suit down over my breasts, noticing his hands have begun to grip into the armrests again. "Fuck—I mean," he loosens a rough exhale. "I would have to see what I can do. I could probably figure something out for her."

I slowly grind my ass up against his lap, my head leaning back onto his shoulder as he tentatively lowers his lips next to my neck. My breath hitches as his words coast along my skin. "Anything you need me to do, it is done."

I lower my hand down to his, bringing it up to a breast. He wastes no time massaging it as I place his other one on my hip.

"Good. She has until the end of the month for us to think of something."

His hand at my waist grips me tightly as I continue slowly grinding on him to the beat of the club music. He stays silent.

I turn my head to see he's looking down my body, his jaw clenched tight. His hand at my breast has stopped caressing me. "Dex?"

In a flash he pushes me up and off of him, hovering me above his waist as he takes a deep breath in and out. "I can't." He forces out.

I begin to rise up. "I can stop the lapdance if you're not—"

"Fuck, no I don't want you to stop, little jewel." He brings me back onto his lap, keeping me locked in place as I feel him grind against my ass. He exhales raggedly before he stills again. "But if you keep doing that I'm going to make a mess and cum in my pants." He turns his head towards me, brushing his lips against my ear. "And I don't know how pleased I'll be walking out of here with a wet stain on my lap."

His lips brush up against mine as his hand roams down my waist, causing my breath to now hitch. He doesn't close the distance to kiss me, though. As he slowly grinds against me a solution pops into my head, causing a grin to curve my lips.

I lean up from his chest, standing up entirely as I turn to face him. His hands fall away as he looks up at me, his stare turning molten as I lower myself down to my knees. His chest stills and he ceases blinking. "What are you doing?"

I shrug my shoulders as I lift my gaze to him. "It doesn't have to be messy." I bring my hands to his thighs.

He grabs one of my wrists, holding it in place. "Cyn, I—" He stops, hesitating saying what I already know to be true. He works on a swallow. "I've never..."

I nod, tilting my head. "I know."

He shakes his head but releases his grip from my wrist, slowly lowering his hands back down to the armrests again. "I might lose control. And if I'm not quiet—"

"That's what club music is for." I smile sweetly as I go to unbutton his pants. I keep my gaze on him, watching intently to see his reaction. To make sure he wants this. "If you want me to stop though, all you need to do is say the word and I'll stop."

He watches me with a clenched jaw, silently watching as the flames of desire roar to life in his gaze.

Just in case he suddenly went deaf in that split moment, and because I know he's never done this before, I want to make sure. "Dex, I'm going to suck your cock. Are you okay with that?"

He blinks as his chest sinks quickly, the arousal coming from him strong and potent. "Yes. I'm more than okay with that."

I grin at him. "Good. Now," I pull the zipper down, pulling his pants down his waist as he lifts his hips to help me lower them. "Just relax, and let me please you."

The moment my hand lowers to his hard length he releases a rough exhale. I keep my gaze on him as I slip my hand beneath the opening, freeing his cock from his boxer briefs. I wrap my hand around it as he jerks into my hand. I watch as he leans his head back, cursing under his breath as I glide my thumb along the underside of his shaft.

I stroke him slowly to start, keeping my gaze on him to watch his reactions. Pre-cum drips from the tip as I lower my tongue down, gliding it along the pearl-white trail. His fists clench the edge of the armrests.

"How is this?" I ask, licking along his shaft.

"Fucking incredible." He forces out through his rapid breaths.

I lower my mouth over the tip, causing him to groan as I lightly suck him. A wet popping noise sounds as I lift my mouth from him. "Still doing okay?" I ask huskily.

"Okay?" He barks out a harsh laugh. "Fuck, I'm more than okay—"

I lower my mouth back down onto him, taking him deep into my throat this time. His hands grip into the fabric of the armrests as he barks out a curse. The blaring club music deafening his reaction to everyone else around us.

I bring my mouth up and down his shaft, swirling my tongue around his hard length as he jerks into my mouth. I lift my hand up, reaching to bring his hands down when he gets the message, and cups them to my jaw.

Pre-cum spills into my mouth and I greedily swallow it, lifting my eyes up to him watching me with a predatory gaze. I take his cock deep into my mouth, watching his chest rise and fall as I keep my gaze cemented on his.

Claiming what I want. What belongs to me.

I watch his lips part as he moans, feeling his body tense as he nears climaxing. In a flash he pulls my face off of him, taking a shallow breath as he says, "I'm gonna lose control." He shakes his head.

I smirk up at him as I challenge him, coaxing him to lose himself in me. "Then lose control."

It takes him only a split moment for him to stand up, towering over me as he pushes his cock up against my lips. I happily open my mouth as he sheathes himself all the way in. He barks out another groan as he holds my face taught, moving in and out of my mouth as he begins fucking my face.

He humps my face into oblivion, gagging on his cock until shortly after he's spilling himself down my throat. I watch as his face contorts into pleasure, his eyes rolling to the back of his head as he bites his lips. Trying to stifle the moan that sneaks out of his lips anyhow.

He keeps thrusting into my throat, his cock spasming as he cums *hard* into my mouth. His warm seed sweet on my tongue.

Several moments later he finally releases his hold on my face, slowly pulling himself out as his cock bobs in front of my face. He urges me up onto my feet, staring at me. "That was...I—"

I chuckle as I bring my bodysuit back up over my breasts. Finding satisfaction in his utter speechlessness. "You're welcome."

I step away from him as he goes to shove his cock into his pants again, his gaze still anchored on me. I don't even think he's allowed himself a moment to blink.

I grab my things as I open the curtain, turning around to look at him as I say, "Give me a ride home tonight when I'm off?"

He nods his head quickly, working on a swallow. "Of course."

I smile at him before I turn around, walking back out onto the main floor.

Feeling wholly consumed with the satisfaction at getting him so tripped up over his words by giving him his first blow job.

CHAPTER 34

Dexter

I watch as she talks to a man at the bar, flirting with him only to get him to spend money on her. Maybe any other guy would be bothered by this, but I know what she's doing is strictly for work.

And what she does with me...well, that's something no one else is ever going to have.

She rests her hand on his shoulder, his eyes lighting up at her touch. A shiver runs down my spine at the feeling of that same hand being wrapped around my cock just minutes ago. Her mouth taking me all the way down her throat as I fucked her face. Gods, she had me coming so hard it's no wonder I can barely find it in myself to get up from this chair right now.

As if I had just run a marathon, she has my energy spent and drained. It was hers to take, anyway.

"Are you listening?"

"Hmm?" I glance over at Levi beside me, Amelia having gone to a VIP room with a regular of hers.

He gives me a look as he says, "I said, what was the business idea she wanted to talk to you about?"

I lift the bourbon to my lips, my hand trembles slightly as I do. I quickly take a drink and lower the glass back down to the table. "She wants me to see about helping a business that's closing down."

At Levi's silence I look over at him, finding a wide grin on his face as he teases me. "Dude, your hand is trembling like a newborn fawn." He pauses. "You two did something in there, huh?"

"What? No—"

He slaps a hand on my shoulder. "She totally gave you your first BJ."

I quickly shush him. "Lower your fucking voice." The last thing I need is some man listening in to our conversation and thinking he can get that same treatment from her.

I'd cut his hands from his wrists before he ever got the chance to touch what is *mine*.

"Sorry, sorry." Levi leans in closer as he whispers. "So, did you nearly black out?"

I chuckle but even find that taxing. Damn, she really wore me out just from a blowjob. What a beautiful inconvenience. "Almost."

Levi chuckles next to me, slapping his hand on my back. "That's my boy. The shakiness will go away. I had that my first time, too."

"Did it feel like an out of body experience for you, too?" Because, gods. I still feel like I'm floating out of my body.

He leans his head to one side, pondering. "I came really hard my first time, but it didn't feel like that, no. But with her—" A wide grin curves his lips, his refusal at saying her real name in a room full of customers intentional. "Yeah, definitely with her."

I let out a long exhale, rubbing my hand over my face. "I'm fucked."

"Yeah, you are." He leans to grab his whiskey, taking a drink. "But in the best way."

I watch as Cynthia walks away from the man, bringing with her a hundred dollar bill from him. She catches my stare, giving me a wink before she disappears into the locker room.

I feel Levi's gaze on my cheek. "You love her."

I whip my gaze to him, raising my brows. "Okay, you're pushing it now."

I watch as that playfulness on his face falters slightly as a seriousness replaces it. "It's okay to let someone in."

My brows lower themselves down, smoothing out as I understand the underlying message beneath his words. Him and Sawyer know me better than anyone, they both know the relationship I had with my parents.

Or lack thereof.

They know what happened to me when I was younger, and have both let me confide in them about it. The partial reason why I've stayed abstinent all these years.

"You deserve good things, man." He reassures me.

I take his words in, feeling them hit a sensitive spot deep inside my soul. I give him a nod as I clap my hand on his back. "Thanks, man."

And just like that, nothing else needs to be said. Because we both know what I haven't admitted to myself yet.

We both know that he's right. Even if I'm too afraid to accept it right at this moment.

Almost two hours later Cyn exits the club, walking towards my car. I make sure the heat is on low so the car is nice and warm when she steps inside.

She dumps her bag onto the floor by her feet. "Thank gods. My feet are killing me." She slides her slippers off, lifting one foot to her lap as she starts massaging the tired skin.

I drive out of the alleyway, chuckling. "I don't know how you wear those heels in the first place."

"They're actually not as painful as people think they are. Since they're so high, your foot sits kind of flat. Making it more comfortable." She leans back into her seat.

I lift my gaze up to her face, noticing the exhaustion settling there. I instantly want to wrap her into my arms and let her fall asleep on my chest. "Tired?"

She looks over at me, nodding as a yawn escapes her lips. "Though I can't complain. I made really good money tonight." A soft smile lifts her lips. "Partially thanks to you."

I chuckle as I pull up to a four-way intersection, braking as the red hue from the light above casts over us.

"Well, maybe *mostly* thanks to you." She adds on, bringing her other leg up and curling into herself as she leans onto her side, facing me.

I glance over at her, smiling. "You're welcome."

Another yawn slips from her lips. "So, what time are we leaving Monday?"

I drive forward as the light turns green. "Check-in for the hotel I've made reservations for is at four. So, if we want to get there right at check-in, we'd need to leave around one. But I've made myself available for those few days, so we can leave whenever you—"

I look over to see her eyes have shifted closed, her lips left slightly parted open as she breathes slowly and deeply. Ensnared under the spell of sleep.

I smile at her as I lift my hand, caressing my fingers across her cheek as I push her hair away from her face.

"Sleep tight." I say quietly as I continue the silent drive back to her house.

Twenty minutes later I drive down the long driveway to her house, shutting my headlights off and putting the car in park. I look over to see her still sound asleep, resting my hand on her shoulder as I gently try to nudge her awake. "Cyn."

She remains unaffected by the movement.

I lower my hand from her shoulder, grabbing her dance bag before I step out of the car. I grab her keys from inside, fitting it into her front door lock. I push the door open, entering her security code into the keypad before heading upstairs to her room.

I set her dance bag on the floor near her vanity, moving over to her bed and pulling the magenta covers back. I walk back outside and open the passenger side door.

I lower down, scooping Cyn into my arms and cradling her up to my chest. She stirs only briefly to adjust herself to my hold, resting her head below my neck.

I walk her inside and up the stairs, the scent of jasmine strong as she nuzzles herself to my chest. I approach her bed, laying her down on the soft sheets. I remove her slippers from her feet, setting them on the ground before I pull the covers over her.

She immediately curls into the sheets, nuzzling her head onto the plush pillow. I turn around to walk back downstairs when I stop, finding myself unable to leave just yet. So I lower myself down, and sit on the edge of the bed.

I run my hand along her cheek, reveling in her soft skin as it glides along my fingertips. I gaze at her as I watch her sleep, studying the curve of her jaw. The way her chest moves in steady strides with her calm breaths.

What started as a spark of awareness stirs in my chest as I watch her sleep, expanding to every dark crevice in my body as if finally being awakened from a long, long slumber.

Levi's words come back to me again, shining a light on a vulnerability I've denied myself. An intimacy I never allowed myself to explore with another. Not until her.

"I'm afraid to let myself fall for you." I quietly confess to her as I brush her bangs away from her face. A simple gesture I've begun to cherish that gives me an excuse to be able to touch her skin. "But I can't stay away from you, either."

I lower myself down, pressing a kiss to her forehead. I lean away as I whisper, "Sleep tight."

I stand up from the bed to walk out of her bedroom and head back downstairs. Feeling wrong and unnatural with every step I take. I punch in the four digit code to her security system, waiting for the green light to flash on before I see myself out.

Driving myself to a home—that, only until recently, has begun to feel empty inside.

CHAPTER 35

Cynthia

I reach up, stretching my arms out against familiar soft sheets. I push my disheveled hair away from my face, my head against my pillow and not the back of Dex's car seat.

I open my eyes to see Boe in his enclosure, feeling the afternoon sunlight beaming through my window as it warms my back.

I push myself up onto my elbows, wiping the tiredness from my eyes—and, the make-up I feel asleep in, apparently.

Pulling the covers back I cross the room, approaching Boe's tank. "Goodmorning, Boe." I pass his terrarium, heading straight into the bathroom as I take care of my personal needs.

I grab my phone from my nightstand before heading downstairs. Fixing myself a hot coffee as I check my phone.

Dex must've carried me in last night because the last thing I remember is him driving me home from the club. I was so exhausted, it's no wonder I was out like a light.

I take a seat at my kitchen table, setting my coffee down as my fingers hover above my phone.

Why am I struggling to send a text to him? And why do I suddenly find myself second-guessing what the right thing is to say?

Good afternoon. Thanks for bringing my sleeping body inside last night.

I lightly smack my palm on my forehead. I bite my bottom lip as I erase the message and try typing something else.

So, will I be seeing you again tonight?

I erase that message before setting my phone down. What has become of me? I am not some woman that pines over a man, nor do I find them interesting enough to hold conversations with them outside of work.

I take a generous sip of my coffee, hoping to soothe the jitters in my body but it only rattles them up even more.

I pick my phone up, sending a text to a different contact in my phone.

Are you free today? Could really use some girl time. Xoxo

A few minutes later Amelia replies back to me. *I'd loveeee that. Where and what time?*

I just got up, so...how about four? Let's go grab sweet treats from Dazzl-In Bakery?

Perf. I'll see you then. Xoxo

I hover my thumb over my phone screen, tapping on Dex's text thread and typing away.

Because what the fuck am I acting so strange for?

I appreciate you not kidnapping me while I was asleep. And for tucking me into my bed. It was sweet, or whatever.

A few minutes later he replies back. *You're most welcome, or whatever.*

I stick my tongue out at my phone, fighting the smirk that tries to display itself on my face.

I saw that.

My smirk smooths out as I look up at the camera in my kitchen, angled to face my kitchen table and my patio door. Forgetting that it was there in the first place.

I stand up from my seat, walking my mug to the sink and rinsing it off. I stand under the camera, leaning a hand onto my hip as I say outloud, "So much for not being a creep."

I stalk out of the room, feeling the total opposite of annoyed. The incoming message from him only adding to the amusement and...something else that I can't quite place.

That was before you sucked the soul out of my body.

I open the frosted glass door, the miniature golden bells hanging above the door frame tink upon my arrival. Warm notes of cinnamon and baked pastries welcome me as my blush pointed-toed heels click against the hickory floor.

Amelia meets me halfway, throwing her arms around me. "Ugh, I'm so glad that you suggested this." She pulls back. "I will never say no to grabbing a sweet treat."

We both share a laugh as we head up to the steel blue counter. Concrete dome pendant lights hang above glass display cases of baked assortments, ranging from fresh baked bread to cherry-glazed pies. Artificial white wisteria vines hang from the ceiling above rich mahogany bistro chairs and marbled round tables.

A girl with a thick blonde braid approaches the counter with a warm smile on her face. "What can I get for you ladies?"

"I'll take a slice of tiramisu, and a chai tea." I reach into my purse to grab my wallet out. Handing the girl a twenty.

She rings up my order, reaching to hand me my change back.

"Keep it." I insist.

She smiles at me, nodding her head. "Thank you so much." She lowers the money into a tip jar before turning her attention to Amelia. "And what can I get for you?"

"I'll have a slice of banana cream pie and a slice of your black forest cake to go. I'll take a chai tea as well."

The girl rings her up, handing the change over to Amelia when she insists on her keeping it. She smiles warmly before serving us our tea and desserts.

"Awe, how sweet of you to bring Levi a treat." I tease Amelia as we seat ourselves down at a small table.

She rolls her eyes as she brings the ceramic mug to her lips. "I find myself annoyingly kind to him these days." She takes a sip, setting the white mug down. "I guess that is what happens when you fall in love with a mortal man who isn't a raging idiot."

I chuckle as I pick up my fork, scraping a piece of my tiramisu onto it. "I guess so." I put the fork in my mouth.

"Speaking of mortal men," Amelia lifts her amber eyes to me, smirking. "What's the deal with you and Dex? Other than working together to find that pig."

I vaguely shrug my shoulders as I bring the ceramic mug to my lips. "We hang out." Hiding my grin as I peek up at her.

She raises a brow at me. "Don't go all prude on me now, bitch. Just say you're both fucking."

We both share a laugh as I set my mug down. "Well, technically we're just fooling around. We've only managed to get to third base."

Her eyes widen as she grins widely. "Oh, you *really* like him."

I lean my head in closer to her as I whisper. "He's still a virgin."

Amelia gasps so loud that two girls seated near us turn their attention over to our direction. They quickly look away as Amelia leans in closer to me. "Shut the fuck up. That's…" She leans back again. "So hot."

"Right?" I exclaim softly. "I don't think messing around was part of the deal when he said he'd help me in exchange for my time, but it's definitely become a part of it." A grin curves up one side of my face. "I can't say that I'm opposed to it either."

I begin telling Amelia about the times Dex and I have hung out, the night he took me to dinner. Him installing my security systems and proving to me this morning that he does indeed spy on me—at least sometimes.

I watch as Amelia's face lights up with amusement at my words, taking every detail in as if I'm supplying oxygen to her lungs.

"We leave Monday to track Jerome down and—" I pause, giving her a look instead of finishing the sentence. Knowing she gets my drift. "That means we'll be staying in a hotel room together for the night..." My words trail off as I feel the anticipation building within.

Amelia smirks at me as she nods slowly. "And what if he wants you to be his first? Will you do it?"

I've never been someone's first before, the thought of sharing something so personal with another kind of mortifies me. For as long as I've been around, I've had quite my share of experience. Many times I've gone on dates with men, and had to compel them to forget about me days after we had sex. As an effect of being a Succubus, our energy and magnetism is infectious.

Which doesn't always produce the best outcomes.

To say that I've never had a man stalk me at work, or call my phone thirty times in one day just because he couldn't bring himself to stay away from me would be an understatement. During one unfortunate experience, when I finally went to finally compel the man to forget about me—to release him from the shackles of what my seductive energy can do to mortals, he tried to pin me down and have his way with me.

His life ended just as quickly as he'd yanked his pants down that day.

So now, I just compel men to forget about me right after we have sex the first time. It's better this way.

But I'm not blind to how protective Dex has grown towards me, how he watches me when he thinks I'm not looking. I see the look of desire and want in his eyes, but most of all, I see the unending yearning.

He looks at me like he wants to peel me back, layer by layer until he's mastered studying everything there is to learn about me. Both with my body, and my soul.

And truth is, I might just let him.

I look up at Amelia. "Yeah. I would." Because he's not the only one whose longing runs deeper than lust.

Amelia gives me a look. "Then why do you still look conflicted?"

I say nothing as I take the last sip of my chai tea.

Amelia's eyes widen as she says, "You don't just like him. You're falling in love with him."

"I don't know if I would call it *love*." I quickly amend. "More like I...care about him. It's easy to be around him. He makes me feel comfortable." I lower my mug back down, sighing. "It was exciting in the beginning when he would come to the club and watch me dance, drawing me in without even saying a word. I thought that excitement would dwindle the moment he finally spoke to me. But—"

"Your interest in him only grew stronger." Amelia finishes for me.

I tentatively nod my head. "Yeah, I'd say so." I plant my elbows onto the table. "I'm fucked, aren't I?

Amelia laughs as she leans in to place her hands on mine. "That depends entirely on you." She gives my hands a squeeze before leaning back. "We're not meant to settle down. It's not in our blood to submit, we take what we want with no remorse." She pauses. "But I've realized that the right person won't make you feel like you're submitting your power over to them, giving them permission to mold you into what *they* want. The right person will honor your autonomy without squandering it." A soft smile curves her lips. "They'll fuel that internal fire rather than letting it burn out."

I take what she's saying to heart, knowing that she's right. I haven't let myself be in many relationships, but I find myself gravitating towards Dex more than just someone helping me to seek revenge. He's the first person—first man, I've been around in a long time where I don't feel like I'm on that stage, performing to allude to the desire that I confidently wield. The first man I can be around and feel present enough to just be...me.

I give Amelia a soft smile. "Thanks for coming to hang with me. I really needed this."

"Anytime, girl." She says, finishing off her tea. "I do not want to go to work tonight." She sighs. "I'm not in the mood for playing nice and charitable to men."

I laugh at her statement. "If it weren't for Dex's promising appearance tonight, I'd be feeling the same—"

My smile smooths out as a fucking fantastic idea springs to life in my mind.

I bring Amelia's face to mine, kissing her cheek. "Gods, I fucking love you."

Because I know just how to help Pauline now.

CHAPTER 36

Dexter

I have definitely gravitated from casual to full-blown creep. There's no denying it now.

Like the moon to her sun, she's pulled me right into her orbit. Where my life now revolves around hers, irrevocably so.

I watch as a white car pulls up to the curb, a few feet back from the front entrance of the bakery. I step out of my car, fixing the watch on my wrist as I approach the car.

I gently knock on the driver side window with the back of my knuckles, a man jerking his head up to me before rolling his window down a crack. "Can I help you?" The bite of annoyance evident in his tone.

I hand him a stack of twenties—one hundred dollars to be exact. He tentatively takes the money. "She will no longer need your ride for this evening."

He looks up at me, blinking once before nodding. "So be it."

I step back from the vehicle as he rolls his window up, leaving me standing there as he pulls away from the curb. I walk back to my car to wait for her when I see a familiar black car pull up.

I grin widely as Levi pulls up to the curb, putting the car in park before stepping out of the driver's seat. "So, this is our life now?" He pulls me in for a hug, patting his hand on my back.

I chuckle against him before I pull away. "Can you even say you're mad about it?"

He barks out a laugh. "Not even in the slightest."

"Oh look, our chauffeurs have arrived." Amelia says.

I turn to look at her before my gaze travels onto Cyn, her gaze lowering briefly before meeting my face again.

Amelia leans into Levi as he pulls her in, kissing her with no short amount of passion. She pulls away as she taps her hand on his chest. "A treat." She hands him a plastic to-go container of some chocolate dessert.

He takes it, grinning widely. "And if I want a different kind of sweet treat?"

She grins wickedly at him. "If you're a good boy."

"I'm always a good boy." Levi says as he opens the car door for Amelia, sneaking a kiss onto her cheek before she lowers herself down into the car.

They drive away as I approach Cynthia.

She gives me a look as she raises an eyebrow. "Can I assume that you're the reason why my Uber driver just drove away?"

I shrug my shoulders as we walk to my car. "Why pay for an Uber when I'd drive you anywhere you want to go for free?"

A soft noise gets trapped in her throat as I open the passenger door for her. "I suppose." She flutters her lashes as she looks up at me. "I'd much rather be in your company than some stranger's anyway."

She seats herself into the car as I close the door, walking around to the front when I have to fight the silly grin curving up onto my face.

I seat myself down into the car, looking over at her. "So, you do like spending time with me?"

She smirks at me, and I fully expect for her to make a snarky comeback. Instead, she says just one word that has my heart feeling like it's melting from inside my chest. "Yes."

Finding myself slightly unprepared for that answer, I forget how to form words like a newborn learning how to speak for the first time.

I put the car in drive, pulling away from the Dazzl-In Bakery as that warmth in my chest blossoms wider. I nod as I finally find the ability to form words again. "I'm happy to hear that."

Unbeknownst to myself, I lower my right hand down onto her thigh, and keep it there during the drive back to her house.

For an hour now I've had my head propped up against her pillows, my legs crossed at my ankles in front of me as I wait for her to finish getting ready. I'd offered to wait in the living room for her, but she insisted that I could wait in her bedroom. That she'd want my help in picking out an outfit for work tonight.

I'm beginning to think this was just a way to torture me. But even if it was, I fear I still would've willingly fallen into the trap anyhow.

The bathroom door finally opens as she steps out, a towel wrapped around her damp body. My gaze tracks over the droplets of water that cling to her porcelain skin, dripping off the tips of her hair and down her shoulders.

I've never wanted to be a droplet of water so badly.

"So we're just going to—what, show up to wherever Jerome is on Tuesday and kill him?" She walks over to her dresser, opening it up and pulling a thong out. "Do you even know where he's going to be?" She leans down, slipping the pink thong on underneath her towel.

"I know where I want to be."

"What?"

My eyes widen as I shake my head, lifting my gaze back up to hers. Did I really just say that out loud? "I mean, yes I know where he'll be. From what I've gathered, he only has work until four that day. So, we'll just meet the bastard at his residence."

"Easy enough." She opens another drawer, pulling out a white v-neck T-shirt. She drops her towel, pulling the shirt over herself.

I quickly look away. "Um, I can step out."

I turn my gaze back to her as she turns around, facing me now. She shrugs her shoulders as she says, "It's not like you haven't seen me naked already."

I try to keep my gaze on her face when I'm entirely distracted by her hard nipples pressed against her shirt. I have to take a steady breath in and out to settle the boner that has quickly invited itself to the party.

Cyn—thank the fucking universe, severs my beady attention to her perfectly round breasts and walks back into the bathroom. Sparing me twenty minutes of ogling her like Tom when he looks at Toodles Galore.

I should've brought some shades inside. That would probably help my eyes from bulging out of their sockets.

Fuck, when was the last time I even wore shades?

Cyn walks back out, heading into her walk-in closet as she shuffles through the hangers. She comes back out a few minutes later with basically floss on. "What about this for tonight?"

I stare for a few moments before rubbing my hands over my face, wiping the vile thoughts from my virgin mind as I stand up, walking to the opposite side of the room. "Yes."

She raises a skeptical brow. "That doesn't sound like a confident yes to me." She retorts.

I grip one hand around a wood poster, leaning my other hand onto her magenta sheets. "That is *very* nice." I remark enthusiastically. "Happy?"

She scoffs at me as she rolls her eyes, stepping back into the walk-in closet. "Fine. I'll find something else."

Yes, please do. I cannot stand here and contain myself while you're dressed in a skinny thong with basically a thread of fabric to cover your nipples.

She comes back out moments later and it feels like my heart has stopped beating inside my chest.

"Okay, what about this one?"

I lean away from the four-poster bed, slowly walking towards her as I take in every detail. A tube top fashioned from black fishnet material, a matching pair of bottoms that go to mid thigh. Wearing a black latex thong underneath, with nothing covering her breasts.

I nod slowly as I meet her in the doorway, lifting my hand to touch the band beneath her breasts. My words low and heavy as I speak. "Definitely this one."

I don't know what it is, but fishnet is gonna do it for me every single time. But something about how *she* looks in it has me full blown possessed.

Her gaze lowers down to my hand as I travel it down her sternum, her skin twitching as I graze the tip of my finger down her belly.

She grabs my hand, warning me even through the disappointment in her tone. She wants me to keep touching her. "I have to be at work soon, so we unfortunately don't have time for that right now."

I raise my hand up to her neck, pushing her damp hair back as I lift her gaze up to me. "Another time."

She watches me with the same hunger in her eyes that I know is reflected in my own. "Yes." She glances downwards. "Another time."

I hesitate before stepping back, seating myself back down onto her bed as I give her space to finish getting ready.

Keeping my hands firmly cemented to my thighs because if I don't, there's a good chance I'll lock us both in this room. And neither of us will leave until I've explored every crevice of her perfect body.

CHAPTER 37

I bring the bourbon to my lips, drinking the last bit that's left as I cross my ankle over my knee. Leaning back into my seat as I wait for her to get called up on stage.

A waitress with long black hair comes over to me, leaning down to grab my empty glass. "Can I get you another, sir?"

I shake my head, handing it to her. "That's okay, thank you." I go into my wallet and pull out fifty dollars, handing it to her. "Keep the change."

"Thank you so much." She says before walking away.

"I would give anything to hit that."

A calm annoyance spikes my nerves as the man takes the empty seat next to me. Of course, when Levi steps away to use the restroom a man thinks it's an invitation for him to sit and talk to me. And to think that the women here have to deal with men all night long.

Gods, I can't even imagine.

I glance at the chain around his neck, watching the way he subtly fixes it. Either he's sporting fake gold because he doesn't want his real shit stolen, or he can't afford it but thinks no one will notice that it's fake.

Judging by the way he's slightly puffing his chest out, I'd guess the latter.

At the sound of the DJ announcing Cyn's arrival, I turn my gaze back to the stage. Hoping if I ignore him he'll just go away.

I find out fairly quickly that I won't be so lucky in that regard.

"Ah, there she is. *Pole Princess.*" He chuckles and I suddenly feel every nerve in my body on high alert. "You here to see her, too?"

I nod my head. "That would be why I'm seated here and not at the bar."

He laughs again, my attempt at being short and choppy doing the exact opposite of what I'd hoped.

Cyn begins her stage performance, starting on the pole. She transitions into different types of moves that I have no clue how she manages to make look so graceful. Like the pole is her medium, and she's just using it to demonstrate the art that is her.

"I bought a dance with her once. She didn't say much but man, had my dick hard just watching her. I wanted to feel her up so bad."

My focus is taken away from Cyn's performance and has now made the man next to me the focal point of my attention.

"I mean, look at her." He leans in closer to me and it takes every bit of self restraint to not choke him the fuck out.

My hands on the armrest grip the edge of it, sinking my fingertips into the leather. He's got one chance to redeem—

"The things I would do to her. I would rape that tight little body."

I clench my jaw shut as everything inside of me boils over into an unending rage. Repulsion roils through me at how confidently he could talk about doing that to her—to *anyone* for that matter. How dare he speak about her in that manner, talk about *her* at all. He'll never get the chance to even get near—

It would be so quick and easy to crack his neck right now, stifling the vile words coming out of his mouth about her. To my incredible disadvantage, I can't exactly do that in a packed club.

So, I improvise.

I turn to look at him, forcing a fake grin. "What if I told you that I had an escort waiting for me? Ready to have some fun?"

A smug grin curves his lips. "Then what are we doing still sitting here?"

He stands up from his seat as I do the same. I glance over at the stage, seeing Cyn is looking over at me. I give her a look before turning my back on the stage. Walking outside with the man.

But not before Levi across the club catches me leaving, a curt nod at the silent understanding.

We step around to the back alleyway where my car is parked. The moment that I know we're clear of anyone seeing us, my restraint breaks loose.

I strike him in the face, sending him stumbling backwards. He puts his hand up to his nose, blood dripping down his lips as he spats, "What's your fucking problem?"

I don't give him a chance to utter another word as I hit him again. Gruesome thoughts of what he'd be capable of if he ever had the chance to subdue her rage in my mind. Fueling the disgust churning through my blood. I hit him again, and again, and again.

I grab his bruised and bloodied face, his mouth limply parted open as I whisper in his ear, "You will *never* get the chance to speak about her ever again."

I spit in his face before pushing him to the ground. I jump on him, striking him in the face until I feel Levi's hands yanking my arm back. Pulling me back up onto my feet and pulling me out of the fog of rage.

"He's dead, bro. He's gone."

My chest rises and falls to the quickness of my breaths, looking down at the man bleeding on the ground. His punishment was not nearly bloody enough for what he could've done to her.

I slowly look at Levi, nodding my head after several moments of silence stretching between us. I gather myself, taking in the whiff of trash from the dumpster nearby. The potent smell of metallic on the concrete beneath our feet.

The haze of anger lifts as I center back into my body.

"Let's get him out of here before anyone sees."

I flex my hands once, the aching bite of my knuckles sending sharp bolts of pain through my hand. But I mentally set it aside while we take care of this.

Levi and I both lower down to either side of the man, lifting him up by his shoulders and his ankles. We load him up into my trunk, and drive him over to the funeral home to dispose of him.

And the feeling of shame never surfaces, nor does the guilt for what I've done.

CHAPTER 38

Cynthia

"Janice!" I yell out, rushing through the sea of people crowding the main floor.

Janice turns around, half of her honey brown hair pulled back into a clip as it flows in loose curls down her back. As soon as I catch up with her she raises a brow at me. "Something tells me you're going to explain why you have that look in your eyes right now."

I bring my hands up to my chest, connecting them in a prayer stance as I narrow my chin. "I wanted to talk to you about possibly holding an event."

She tilts her head as her green eyes hone in on me. "What kind of an event?"

I bite my inner lip. "I want to hold a charity event."

She blinks at me once. "A charity?" She repeats, sounding like she's completely done with my shit.

"Yes. See, I have this friend—well, this woman that owns a small business that's forced to close up. And I really want to help and I thought why not have a charity night!"

She stares at me as if I've lost my mind. And hell, maybe I have.

"I know the club has to make ends meet each night, but I'd use whatever I made for the event to put towards helping to keep her small business open. I could market it online and bring even more traffic in. It could be a win-win for everyone."

She sighs. "I'm not promising anything, but I'll think about it."

I squeal as I say, "Thank you!"

The club owner smiles at me before she walks away.

I turn around, going back out to the main floor to look for Dex and tell him what my idea is. But quickly remember that he walked out with that look on his face, with an unknown man I didn't recognize.

Even though his body language insinuated he was calm, I knew better from the look in his eyes. He was *fuming* on the inside.

I grab my phone, sending him a text. *No interest in staying for the full show?*

I wait for a response but get none, feeling a worried knot form in the pit of my stomach. Did something happen with him and that man? Aside from Dex not being alone tonight, I know he can handle himself without Levi.

For the first time I feel a dart of worry slither its way up to my chest, settling itself over my heart.

I look down at my phone again, tapping my heel to the carpet as I wonder if I should send another text. But instead of prying, I lock my phone and try to set the worry aside.

But it follows me like a silent wraith throughout my entire shift.

CHAPTER 39

Dexter

I lean up against the metal table, listening to the cremation chamber start up as the man burns inside of it.

Levi stands next to me, looking over at me. "So, what did he say about her?"

I shake my head, looking at him. "How'd you know?"

"Because you're calculated, methodical in your pursuits, Dex. But tonight, you were sloppy." He narrows his gaze briefly. "There's only one reason why you would've switched up so fast."

I turn my gaze away, sighing. "He said he wanted to rape her." I shake my head. "He deserved nothing less."

A beat of silence passes between us. "I'm not disagreeing with that."

We both stand there for a small eternity until Levi breaks the silence. "Does she know you love her?"

I remain silent for a moment until I push away from the table. Rubbing my hands through my hair, pushing the jet-black strands away from my forehead.

Levi steps in front of me, resting a hand on my shoulder. "It's me, man."

I shift my gaze to him, seeing the earnestness in his brown eyes.

"You can't bottle this shit up. Talk to me."

I want to laugh at him for saying that, because he knew it'd be the one thing that would both piss me off and cut straight to my core. I've lived so much of my life being alone, keeping to myself that I still find it challenging sometimes to open up. Forgetting that I have the few people around me that make it safe to do so.

I think what actually makes me afraid to have fallen for Cyn so hard is how easy she made it for me to get close to her. How even through my own fears, I still fell in love with her.

I sigh slowly. "It's different this time. I thought I knew love before with—" I cut myself off, and the look in Levi's face tells me he knows where I was headed with that sentence. "Despite what she is, she's warm and kind. And—gods, I'm afraid because I've never fallen so quickly and so deeply like this before. There are things that I would do—*have* done for her that I've never done for anyone else before. I just..." I trail off before I force myself to finish the sentence. "I'm the guy who retreats into the shadows, seeing and knowing everyone else around me. Not the guy that actually gets seen."

A soft smile forms on his face, an expression I don't see too often. "Sometimes we meet someone who pulls us out of our comfort zones, where we have no other choice but to break the iced-over surface that has kept us drowning in our trauma, and come up for air."

He shrugs his shoulders. "You start shaking like a leaf on a tree as your body regulates its internal temperature. Your teeth chatter together, and you might even try to speed up the process by rubbing your hands over your arms. But sooner or later, your internal temperature regulates and you stop shaking. Your hands lower down and your body calms." He rests a hand on my shoulder. "Meeting Cynthia is like that. Because even though logically you know you love her, your past triggers your nervous system to believe it's not safe to get so close again."

I let his words wrap themselves around the jitters clinging to my bones, a residence they have occupied for years.

Levi brings me in for a hug as I wrap my arms around him. "There are people out there that want to get to know you because they care about you. Don't let your past win by making you believe that genuine connections don't exist."

A tremor works its way through me at the implication beneath his words. Because as I stand here now, I find myself wanting to put distance between us. To pull away from this hug and dead the conversation. Because as sad as it sounds, intimacy and acceptance was a foreign concept growing up. Let alone a warm hug.

I pat my hand on his back, my voice rough against his shoulder. "I appreciate you, man. Thank you."

Levi pulls away, softly grinning as he nods. "Anytime, brother."

As we go ahead and shut everything down once the body has finished cremating, I settle into my car feeling lighter than I had when I originally stepped into it.

I pull out my phone, seeing that Cyn texted me some time ago. I read it, then promptly sent her a response.

Sorry, something came up. I will still be there to pick you up at two, and take you home tonight. I promise I'll make it up to you.

Because Levi was right about one thing. Even when the haunts of my past come back up to try and pull me back, none of it is a match for the way Cyn draws me in.

And I have no desire to resist the pull anymore.

CHAPTER 40

Cynthia

After I get everyone's tip outs taken care of, I make my way to the club's back exit door. The cool night air kisses my face as I step outside.

My gaze lifts from a glass bottle on the concrete to Dex standing in front of the passenger door. I lower down, grab it and toss it into the recycling bin literally four feet away.

Why do mortals insist on being so damn inconsiderate?

"Good evening, Ms. Monroe." Dex says as I approach him, his hand lowering down to the door handle. He enthusiastically bows his head as he opens the door.

A laugh slips out of me like warm honey. "We're addressing me by my last name now?"

He bows his head again, causing another airy laugh from me. "Is that a problem, Ms. Monroe?"

I shake my head as I seat myself down into the passenger seat. "Not at all."

"Good." He says before he closes the door. He gets into the driver seat and looks over at me. "Are you ready to be escorted back home, ma'am?" A grin curves up one side of his handsome face. That damn dimple making an appearance.

I raise a brow at him. "Where else were you going to take me?"

The chuckle that escapes his lips sends a twinge of heat to blossom in my navel, heightened by his piercing gaze.

He glances down as my stomach makes an obnoxious grumbling noise.

"Or we could make a pit stop for tacos again?" I ask.

The grin on his face deepens as he nods. "Of course."

He drives out of the alleyway, driving the short distance to the food truck parked down the street. He comes around to open my car door and I step out. "Thank you."

"You're welcome."

I lower my gaze to his hand, noticing the distinct difference from the other one. His knuckles swollen and peppered with bruises.

"What happened to your hand?"

He says nothing as we walk up to the window. "I had some unexpected business to handle." He looks over at me, flashing me a grin. "It's nothing to worry about."

I pull my gaze away from him, turning it to the gentleman in the truck. I place my order, Dex doing the same after me. He pulls his wallet out of his pocket and I notice the subtle jerk he makes.

"Doesn't seem like nothing." I muse.

He pays for our food, carrying our items to the same table we sat at last time. I—like last time, chow down while barely saying a word. It isn't until I've finished my last beef taco that I press on. "Who did you beat up?"

"Cyn." He warns as he lowers his soda back down. Wiping his hands with a napkin.

I grab his wrist, pulling it towards me as I examine his hand. I expect for him to pull away from me, but instead he lets me study his knuckles.

When I think back to tonight, how he got up and walked away with some strange man, my assumptions settle as the truth becomes apparent. "It was that guy you were sitting next to tonight." I lower his hand back down.

His jaw clenches for a brief moment before admitting, "Yes."

My brows knit together. "Why him? Did your boss put a hit on him or something?"

He shakes his head. "No, Sawyer had nothing to do with me handling him."

I take note of his use of words, and also his vagueness in answers. "Why'd you go after him?"

That line of obscurity finally vanishes as he looks me dead in my face and says, "Because he threatened to hurt you."

I don't have to ask him what exactly was said that gave him that indication. I've worked in the industry for long enough to know that most things that come out of men's mouths about the dancers are usually not of a kind, genuine nature. So, I don't pry any further.

Because I know with full certainty that Dex killed that man tonight, and wouldn't have handled the situation any differently on my behalf. He may have once been someone that just watched from afar, but that quickly changed the moment I asked for his help and inserted myself into his life.

My gaze narrows for a beat of silence, tracing the curve of his lips. "Did you make it hurt?" My words barely above a whisper as I lift my gaze back up to him.

Our hands flat on the table inch closer to each other, his index finger lifting to slowly caress mine. The simple touch electrifies every nerve in my body. "Yes." The loss of sympathy is evident in his tone.

A faint smirk curves up my lips. "Good."

I pull back from him, standing up from the table as I tousle his hair. "Ready?"

He graces me with a shy smile before getting up, throwing our trash out before escorting me back to the car.

We both seat ourselves inside his car and drive away from the taco truck. His swollen, warm hand finds its way to my thigh, cementing itself there as he traces idle circles over my leggings. His bruised knuckles a testament to his fierce loyalty over me, a hint at his obsession to keep me safe.

And a dark, wicked part of myself—a being whose inner framework is to never allow submission to anyone, clings to the show of his dominance.

CHAPTER 41

"So, that's it?" I ask, pouring myself another glass of sweet red wine.

Dex tilts his head. "Were you anticipating our plan to be a lot more complex?"

I chuckle as I seat myself back down next to him, angling my body to face him as I curl my legs underneath me. "I just didn't think it would be so straight forward." I bring the wine glass to my lips.

He chuckles, the sound causing my belly to do all kinds of flips inside. "Fortunately for us, it will be straightforward. We'll just need to wait until he's off work on Tuesday to do it. I'd rather not be in the area when the news puts out a missing persons report for him." He brings his bourbon to his lips.

He's taking a sip of his drink and I'm instantly turned on like a cat in heat. My thoughts betraying my self restraint by practically begging me to put my ass in his lap.

What would he do with it? Would he just get off to humping me like before? Or would he finally slip my shorts down and slip his cock inside of—

Okay, I need to chill the fuck out.

I nod my head, forcing my sudden horny-crazed self to simmer down. I'm acting like *I'm* the virgin here with how badly I want to climb him like a tree. "That's probably best. And you've already made reservations for our stay Monday?"

He nods. "I reserved a room with two beds. We'll stay overnight, and return as soon as he's in our possession. We'll take him to the funeral home that night."

A tang of disappointment flashes inside of me. *Two* beds? I want to ask if that's really necessary, but I quickly understand. He's a virgin, and even though we fool around, having sex is a big deal for someone who's never done that before. I know the importance and vulnerability that comes with doing it for the first time.

Even as a Succubus who's fluent in the art of seduction and sex, I would never pressure someone to engage in something they weren't ready for. So, I'll let him lead the way with this.

I take another drink of my wine before setting it down on the tray on my ottoman. "Sounds like a date."

He raises a brow. "Have you previously been on a date where you both spent it murdering a man together?"

I laugh as I finger a loose hair back from my cheek. "Maybe I have." I flash a grin at him. "There's still much to me you don't know about."

His arm on the back of the couch bends at the elbow, lifting his hand to my face. His fingers snake themselves through my hair as his voice lowers a notch. "Tell me something I don't know, then."

I lean into his touch, vaguely shrugging a shoulder. "I like to shop."

A half-smirk teases up his lips. "I already knew that." His gaze narrows to my lips. "Tell me something real." Slowly trailing that glacial gaze back up to meet mine.

I loosen a breath as I think of something to say. The first real thing I can think of popping in my head. "I'm kind of a loner. Outside of work and occasionally meeting up with Amelia, I basically keep to myself." I lean myself down, grabbing my wine glass as his fingers slip from my hair. Once I right myself back up against the couch, his fingers go right back to gently touching my hair.

"Does that bother you?" The slight furrow in his brows telling me his question is genuine.

I shake my head. "Not really. I enjoy being by myself. I think that's why I bought a house secluded in the woods." A laugh slips out of me before I lift the wine glass to my lips, taking a sip. "There was a time when the idea of intimacy with another—platonic or more, felt like a chore because of the work I do. Being in the industry can make it difficult to separate yourself from this idea of sex or intimacy feeling performative. It can make it challenging to actually feel real pleasure that comes from *real* intimacy."

He keeps his steady gaze on me as he drinks in my words. "And what changed? How did you get past that hurdle of it feeling performative?"

"Honestly?" I begin. "I've never been one to throw myself into relationships, let alone let a man sleep with me more than once." A moment of silence passes between us as I admit something I don't think I truly internalized until this moment. "It was the night in the hot tub."

I watch him work on a swallow as his breathing slows.

"I don't think I really recognized that intimacy no longer felt performative until the night in your hot tub. For the first time in a long time, the intimacy genuinely felt enjoyable. There were no thoughts of performing—*are* no thoughts of performing when I'm with you." A faint grin curves my lips. "We didn't have sex and it was the most turned on I'd been in a long time. The most present I'd been with someone else."

His fingers in my hair slow as he watches me with an intensity that makes my insides do cartwheels. His hand lowers to my neck, splaying his fingers along the underside of my jaw as he vows, "You never have to perform when you're with me. Whether dancing on stage or fully clothed beside me, you will always have my undivided attention."

I lean into his touch, fluttering my lashes. A grin curves my lips as I notice his eyes have drifted to them again. "Can I ask you a question now?"

His attention on my lips remains there as he hums his response.

"Do you want to kiss me?" My voice barely above a whisper.

That gets him to finally lift his gaze up to me, his voice coming out in a low rumble. "More than anything."

His hand on my neck brings my face to his, crashing my lips into his as he tilts his head to deepen the kiss. I bring my hands to his hair, running my fingers through his dark strands as he lowers me down to my back.

I part my lips open for him as our tongues explore each other. His hands move to my waist as he presses himself into me, feeling his hard cock through his pants. I go to lower a hand down to touch him when he grabs my wrist.

He brings my hand above my head, pinning it there as he lifts his mouth long enough to whisper, "Let me touch you this time." He brings my other hand above my head, his heavy hand pinning both of my wrists. "Let me learn your body."

My stomach dips as his other hand lowers to my navel, slipping itself beneath my silk shorts and slowly slipping a finger down my pussy. My body jerks as he rubs me, slowly and tortuously.

He presses a kiss to my neck, feeling a wicked grin curve itself along my heated skin. "Your heart rate increases when I kiss you like this." He kisses the skin right above my jumping pulse. He brings his thumb to my clit, slowly rubbing me as a moan slips out of my lips. "It thrums even quicker when I touch you like this."

He slips a finger in, pumping me slowly as my legs fall to the sides, widening myself for him.

I writhe against his hand, against the hardness I feel beneath his pants. He groans as he continues fingering me.

"You're already so wet for me. It makes my dick fucking ache." He says as he lowers his hands caging my wrists above my head. "Keep these here."

I nod my agreement as he glides his fingers along the hem of my shirt. Slowly lifting it up as I jerk into his touch.

He lifts my shirt up to my chest, exposing my breasts and caressing a thumb over a hardened nipple.

"Please—" I whisper before a moan slips from my lips, bowing my head back as Dex increases his pace pumping in and out of me. My orgasm building with it.

He presses a kiss to my nipple as I cry out. "Mmm. You're so polite for me, too." His tongue flicks out as he looks up at me, locking gazes as he swirls it around the hardened flesh. Any nervousness he had with touching me the first time has completely disappeared now. "I think as your reward I'll let this pretty pussy cum for me."

He closes his mouth over my nipple, sucking as he pumps his finger in and out of me. His thumb rubbing my clit as I writhe against him. I cry out in pleasure as every nerve in my body lights up, fueling my orgasm as it sends me over the edge. A pleasure that is far different from what I perform on the internet.

What he does to my body, it feels like a spark lighting me up from the inside out. And it feels fucking *amazing*.

He lifts his lips from me, hovering his face over mine as he watches me come undone.

"Cum for me, little jewel. It's just me and you."

My gaze locks onto his, and it burns straight to my soul. "Us," I whisper. "Me and you." A cry wrings from my lips.

I writhe against his finger as I ride my orgasm into oblivion, melting into the couch when my body is finally sated. When I'm finished, he descends his finger from me, then leans down to kiss me softly. His lips continue pressing soft kisses to mine as I feel his hands move to my shirt, pulling it back down over my belly.

At some point he turns me onto my side as he lays down behind me, pulling me close to his chest as he lays the golden blanket over us. And with little effort, I fell deeply asleep in his arms.

CHAPTER 42

I woke up the next day to Dex's arm tucked behind his head, his other hand resting on his lower abdomen. I blink the tiredness from my eyes as I slowly lift myself from the couch, sneaking off of it without stirring him awake.

I grab my phone, seeing the time in the top right corner read twelve-fifty. I grab our glasses from last night and walk them into the kitchen.

I rinse them off before setting them into the dishwasher, heading upstairs to my bathroom to take care of my personal needs and freshen up.

I spit the toothpaste into the sink before setting my toothbrush into the holder, shutting off the light and walking into my bedroom. I open my phone and check my notifications, seeing I got one from my camgirl site. I open the app, cursing under my breath.

Shit, it's Sunday Funday. And I still haven't taken a video yet.

I push my hair away from my cheek, looking over at the doorway. Every Sunday I usually have a video uploaded in the morning as my *Sunday Funday* special. It's usually a video of me fingering myself, or playing with some kind of sex toy. To my surprise it is by far one of the highest selling content that I make.

Probably because most people have off work on Sundays. So what do you do when you're laying around in bed anyway? You scroll.

I lean my head out of the doorway, hearing complete silence from downstairs. I'm sure I could just take something real quick before Dex wakes up. Though I don't need to be secretive about it, I know he's supportive of what I do.

I close my door until only a crack is keeping it from shutting all the way. I grab my tripod and set it in front of my bed, grabbing my digital camera and placing it into the holster. I seat myself onto my bed, and press record.

Usually it takes me a few minutes to get into the *groove*, in which I delete that part out anyway. I hike my legs up, bending at the knees as I warm up.

But thoughts of last night creep back into my mind, making it easy to get myself worked up as I feel myself getting wet already. I bring my hands to my shorts, slipping them off and exposing my pussy to the camera. I lift my shirt up and over my head, completely naked on my bed.

I rub my finger through my wetness before rubbing my clit. "I'm so wet." I say quietly to the camera.

I slip my finger inside as I hear my door creak open.

My eyes widen slightly as Dex walks into my bedroom, watching me with a hunger in his gaze. He takes the chair at the vanity table, turning it around as he seats himself down into it.

"What are you doing?" I blurt out, forgetting I'm still recording.

"I was rudely interrupted last night from watching my favorite show at the club." He lowers his gaze down. "So I'm staying to watch this one."

My hand stills as I bark out a laugh. "Are you—"

"Don't stop." He urges, his voice nothing short of a commanding presence. And I find myself willing to listen. "Keep going." He encourages.

He moves his hands to his pants, my gaze tracking down to his movements. I take notice of the hardness beneath as he grabs himself, letting out a soft groan.

He ensnares my full attention as he unbuttons his pants, pulling them down his legs. His cock bobbing out of his boxer briefs as he pulls those down too. I quickly regain my pace, pumping my finger in and out. He palms himself as he widens his legs.

"Gods, I love to watch you touch yourself." I moan out as wetness pools out of me. My gaze lifts back to the camera even though my words are strictly meant for Dex.

I lower my gaze to watch him stroke himself, slowly to start. His gaze alternates from me to my pussy, reminding me what he said last night. The truths I uttered as well.

That when we're together, it's just me and him.

He pumps himself harder, pre-cum glistening at the tip of his cock. How badly I want to lick it off of him right now.

We both continue touching ourselves, rolling my head back as I come close to climaxing but forcing myself to keep my gaze on him nonetheless. I want to watch him cum.

He pumps himself faster as I do the same, crying out as release finds me. Glancing up at the camera as I cum on my fingers before lowering my attention back down to Dex.

He presses his lips together to stifle the moans I know want to burst out. Cum shoots out of the tip, spilling onto his abdomen as his chest rises and falls quickly. He jerks into his palm, leaning his head back until his dick goes limp in his hand.

I keep my gaze on the camera for a few more moments before I stop the recording, standing up from my bed.

I walk over to Dex, lifting his gaze up to me. He lowers a hand to my navel, trailing a finger down my skin until he lowers it to my pussy. I moan softly as he runs it through my wetness before bringing it to his lips.

I do the same to him and trail my finger along the trail of cum on his lower abdomen, his gaze cemented on mine as he watches me bring my finger to my lips. Tasting him as he tastes me.

My lips make a popping noise as I release my finger from my lips. "Thanks for joining."

He watches me like he's the predator and I'm his prey. And for a moment, he doesn't respond. His finger tentatively lowers from his mouth, as if he can't believe he's tasting me for the first time. That fire in his eyes only intensifies as he says gruffly, "Anytime."

He gets up from the chair as we both walk into my bathroom, cleaning ourselves up. "I just have to upload that onto my computer and then I'll be free."

Dex nods his head. "I'll make us some coffee in the meantime."

He walks out of the bathroom as I call out for him. "Dex."

He turns around, stepping towards me.

"It truly doesn't bother you what I do?"

Usually men say they have no problem with women doing sexwork for a living. Until weeks later they suddenly start acting cold and resentful towards you. Giving you the cold shoulder, expecting you to try and figure out what their hissy fit is for. It's hard to come by someone that actually supports sexworkers, but Dex has given me no indication he's bothered by it.

Even if he were, I'd still be doing sexwork because it's how *I* choose to make money. I'll never let a man talk me out of what makes me feel powerful and in full control of my own bodily autonomy.

He stands there, staring at me for a moment before closing the distance between us. Tiny bumps raise along the back of my neck as he caresses a hand to my cheek. "Like I said. You never have to perform, or be something that you're not when you're around me." He lowers his hand. "I do not pick and choose the parts of you I care for and accept. And I have no intention of making you compromise with anything that makes you feel whole."

He walks out of the room as I stand there watching him leave, finding myself clinging to his every word as he makes his way downstairs.

Because I know with full confidence that he meant every word.

CHAPTER 43

Dexter

After Cyn and I shared coffee and breakfast together, it was time for me to return home to get ready for the day and tend to some business with Sawyer.

Unfortunately.

I wanted nothing more than to spend the next several hours snuggling with her on the couch, wrapping my arms around her and smelling her sweet jasmine-scented skin. But I didn't bring an overnight bag—as I hadn't planned to spend the night, so therefore I didn't have a change of clothes or most importantly, a toothbrush.

Hopefully I didn't have bad breath around her. I checked my breath when she wasn't looking and smelt nothing other than coffee. Hopefully I wasn't wrong in my assessment.

I open the front door, closing it behind me and slipping my shoes off on the antique entryway rug.

I walk across the marbled floor and head up the curved iron staircase. I catch my reflection in the large iron vintage mirror hanging above a half-moon table, a vase of chrysanthemums partially blocking the left corner of the mirror. Sconces mounted on either side of the mirror against cream colored walls.

I walk down the hallway until I come to a mahogany door, pushing it open to see Sawyer sitting behind his executive desk. He looks up, flicking his amber gaze to the manilla folder in my hands. "What did you find?"

I set the folder on his desk, Sawyer flipping it open as I debrief the contents of what's inside.

He closes the file, setting it aside. Sunlight from the nearby window glints off of his silver rings as he flexes his hand, lifting a thumb to crack his knuckles. He leans back into his leather chair, folding his hands on his lap as he says calmly, "Alert me to any new developments. I want to keep a close eye on their whereabouts."

I nod. "Understood."

He lifts his stern gaze up to me again. "When do you leave?"

"Monday afternoon."

He nods slowly. "Keep it clean. Don't draw any unnecessary attention." He opens a bottom drawer, setting the file into it before locking it again. "I'll see you Wednesday."

I nod my agreement before walking out of his office, ending our brief meeting.

When Cyn came to me about Jerome, I let Sawyer know the magnitude of my relationship with her. Not the part of our intimacy, but about helping her track down the man responsible for stealing and leaking her content. If there's anything I've learned from working side-by-side with the boss of The Deimari Mafia, it's that he wants to be in the loop about everything. He hates surprises and—most importantly, wants to make sure no decision puts his family's life in jeopardy.

I kind of can't blame him for that. This isn't a lifestyle that most can stomach, bringing with it an element of danger that's sometimes unavoidable. Most of his motives are centered around keeping his family safe, and he especially takes protecting Priscilla very seriously.

I think that's why he's accepting of this hit Cyn and I are placing on Jerome. Because if the roles were reversed for him, he'd handle it no differently.

After I packed some clothes and other necessities into a black duffel bag, I retreated to my basement. Letting the silence of the space around me quiet my mind as I make the final touches on my drawing.

I stand back from the large canvas, roaming over the entirety of it as I check for any imperfections. After I fix a few areas I look at the time in the top right corner of my phone. Eleven-twenty. Cyn would've just gotten to work a few hours ago.

I hope she's having a good night.

I open up our text thread, sending a message to her. *How is your night going?*

She must've already had her phone in her hands because she sends a reply a few moments later. *Lame. I'm ready to go home.*

I chuckle to myself. *Are the frat guys being selfish with their money?*

I can practically feel the glare in her response. *As if they aren't always.*

The grin on my lips stays as I go into my banking app, sending a wire transfer to Cyn's bank account. The notification for my deposit pops up, alerting me that my transfer of eight hundred dollars was successful.

How about now?

She heart reacts to my message. *This is why I keep you around. ;)* A black heart emoji at the end of her text.

Is that the only reason?

It takes her a few minutes to reply, but when she does, that silly grin on my face widens. *No. Xoxo*

I lower myself back down into my chair, leaning my calves on the edge of my table. *Are you all packed and ready for tomorrow?*

She replies back. *......no*

Why haven't you packed yet?

Because I've been busy. I can practically hear the attitude.

Busy with what? You don't go in for work until nine-thirty. You had all day after I left to pack.

I might have been sleepy, and taken a nap.

I raise a brow at my phone. *For three hours?*

......possibly.

I bark out a laugh as I shake my head. *I'll be there at two to pick you up. We're getting your bag packed tonight after work.*

Fine. Whatever you say.

Her words have the opposite effect of what she probably intended. A chill races down my spine at the heated promise. *Don't tempt me.*

Tempt you how? A black heart emoji at the end of her text.

Oh, this woman is trouble. *Finish your shift and I'll see you later.*

Yes, sir. ;)

Heat rushes to both of my heads when I read that text. I set my phone down and get myself together.

This woman will be both the awakening, and the death of me.

CHAPTER 44

Cynthia

"Awe, you guys are all matching." I hook my bare leg over my knee, bringing my hands together as I smirk at the men seated on the couch in front of me. "My girlfriends and I do that, too."

The four frat boys all turn their heads to look at each other, one of them scoffing at me as another becomes visibly annoyed. "It wasn't planned."

Right. As I'm sure it also wasn't planned for the four of you to have nearly identical hair cuts.

I glance down at their muted light-red shorts, each of them rising above their kneecaps. My gaze lowers to the sandals on their feet, one man's toes longer than mine with overgrown toenails.

He could really hurt someone with those fuckers.

"Do your girlfriends also show off their bodies for money?" The one to the far left asks, a smug grin curving his face.

Awe, I really did hurt his feelings.

When these men asked to buy a VIP room with me, I watched in disgust as they all pulled out their wallets. Each of them chipped in to afford the room, and I noted that they had nothing left in their wallets afterwards.

I maybe would've been a bit more grateful for the money had I not heard them talking badly about Amelia when I was standing behind them with another gentleman.

"You just know that she sleeps with anyone who gives her the time of day. She definitely can't get a good man in her life because of what she does." One of them had said.

"Yeah, she's hot though." Another had remarked.

Oh, how they were so incredibly wrong in their misogynistic assumptions.

So, I took the money and got the room. They think they've bought a room with a woman who won't talk back, but little do they know I'm a misandrist who will have them weeping through their fragile egos after I'm finished with them.

"Yes, because men like you continue to be a constant consumer. Though, most men can actually afford my time without needing to lean on their friends" I lower my hand down, placing it on my chest. "But don't worry," I begin as I tilt my head, frowning slightly. "I understand times can be tough, so I greatly sympathize with those less fortunate than others."

The one on the far left looks at me through bushy eyebrows. I see the tension creep into his jaw as he clenches it.

Gosh, they're so sensitive. I love exploiting it.

"Because we're in college, you know. So we can get *real* jobs one day." The one next to him says, laughing with his friends.

I tilt my head, amusement sparking. "Let me guess....you're all majoring in either finance or criminal justice. Studying to be lawyers, perhaps?"

When he gives me a smug nod, I continue.

"So even when you land a job after college—if you do, that is. You'll still be left with probably eighty to one-hundred thousand dollars in debt. And at the rate you're all going, I can't imagine any woman would want to settle down with men who view women through such an objectifying lens. So that second income that you're wishfully hoping for, to help keep you afloat while you pay back your loans, probably isn't going to pan out the way you hoped it would." I lean down to grab my drink, lifting it to my lips. "So, while you'll barely be hanging by a thread paying back your debt, I'll continue making riches in my skimpy outfits."

He goes to stand up when my Succubus power reaches for him instantly, a reaction I fully expected. He stops and waits for my beck and call, my further instruction. "Sit." I compel him.

He does as I say, seating himself back down. I link my power to the other three men, holding all four of them under my mental grasp.

"Now, tell me why you all *really* bought this VIP tonight."

The one on the far right answers. "We made a bet that whoever got you to do things to them first would get fifty bucks."

I hiss through my teeth. "Only fifty dollars? Sheesh, I think I'm a little offended that you bet so low on me boys."

I stand up from the round-backed chair, walking over to seat myself onto the glass coffee table in front of them. "That is a nice bet. But I think I'd like to make my own now."

I pull out four hundred dollars, setting it down onto the glass surface. "I'll split this between the two of you who share a kiss—no, better yet." A devilish smirk crawls up my lips. "The two who make out with each other. I'm really into tongue action."

I release my power from them, their eyes darting between each other as I notice two of them have put distance between the other.

A sinister laugh escapes my lips. "What's wrong? No interest in making a little cash tonight?" I lean closer to them as I whisper. "I'm sure this could go a long way since—you know, you spent your last dollars on this slut tonight."

The one on the far left tries to get up again when my energetic claws latch onto them all. "No one leaves this room until the money is collected."

He lowers himself back into the seat, confusion and worry rippling on his face. "Why can't I get up?"

I shrug my shoulders. "Because I compelled you, and you have to do what I say until I lift it. But don't worry," I add on. "You will not be afraid."

The five of us sit in silence for what seems like a small eternity. I tap my acrylic nails onto the glass surface. "Don't worry, what happens here will stay here." I smirk. "I'll give you the option you wouldn't have given me. I'll let you choose."

One man seated in the middle with russet brown hair turns to a blonde guy next to him, lowering his voice as if I couldn't hear them. "Bro, we could use the money to go to—"

"I'm not making out with you." The blonde one seethes, puffing his chest out.

The guy with russet hair lowers his voice even further, his words barely audible. "Come one. It wouldn't be the first—"

"Shut up." The blonde seethes, clenching his teeth.

Oh, this is even better than I thought.

They bicker with one another as the two on the ends lean back, whispering to one another. "Bro, did you know about this?" One whispers to the other.

He shakes his head as the russet-haired one in the middle lowers a hand to the other's thigh.

I smell the heightened arousal coming from the blonde man.

"No one else has to know." The russet-haired one says.

They both gaze at each other for a long moment before the blonde man pulls him in, his lips crashing with his. It starts off slow and tentative, but quickly becomes passionate as their lips part open.

The hand on the blonde one's thigh moves to his cock, grabbing him as he groans into his touch.

The two on the ends watch in disbelief.

He jerks into his touch, deepening the kiss before remembering that they aren't alone.

They both quickly pull away from each other, looking at me with lust and shame in their eyes. Looks like they haven't quite come to terms with their sexuality yet.

I clap my hands together before grabbing the money. "Excellent job, boys. I knew you had it in you." I hand them the money as I stand up. "You will not remember that I compelled you at all tonight, that everything you did was of free will."

They stare at me as I begin walking to the door, turning around once more. "Put the money to good use boys. Oh, and feel free to use the room a little longer." I wink at the two in the middle. "There's nothing wrong with being gay. Embrace it."

I exit the VIP room, a few seconds later when my compulsion has completely lifted, I hear their voices stream down the hallway. Mostly in denial that what happened actually did.

I look down at my phone, sending Dex a text. *Come get me now. I'm leaving an hour early.*

I head to the locker room as I meet with Vivianne. "Hi, mama."

She gives me a warm smile as she comes around her desk. "I understand, dear. Just pay me and then you can leave."

"Ugh, thank you. I love you." I pull out my money, handing her tip out to her. "I'll see you Thursday."

She takes the money, nodding her head. "Be safe, dear."

I exit out of her office and go to my locker, changing out of my dance outfit and throwing on a pair of sweat pants and a T-shirt. My phone buzzes and I look down at Dex's reply.

I'm on my way.

CHAPTER 45

Dex raises an eyebrow at me. "We're staying for only one night?"

I look over at him, tilting my head in confusion. "And?"

A chuckle escapes from his lips as he holds my travel bag open. "You've packed *four* different outfits."

Shrugging my shoulders, I grab a pair of silk pajamas and toss those in there, too. "I need to have options."

Since we got back to my place we've been packing up my bag—or rather he's been holding it open, watching me while I stuff things inside of it.

He looks down at the silk pajama set. "You already packed a pair of pajamas."

"That is a set with long-sleeves and pants. This one is a cami and short set." I kneel down next to him, assessing what I've put in already. "I may get warm and want to change."

He graces me with another one of his soft chuckles, breathy and rich like the bourbon he's been drinking.

I move to my bathroom to pack in all of my feminine toiletries. Shoving my hair dryer, straightener, skin care and body lotion before zippering it up.

"There. All packed." I drop the oversized black bag to the ground as it makes a generous thud.

I jump up onto my bed, sprawling out as I lower myself beneath the covers. "This is going to be so fun." A surge of giddiness bursting through me.

At Dex's silence I look over at him, noticing him still standing there. I pat the spot next to me. "You can stand there all night if you want. Or you can be a normal person like me and get some sleep?"

I watch his gaze move to where my hand is, and become wholly aware of one realization.

He's never slept in my bed before.

After what I assume is him internally battling with a mild freak-out session, he finally comes around to the other side and pulls the covers back. He lifts his shirt off and climbs into bed.

I turn onto my side to face him, the bed dipping beneath him as I tuck a hand underneath my pillow. "Have you ever slept next to a girl before?"

He turns to face me, leaning his head against the pillow as he shakes his head. "This would be the first."

Something inside of me both lights up and melts at his response. Feeling flattered that I'm the first one to share this experience with him. "Well, I promise I'll keep my paws to myself." A yawn escapes from my lips.

He chuckles as he lowers a hand beneath his pillow, his fingers bumping into mine. He reaches out and curls his hand over mine. "Goodnight, Cyn.

I close my eyes as I grin into my pillow, the warmth of his skin settling against mine. The heat of his body cradling me like a cocoon beneath the covers. "Goodnight, Dex."

Knowing that I'm safe in his presence, it takes me no time to fall asleep. And when I wake up in the morning, I feel the weight of his hand still holding mine.

I lean the car seat back, hiking my knees up to my chest as I open the window a crack. Fresh air rushing in, blowing the wispy strands of my bangs back. I lower my hand into the plastic bag, pulling out a crispy hot chip. I plop it in my mouth as Dex lowers his hand inside.

I look over at him. "You said you didn't want any."

He plops a chip into his mouth. "I lied."

I roll my eyes as I turn the radio on. "I like you and all but I cannot spend the next two and a half hours driving in silence."

That gets him to look over at me, flashing me a grin as he asks, "You like me?"

A sudden weight drops down to the pit of my stomach. I hide my own shock that I said that by rolling my eyes at him—again, as I toss another chip into my mouth. "Whatever. You know what I meant."

That smirk on his face only grows as I flip through the music, bored with everything that's playing. When I notice he has an aux cord I grab it, plugging it into my phone.

I flip through my music playlists, choosing a song. I set my phone down as the music starts building up.

He looks over at me as I start singing my heart out to the song, watching me as if he wants to join in but just won't let himself.

I start dancing in my seat as I let the music carry me, not giving a damn about how I look. To my surprise, minutes later, I hear a voice chiming in with mine.

I look up at him as he belts out the lyrics, wringing a full-bellied laugh from me. He keeps singing completely off key as I chime back in with him.

For the remainder of the car ride there, we laugh and sing our hearts out.

CHAPTER 46

Dexter

I carry both of our bags to the front counter, the chandelier high above us adding to the luxurious aesthetic of the hotel.

"Good afternoon, how may I help you?" The clerk behind the marbled counters asks. Her dark hair pulled back into a sleek bun.

"Reservation for Lacroix." I say as I set our things on the ground.

The clerk's green eyes roam over her computer screen as I look over at Cynthia. Her curious gaze has wandered over to the glass doors at the opposite end of the hotel.

I turn my gaze back to the clerk when a worried look flashes across her face. "Yes, we do have your reservation here, Mr. Lacroix. There does seem to be a bit of a booking error that is completely on our end, and we've had to accommodate your room for a different one."

That brings Cynthia's attention back over.

"As long as it's the same kind of suite, that will be fine." I say as I lower down to grab our belongings.

"Yes—see, that is the issue here." The clerk bites her inner lip. "It appears we have run into some plumping issues in the suite we booked you for. So we've had to switch you to a suite of the same size, just a one bedroom instead of a two."

It was easy not to fool around with Cyn last night because she wasn't the only one who was tired. I was beat, and honestly...it was really nice to just sleep next to her.

But I booked a two bedroom for a reason. So I could keep *my* paws to myself. But you're telling me that now we have to share one bed together, *and* have to somehow find a way to kill the time together until tomorrow?

I'm in deep shit. Horny, deep shit.

"That will be fine, thank you." Cyn says for me, my tongue suddenly heavy in my mouth.

I nod my head to the clerk as she hands our key cards to Cyn. I grab our bags and we head to the nearest elevator.

The stainless steel doors part open as we step inside, revealing tall vertical walls with shiny, reflective metal. I lean my back up against the metal railing while Cyn pushes the silver button for the eighth floor. The space around the button turns yellow and the elevator begins to rise.

Cyn turns around, giving me one of her infamous looks that tells me she's about to try and push my buttons. "A two bed suite was unnecessary anyway."

"It was necessary." I counter as I fix my attention on the wall, dropping our bags.

I see myself reflected back with little to no restrictions, as if I'm looking at myself through a mirror. I lower my gaze back to her when I feel her approach me.

She raises a brow. "Does this mean you're going to be weird and say you'll sleep on the floor now?"

I lean my head closer to her, tilting it. "And if I did?"

She laughs as she pats my shoulder.

Pats me as if I'm a dog or something. Though at this rate I might as well be one. Like a damn mutt, my loyalty extends to her and her only. My life now revolves around being faithful to her, serving and protecting her.

Hell, I'd probably roll around and beg for a treat if she asked me to.

"There's no reason why you can't sleep in a perfectly good bed with me." She goes to turn back around before I grab her arm, twirling her back to face me.

I lower my face to hers as her breath catches in her chest. Sending a coil of heated delight over my skin at her reaction. A darkness welled deep inside of me begs to be released. "I will make one thing clear while we're here, little jewel." I pull her closer until our lips are almost touching. "I need to focus while we're here." I loosen a breath. "If we're going to pull this off, I can't get distracted. And if I lay in that bed with you, feeling your soft body touch mine—"

A deep growl gets trapped behind my teeth. My voice dropping as I say, "We'll never leave that room."

Her gaze lowers to my lips, loosening a trembling breath. I take one whiff and smell her arousal.

Gods, I want to fucking taste it—

No, cut that shit out. We need to focus.

I release her arm, lowering to grab our bags when the elevator dings the arrival to our floor. She steps back from me as we both step out of the elevator.

Thank fuck.

We head down the hallway, approaching our suite on the right-hand side. Cyn presses the key card up to the door sensor, a green light flashing before she pushes the door open.

"This is nice." She coos. We both walk inside and explore the suite.

As soon as you step in you're greeted with a short hallway leading you to an open concept. Through a room on the right hand side is the bathroom, adorned with a white clawfoot tub and a stand up shower at the far wall. Two sinks next to each other beneath a large mirror.

I set our things down in the main room, looking up at the floor to ceiling windows throughout. My gaze lowers to the ivory lounge chair situated next to a wide table before moving over to the king sized bed.

Cyn appears next to me, catching where my gaze has gone. I look over at her.

Just for sleeping. The words in my head sound like a weak, brittle vow.

I drop our bags down next to the bed, going into the bathroom and turning on the lights. I scope out the room before Cyn breaks the silence.

"Are you really checking the rooms right now?"

I give a final glance over before turning the light off, stepping back into the main room. "One can never be too sure." I assess the rest of the suite.

She scoffs at me. "A little excessive."

I approach her, and unbeknownst to myself I find myself reaching out for her. Tucking her hair back behind her ear. "Nothing is ever excessive when it comes to you."

We both stand there for a small eternity as I lower my fingers down her neck, her chest rising at tiny bumps raise along her skin. I want to kiss her again, kiss her a thousand more times.

But my desire for her is too strong right now, and I can't be sure that I'll be disciplined enough to end it with one kiss.

Tension thickens in the air between us before she takes an unsteady breath in, blowing it out. "Well, I don't know about you. But I'm starving." She steps back from me and walks over to her bag.

This woman is always hungry. I oddly find it cute.

"I saw there was a restaurant downstairs." She grabs it, lifting it up onto the bed. "I'm gonna change, but when I'm finished, I hope you'll be on board with getting some grub."

I nod, softly chuckling. "Of course."

She slips off into the bathroom to freshen up and change, leaving me out here to wait for her.

Like the good dog that I am.

CHAPTER 47

I bring the glass of bourbon to my lips, notes of clove and cinnamon settling on my tongue. I rest my arm on the back of the red tufted sectional as the waitress delivers another round of drinks, setting them down onto the wood table. "Can I get you two anything else?"

I look over at Cyn as she shakes her head. "Thank you."

The kind waitress dips her head into a quick bow before excusing herself from our section.

What we thought was a restaurant was more of a jazz-inspired lounge. A large open space with dim lighting throughout, giving the ashen walls a red and golden hue. Carved into the brick walls are deep arches revealing tall windows that showcase the clear night sky. At the far wall ahead of us guests crowd around a U-shaped counter, the bartender behind it moving with the grace of a cat as he fulfills drink orders. A small group of women lean in towards one another as they pass excited stares at the handsome man.

"It's really busy for a Monday night." Cyn remarks as she brings her margarita to her lips, the salt on the rim caught between her red lips. She looks up at me through darkened lashes with winged black liner on the crease of her eyelids.

After she steals a sip she licks the salt from her lips, careful not to smudge her lipstick. My discipline fails me as I lower my gaze, watching her hook her leg over her knee, baring half of her porcelain thigh to me.

I refocus my gaze. "When I booked our reservation, I was made aware a convention was going on this week." I take another drink before setting my bourbon down onto the table. "If it's too much we can go back to the room."

"No, it's fine." She says quickly. She begins to do a little happy dance in her seat as she sips her drink. "The vibes are immaculate in here."

I chuckle as I silently admire her, a flush of warmth settling in my chest that has nothing to do with the alcohol. "Yeah, it is pretty nice in here."

But you look far nicer, I almost say.

Tonight she's wearing this tight fitting, strappy black dress. The velvet material shapes her body like an hourglass, accentuated by a pair of close-toed, black high heels on her feet. When she came out of the bathroom fully dressed, I nearly fell to my knees in awe. While my foolish, starstruck heart was beating a mile a minute, I had to keep my legs from trembling like twin branches being hurled against a windstorm.

"Come on." She says, pulling me from my thoughts as she stands up from her seat. Her dress smooths out, laying like silk against her body as she steps in front of me.

I raise a brow as she holds a hand out for me.

She huffs out an exaggerated exhale as she grabs my hand, hurling me up onto my feet. "I want to dance." She turns around, pulling us out of the section when I gently haul her back.

She whips her gaze up to mine, and that quick rush of annoyance in her gaze radiates a wicked heat along my bones. And gods, a day doesn't go by that I don't thank the universe for bestowing upon me with such a fiery woman.

I reach for our drinks, placing hers in her hand. "These come with us then. I don't trust anyone here to leave these unattended."

That annoyance in her gaze melts into a softness I've never seen before. She stares at me for only a few seconds, and in those silent moments, the rest of the establishment fades away into a void of nothingness.

Because when we're together, it's just us. Enthrallingly, and consumingly so.

A wide smirk curves her lips as mischief dances in her eyes. "Fine." She brings the glass to her lips and starts chugging the margarita.

I tug the glass away from her lips, my brows raised. "Are you trying to get sick later this evening?"

She snorts out a laugh, and it soothes my sudden concern. "I have a high tolerance, remember?" She winks.

"And I don't want to carry this around, so—" She brings the margarita to her lips again. "I'm going to finish it off."

I watch in shock as she downs the entire drink, setting the empty glass on the table. "Come on." She says as she glances at my bourbon. She makes a pouty face at me as she tempts me. "Unless you can't hang." She turns on her heels and walks out of my reach, through the open archway and out to the dancefloor.

Oh, she's tempting me alright.

I down the last half of my drink, setting the glass down before submerging myself into the crowd of people as I go in search of her.

Like a moth to a flame, I find her within seconds and stalk over to her. She turns around, swaying her hips as she winks at me. She presses her manicured hands on her body like she's enchanting me into her trap.

And I willingly allow myself to fall prisoner to it.

I stand behind her, stuck there like a statue as my senses remain on high alert. The ceiling above us is decorated with silver discoballs, tiny slivers of light reflecting out but leaving the dancefloor mostly dimmed.

A woman in front of Cyn backs into her, pushing her right into my chest. I quickly reach my hand out to steady her, my hand gripping her hip.

The woman quickly turns around and apologizes. "I'm so sorry!" Her lithe hand raised up to her mouth.

"It's fine." Cyn says before the woman merges through the sea of bodies, leaving us.

I go to remove my hand from her hip but Cyn grabs my wrist and pushes my hand back down. I take a shaky breath in as I let my fingertips glide up the soft velvet, feeling the rise in her chest against mine as I obey her command.

The breath in my lungs slows to an almost nothingness as I realize just how close she is to me right now. The curve of her ass pressed right up against me.

My chest sinks as I loosen my breath, trying to contain that desire raging within. I lower my gaze to my hand still on her hip, watching as I lower it a few inches down until my fingers are brushing her thigh.

I play with the hem of her dress, trailing a finger beneath the fabric then stopping when she gasps at my touch. I can't do what I want to her here, not with—

My attention is quickly snagged from my thoughts as she begins slowly rolling her hips to the music. Rolling her hips *into* me.

I lower my head to her ear, pressing my fingers into her hip to steady her. Or rather, to steady myself. "What are you doing?"

She turns her head to the side, her lips tauntingly inches from mine as she whispers, "Dancing."

She faces forward again as she continues dancing on me. The song changes and her ass continues slowly grinding into me, matching the sensual beat of the music. I know she feels me rock hard beneath my pants, feels the way my chest has stilled completely against her back.

I lift my gaze up to the sea of bodies around us, everyone lost in their own worlds to chance a glance over at us. I work on a swallow as I loosen my grip on her hip, and move my hips with hers as I let go to this moment—*our* moment of feverish bliss.

The bass to the song is no match for the buzzing in my ears, the throbbing in my dick as she dips low to the ground and brings herself back up. Slowly gliding her ass up into me.

Fuck, she's so good to me.

I grip my hand into her hip again, pressing her closer to me as I move my other hand down to her navel. I feel her breath hitch, and I almost wish someone would turn around and look at how beautiful she looks dancing on me right now.

That resistance to seize the moment—seize what I *need*, evades me completely.

I lower my head down to her neck, my lips pressed up to her ear. "I should have my way with you right here, in front of all of these people."

Her pulse begins to race against my lips. I grin in response as my blood thrums with wicked delight.

She continues grinding into me as I whisper, "Take them off."

Her breath hitches in response, and it wakes up every last sleepy nerve. "What?"

My hand on her navel lowers down, my index finger touching her over the dress. I slowly caress side to side as I rumble against her ear. "You know what. Give them to me."

She slows her pace down as she slips her hands beneath her dress, bending down at the waist as she lowers a black lace thong down her perfect legs. Her ass presses right into my hard cock, and I suddenly want to know what it's like to see her on all fours, caged beneath my body while I ram my dick inside of her as I whisper sweet promises in her ear.

"Fuck," I mutter beneath my breath, gripping her hips with both hands now.

She slowly brings herself back up, lowering her thong into my hand as her back presses into my chest again. She turns her head as she asks in a breathy voice. "Happy?"

I grip them in my hands before tucking them into my pants. "Extremely." I groan.

I feel pre-cum bead at the tip of my cock, begging to be released. And there's no self-control left in me now that's able to wait until we get back to the room.

I guide her to keep rocking against me, my need turning feral as my orgasm climbs hotly to the surface. Fuck, she gets me going with little to no effort. All she has to do is just touch me and I'm raging with desire.

I feel my body tense up as she keeps going, teasing me to the edge. "You like that?" She asks in a breathy tone.

"Mmm. You know I do." My voice rumbling against her skin.

She gasps as I grip her hips, rocking against her. The thought of sinking my dick deep inside of her tight little pussy has me spilling inside of my pants. I try to keep my whimpering at bay, my eyes from shutting closed as hot release finds me on the dancefloor. And I swear I hear a soft moan slip from her lips as I cum against her.

After I've finished and my grip on her hips releases, she turns around, lowering a hand to the wetness beneath. I groan at her touch, my hips jerking as she grins up at me. "Good thing you're wearing black." She says before she abruptly pulls away from me, and slips herself through the crowd. Vanishing from my line of sight entirely.

The laugh that was about to slip from my lips dies on the tip of my tongue as I leave the dancefloor and follow in search of her. What a devious, pretty little thing she is to make me cum in public and then make me chase after her afterwards.

A game of cat and mouse that I'll always *thoroughly* enjoy playing into.

Thank fuck it's too dark in here for the wet spot on my pants to be all that visible. I hurry past bodies standing around full sections and find her leaving through the glass doors. When she looks back to see me right on her tail, she hurries down the brightly lit main lobby, rushing over to the elevator at the end of the hall.

Seconds after she slips through I hold my hand out, halting the shiny steel elevator doors from closing in on me. She looks up at me with anticipation in her eyes as I advance on her, pushing her back into the metal railing as the doors close behind us.

I capture her lips with mine as I hike her leg up, wrapping it around me as I press my body flush against hers. Her breathy moan gets trapped in my mouth as I grind into her, nowhere near finished with her yet.

My hand lowers to her thigh, her skin as soft as silk beneath my touch. I lift my hand up higher until I'm cupping her ass.

That cage I've sheltered myself in for years breaks wide open. Leaving nothing left behind but a feral, unrelenting beast.

I bring my fingers to her pussy, rubbing the wetness gathering there. I circle my thumb around her clit. "I need this pretty pussy to be ready for me. Because tonight, I'm not satisfied with just touching her."

She gasps as I slip my finger inside of her, stretching what's been made for *me*. I grin against her neck as I say roughly, "I need to fucking taste her."

The elevator chimes behind us, the doors opening up as I haul her up. Hiking her legs around my waist as I carry her down the hall. Her hands on my face bring my lips to hers as I press her up against the hallway wall, lowering my hand to my pocket.

I quickly pull out the key, pressing it up to the sensor as I hurry us both inside. The ferocity of my impatience to touch her, to taste her on my lips leaves my mind dizzy with untamed need. My nerves firing with the potency of electricity raging along my body.

I walk us over to the bed, dumping her body onto the silk sheets. She looks up at me as she balances her weight on her elbows, her face flushed and—*fuck,* it makes me ache.

I unbutton my pants, lowering them down my waist. "Are you going to be a good girl for me tonight?"

She nods eagerly as she tracks my movements. "Yes, sir."

That primitive darkness that's laid untouched, unprovoked for a long time floods to the surface. Wrapping and coiling itself around every tether of uncertainty, breathing life into the intimacy I've longed denied myself. And by the fire in her gaze, I don't have to wonder if she'll willingly fuel that craving.

She wants this as badly as I do.

I bring her head to my cock, pressing her cheek up against the damp release on my boxer briefs. "Feel that, little jewel?" I shift her head, pressing her lips there. "That's what you do to me."

She goes to lick me when I pull her face away, shoving my briefs down and lifting my shirt off. She stares at me with a hunger in her gaze that I want to fuel, that I want to feed for the rest of my life.

I palm myself as I lower down to my knees, pulling her close to the edge of the bed. I hike her dress up to her belly, my voice full of sinister smoke. "Take your dress off."

She does what I ask, lifting her dress up over her head and tossing it nearby. My gaze cements itself on her perfect breasts. My cock twitching in my palm as I press a kiss to her hard nipple, her back bowing into me.

I groan my yearning as I lower myself down, kissing her navel before gripping her legs and spreading them wide open. She leans back onto her elbows to hold herself up as I push her legs back, completely exposing herself to me. I stare down at her pussy, glistening and waiting for me to taste her. The worry of how good I'll be my first time no longer playing a role in my thoughts.

Because right now, I'm being guided solely by pure, primal need.

I press a kiss between her pussy lips, wringing a moan from her. A tight shiver runs down my back as her wetness coats my lips. I lick her sweet nectar as I growl. "Fuck."

I grip her hips as I descend my mouth on her.

CHAPTER 48

Cynthia

I'm not sure when exactly I brought this side of Dex out, but I'm thanking the fucking universe for finally showing me this other side of him.

Unrelenting, unforgiving in his pursuit to please me.

As his mouth descended on me he went right to tasting me. Rubbing his tongue along my entrance, licking and drinking everything I had to give to him. Exploring and learning my body, watching me with a steady gaze as he figured out what made my body jerk, my legs twitch as I come apart.

I cry out as he lowers his tongue inside of me, moving it in and out as I spill myself onto him. I feel my orgasm build hotly within me as he rubs his thumb over my clit.

I cry out. "Suck my clit."

He continues dipping his tongue in and out of me, as if he can't seem to pull himself away. And when I catch a glance down at him, I realize by the way his eyes are nearly rolling in the back of his head that he can't.

"Finger me while you suck my clit." I order him.

A grin curves up his lips as he finally does what I say. His tongue descends out of my pussy as he begins twirling it around my clit, sucking the sensitive flesh as he lowers a finger inside of me.

"*Yes.*" I hiss out, writhing against him.

He pumps his finger in and out with a delicious pace, wetness dripping out of me as my orgasm teeters the surface. I cry out as I climax, watching him as he continues sucking my clit. I bring both of my hands to his head, holding him as I rock against his mouth and finger.

I scream out his name as I ride my orgasm, falling limp to the bed several long moments later. He slowly descends his finger out of me as he releases his mouth from my clit.

He starts devouring everything that I have, drinking every last drop that drips from me. I gasp as a groan gets trapped between his lips.

When he's finally finished, he hovers above me as he presses a kiss to my lips. He lowers down to kiss my neck, wringing a breathy moan from me.

"So what do I taste like?" I whisper.

He lifts his head up from my neck, hovering his lips above mine as he vows with absolute certainty, "Like mine."

His oath leaves a heated brand along my skin, one that I don't ever want to be parted from.

He goes to kiss my lips when I stop him, whispering huskily, "Turn me around."

He leans back, tilting his head at my request.

I lower myself down onto the bed. He sits back, watching me turn my body so my head is laying at the edge of the bed. I bring my legs up, bending at the knees. "I'm not finished with you."

His piercing blue eyes slowly roam over my body before cementing his gaze on my pussy laid bare for him again.

"Taste me, while I taste you."

His gaze drifts back down to me, noticing I've leaned my head slightly off the bed now. I watch his chest sink suddenly as he releases a staggering breath. He stands up, towering over me as his cock bobs in front of my mouth.

I expect him to hesitate, to ask me if I'm sure. But whatever part of him that's broken wide open has him acting out the darkest parts of him. The part of him I want to find safety in me.

And me alone.

I part my lips as he angles his hips down, pressing the tip of his cock to my mouth. His hands move to the sides of my face, his fingers splaying along my jaw as he slowly thrusts himself in, inch by inch.

He barks out a curse, a tremor running along his hands as he thrusts all the way to the hilt.

Sheathing himself down my throat.

He keeps his pace slow to start as I take him greedily. One of his hands lowers to my hair, bunching it up and gripping it as he quickens his pace. "Fuck," he whimpers. "You feel so good."

He looks down at me as I twirl my tongue around his length as take him. "You're going to take every last drop as I fuck your face. Understood?" His voice hovering above a growl.

I hum my agreement as I bring his hands away from my face, lowering them to my breasts. He lets out a ragged breath as he lowers himself down, sucking on a hard nipple. He stays there for only a moment until he lowers himself all the way down. His lips exploring my pussy once again.

His hands grips my thighs, spreading me wide open for him as he quickens his pace, his cock jackhammering into my throat. I bring my hands to his thighs, urging him to go faster, that I can take him. He moans against me as he obeys my silent command.

I gag on his cock as he fucks my face with no restraint. I lower a hand to his balls, gently squeezing them as he curses against me. A whimper escapes from his lips and the sound has me reeling.

His tongue on my pussy descends down lower, and my moan gets trapped against him as he rims the hole below.

Gods, where did he learn this? I didn't expect this from a virgin. But fuck, I—

He sinks a finger deep inside of me, not even easing his way in. But he doesn't have to. I'm already soaked for him.

I moan against his cock as he spills pre-cum down my throat, my throat constricting as I swallow.

"Fuck," He curses as he wraps his arms around my waist, hauling me up against his chest.

I feel us moving until a moment later, I feel my back press up against a hard wall. Dex holding me up as if I weigh no heavier than a feather.

I feel him tense up as he bucks into my mouth. He wraps my legs around his neck as he licks me. "Show me who this pussy is wet for. Cum for me, little jewel."

My orgasm breaks the surface as I cum, Dex drinking every last drop of me. His lips sloppily roam over my pussy as he licks me dry. Shortly after I feel him pulsate in my mouth, spilling his hot seed down my throat as he bucks into me.

"Take it. Fuck—*please*, take it." He whimpers as he holds me up.

I swallow every last drop of him, reveling in the way his body trembles around my lips. He curses under his breath again before walking us back over to the bed. Gently unsheathing himself from my mouth before laying me down on the bed.

He jerks himself off, angling his cock for my mouth as the last of him shoots out. I lick his cum off my lips as I look up at him, staring straight into his soul.

He grips the back of my head, hiking me up onto my knees and kisses me. Tasting himself on my lips.

I pull him down onto me and he obeys. Bringing my arms around his neck, we continue kissing long after his tongue has licked himself from me.

I feel his cock rub against my pussy and writhe into him, wanting him to fill me so badly. "Dex." I whisper.

He looks down at me, seeing the need in my eyes. He knows what I'm about to say, that he can fill me if he wants to. That I'll take every inch of him, if he's ready.

His chest rises and falls as he rubs himself against me, that tether of control visibly slipping. I let him take the reins, showing me what he wants. But after a few moments, I see the hesitation in his eyes. The nerves of having sex for the first time spike in his expression.

I visibly see him begin to battle with it internally. So, I grab his face, stilling myself on the bed. "Hey, it's okay." I whisper before kissing him slowly. Pulling back and keeping his attention on me. "I like touching you just like this. We don't need to change a thing."

I watch that battle within himself lessen, the worry and hesitation in his eyes fading as he takes a deep breath in. Exhaling the shakiness from his body.

"Just kiss me, and think of nothing else." I say, smiling as I caress my thumb along his cheek. "It's just us."

He leans into my touch before he brings his lips back down to mine. His body melts against mine as he kisses me with a passion I've never felt before.

Like my lips are a temple he's vowed to devote himself to eternally.

His calloused hands roam over my shoulders, then down my sides before he's cupping my breasts. I gasp as he lightly traces my hardened nipple. Slowly, torturously touching me as my fingers run through his hair, my back bowing at his unhurried touch.

And in his exploration, I've never felt more alive.

CHAPTER 49

"Room service." A feminine voice says through the door.

I hear his feet padding along the carpet, unlocking the door and quietly pulling it open. The sound of a crisp bill and a metal tray follows.

"Thank you." He whispers before closing the door.

I peel my eyes open to vertical blinds drawn over the floor to ceiling windows, blocking out the sunlight trying to filter in. I feel the mattress dip behind me before an arm wraps around my waist.

I stir awake and turn to face him, wiping the sleep from my eyes. Before I can open my mouth the smell of sweet syrup and fresh strawberries wafts towards me, followed by the smell of rich coffee.

A sleepy smile curves up my face. "Are those pancakes I smell?"

He chuckles, pressing a soft kiss to my forehead. "Maybe." A grin pressing into my skin.

I lift my head up, looking behind him to see a tray of pancakes with fresh strawberries on top, sprinkled with a dusting of powdered sugar. A plate of bacon and scrambled eggs lies next to it, followed by a pitcher of coffee.

I lower my head back down. "How'd you know I loved strawberry pancakes?"

He vaguely shrugs his shoulders. "Lucky guess."

I raise an eyebrow at him.

He pauses before admitting, "I may have seen you making them one morning."

I smirk at him as I shake my head. "Such a creep."

"Whatever." He says before he leans in to kiss me.

I bring my hands to his face, running my fingers through his hair as he deepens the kiss. Several moments later he pulls away. "I'm afraid if we go any further we will never leave this bed. And, unfortunately for him, we have an asshole to take care of today."

I giggle softly. "You're probably right." I free my fingers from his disheveled hair. Leaning up onto my knees before climbing over him.

His shirt falls to my mid-thigh when I stand up, fitting me like a loose dress. I pick up the pitcher, pouring some coffee into a white ceramic mug before grabbing the plate of pancakes.

I get back into bed, taking a sip of coffee before setting it onto the nightstand. I glance over at him to see him staring at me. "What?"

A goofy smile is fitted on his face. He shakes his head as he says, "Nothing." He turns to pour himself a cup of coffee, grabbing the other plate and leaning himself back.

"Have you been to The Sixth Ward before?" I ask through bites of my breakfast.

He shakes his head. "I tend to stay close to The Pleasure District."

"How come?"

He looks over at me, swallowing a piece of bacon. "Some Districts are ruled by different governing families. Or rather, governed by their respective mob." He dips his fork into the scrambled eggs. "The Deimari Mafia isn't the only affiliation around. While we govern our respective territory, other mobs—like The Croshick's, govern their own territory of the city." He brings the fork to his mouth, continuing after he's finished chewing. "In the past, feuds have arisen amongst the two families. Usually for drawing unwanted attention or stepping out of line in their turf. But now we've come to an agreement: keep to our territories, nobody gets dealt with."

I plop a strawberry into my mouth. "So what part of the city do they oversee?"

He sets his cleared plate down onto the tray, grabbing the cloth napkins. "Westpoint." He wipes his mouth with one before lifting the other one to my lips.

He wipes the corner of my mouth, lifting his gaze to me as he pulls it away. "You had syrup on your face." He says before setting the napkin down.

"Thanks." Is all I manage to say as he takes my finished plate from me, setting it onto the tray. "So, what would've happened if Jerome was in Westpoint? Would we still have gone out to get him?"

He gets up and walks over to his duffel bag, grabbing it and setting it onto the bed. He remains silent for a moment before lifting his gaze to meet mine. "I would've drawn him out one way or another. Or if I had to, I would've damned the agreement for you."

I watch him pull out some clean clothes, setting them onto the off-white sheets before zippering it closed. There's something so simple in the act, yet I can't take my eyes off of him.

He catches my stare and smirks. "Don't do that."

I ask innocently. "Do what?" Tilting my head as I bat my lashes at him.

"That." He comes around to lean closer to me, pulling my face close to his. He kisses me, quick and simple. As if he's been doing it for his entire life but it shares just as much enthusiasm as he did the first time.

He stands up right again. "We have two hours until we have to check out."

My eyes widen as I look over at my phone on the nightstand, tapping the screen. "It's two o'clock already?!"

A deep rumble of a chuckle draws my attention back to him. "We were up pretty late last night, little jewel."

Heat pools itself down low.

"I wanted you to get your rest." He starts walking away, taking his clean clothes with him. "You can shower after, or join me if you'd like."

I stare after him as I watch him lean into the shower to turn the water on, the door wide open. With his back towards me he begins lifting his shirt off, dropping it to the ground. When he lowers his sweatpants down all I see is a perfectly sculpted ass.

Wait—when did he put those sweatpants on?

He opens the glass door, stepping into the standing shower as I shove the covers off of me. I pad over to the bathroom, watching him lift his hands to push the water back from his face. The muscles in his arms and back tightening, constricting in the most appeasing ways.

I lift his shirt off my body, pulling the glass door open to step inside. The moment I close the shower door behind me he advances on me.

He pulls me flush against him, his hard length pressing against my lower belly. His strong hands cup my jaw as he grinds into me, neediness evident in his pace.

He backs me into the tiled wall, lifting one of my legs up as he palms his cock with his other hand.

He teases my entrance, rubbing the head along my glistening pussy and I'm instantly reminded of that night in his hot tub. "It would be so easy to slip myself inside right now." Hearing the slight tremble in his words makes my insides do all kinds of flips. "You're already prepped for my cock."

For a virgin he sure talks dirty. I fucking love it.

"Then do it." I coax him, lifting my gaze up to his.

He rubs his cock through my lips, his hand keeping my leg up gripping into my skin as he barks out a curse. "I won't stop once I'm inside of you." He moves that hand from his cock to my throat, gripping the sides of it. "I could fuck you right now, lose my virginity to you in this moment. I want *nothing* more than that. But I—"

He rocks his hips into me, his cock sliding up and rubbing along my clit. I glance down and watch as pre-cum glistens the tip, trapped against my belly.

"Not yet." He stammers as he lowers his lips down to my neck, running his tongue along my skin as he keeps rocking into me. "I won't claim you until I can have your full undivided attention. Until absolutely nothing is standing in our way from me taking you over and over again." He rumbles against my skin. The heated promise of his words running through me like molten lava.

My pussy slides against his cock as I moan through the pleasure building inside of me.

"So for now, make me beg for it." He demands as he lowers himself down to his knees. Lifting my leg and hooking it around his shoulder. "Make me earn your body, earn *you*. And only when I'm shaking with need for you, only when you need me as badly as I need you, do I get to fill you."

I cry out in pleasure as he flicks his tongue out, gliding it through my wetness. "Because you will not just be my first, little jewel."

I look down and fixate on the sight of him. This strong, protective and slightly unhinged man kneeling before *me*. A reverence so bright in his eyes that it would put a god's most loyal devotee to shame.

"You will be my last."

His mouth closes over my clit as he sucks and licks me into sweet oblivion. My head leans back as I arch into him, writhing against his lips. I look down and watch him lower a hand to his cock, dripping with anticipation.

He strokes himself as my orgasm builds quickly, leaving me little room to catch my breath before I'm climaxing hard against his tongue. I scream out his name as I use his mouth to ride my release. Seconds later, his moan is trapped against my pussy as he's spilling himself into his hand. Cum shoots out onto the tiled wall behind me, and drips down his wrist.

After minutes of him making sure every last drop of me has been devoured by him, he pulls away and lowers my trembling leg down. He stands himself upright, pressing a kiss to my lips.

He pulls away and grabs the bottle of shampoo I put in here yesterday. Flipping the lid and dumping some into the palm of his hand. He lathers it up before gesturing for me to turn around. I smile, doing as he asks.

He begins lathering the soap in my hair, paying attention to my roots. And as I stand there letting him care for me in a way that no man ever has before, I begin to feel sorry for anyone who doesn't get to experience this level of devotion that I know whole-heartedly belongs to me.

CHAPTER 50

The steel elevator doors open up as Dex and I step out into the main lobby, his hands full carrying our luggage as we walk up to the front desk.

He places our bags down as he speaks with the clerk. His attention is momentarily distracted to his pocket, reaching down and pulling out his phone. I watch as his brows furrow briefly at his screen.

"What?" I ask, trying to look over his shoulder.

He shakes his head, shoving his phone back down into his pocket. He leans over, giving me a kiss on the top of my head. "Nothing. Probably just the wrong number."

He continues with the check out process while another attendant grabs his keys, exiting out of the front door to pull his car around.

I look over to see a silver bathroom sign hanging nearby, leading to an open hallway. I knew I should have used the bathroom before we left the room. "I need to pee. I'll be right back."

He glances over at me. "I'll be here." A soft smile gracing his lips.

I walk the short distance to the hallway, turning the corner. My mary-jane heels click against the tiled floor as I enter the women's bathroom, heading straight for an open stall. The bathroom eerily quiet, empty aside from myself.

I finish using the bathroom and turn the water from the faucet on. Washing my hands with some cherry-blossom scented soap. As I wave them under a motion-detected paper towel machine, I hear someone enter the bathroom.

I swipe the paper towel, drying my hands before an awareness heightens my senses, raising the hairs along the back of my neck. I inhale—

And smell not the pheromones of a woman, but a man.

As soon as I move to turn around to defend myself, I feel strong arms wrap around me, caging my back to a hard chest.

One of his hands cups my mouth as I feel a sharp pinch in my neck. I try to scream as I look down to see the barrel of a needle protruding from my skin.

Not even a full second later I go to shapeshift into my Succubus form, elongating my claws when—

I feel the numbing effects briskly take over. Within mere seconds, I can't move at all.

He lowers his hand to stuff a damp rag into my mouth, my eyes widening in horror as I taste what's lingering on the cotton rag. Alarm bells go off in my head.

They know.

"Don't worry, this will all be over soon."

I feel a heavy hand hit me on the back of my head before everything turns dark.

CHAPTER 51

Dexter

She was out of my sight for less than two minutes. That's all it took for her to be taken from me.

Two fucking minutes.

He knew we were coming this whole time, and if I had been more alert, more on guard, I would've realized that the text sent to me wasn't meant for someone else. It was meant for me.

Thanks for making my job easier.

That's it, all that was said. A warning that he was already here, and was already waiting for her.

But thankfully, I am never without a back-up plan, and help is never far away.

The bastard knew taking her in a public place would leave me at a disadvantage. Where a normal person would've frantically asked the front desk attendants to call for the police, I was left with no choice but to walk out of here as if nothing happened. Because the only thing that having police here will do for me is get in my way.

And make it extremely difficult for me to do what I want to him, which will be nothing short of bloody.

It took every ounce of strength inside of me to remain calm, and exit the building. But as soon as I made it to my car, I quickly dumped Cyn and I's luggage into the passenger seat before pulling my phone out of my pocket. I pull up the hotel's wifi, hacking my way into their security cameras at lightning speed. I pull up the ones for the front and back of the building, catching a white man with brown hair walking out of a back door, carrying a blue haired woman in his arms.

Anger fuels to life as I continue watching, witnessing the car he tosses her into—

Tosses, not places. A violent wave of anger churns in my blood and threatens to boil me over. But I can't. I have to focus on getting to her.

I watch the captured footage from not even ten minutes ago as he seats himself into a yellow car, closing the door before he quickly drives away, but not fast enough to draw unnecessary attention to himself. I catch his license plate as he turns out of the alley.

I screenshot it, closing out the security feed as I send a text. *Something's happened. I need you out here.*

I send my location to Levi, fitting my key into the ignition as I drive out of the parking lot. He texts back not even thirty seconds later.

I'm already on my way.

Jerome made a big fucking mistake taking her, and he's going to find out just how big of a mistake that was.

Because I have never been a violent man for the sake of violence, but if it ensures that she's safe in my arms, I'll gladly become the villain for her.

CHAPTER 52

Cynthia

I wake up to the putrid smell of cigarettes, the smoke clinging to the enclosed space around me.

I reach my hand up to soothe the ache at the back of my head—

My eyes spring open, staring straight up at the roof of a vehicle. I lift my gaze up to the man in the front seat, immediately trying to lift myself up but I can't.

Aside from the movement in my eyes, I have absolutely no function in any part of my body. There's only one drug, one herb that can render a Succubus—*any* demon, for that matter, completely paralyzed.

Nettleshade.

He looks back at me, a set of dark eyes creasing at the corners as a smirk curves his lips. "You're awake already."

He turns his gaze back to the road. "Don't attempt to move. You won't regain function in your body for at least another three hours."

Anger seethes hotly through me. I try to thrash against my own body, trying to will myself to get up and rake my claws through this man's eyes.

"I'm sure you have many questions, so for starters: I'm Jerome. Pronounced Jair-OH-mee. I know, many people mistake it for Jer-OME." A light, airy laugh escapes him as he presses a cigarette to his lips, taking a hit before tossing it out the window. "And you, gods." He turns back around, roaming those sick eyes over my body. "You go by many names. Virtual Vixen, Sapphire." He pauses. "Cynthia Monroe."

A nervous chill travels down my spine, sinking itself to the pit of my stomach.

"I assume by now your boyfriend is probably trying to track down the vehicle I dragged you away in."

With my head turned slightly towards him, all I can see is the warm glow of the setting sun reflecting itself off of his fair-skinned face. Highlighting the angular planes in his jaw, the scruffy beard on his chin. I glance down at my body, my legs angled towards the front seats.

"I'm afraid he'll be terribly misled when he realizes that I paid a friend of mine to switch vehicles with me two hours ago." He glances back at me, giving me a smug grin that is anything but friendly. "What you both failed to realize is that there's a whole network of us. We've known what you and your little friend are for a little while now."

That thread of worry coils itself deeper in my stomach. Who is—

"Your boyfriend is valuable too, you know. Being Sawyer's right-hand man and all." He pauses, his voice lowering. "But you're worth a far prettier price."

If I had feeling in my body right now, I'd know with full certainty that the chuckle that slipped from his mouth would've skittered an uneasy awareness over my skin.

"Adrian was the first one to attempt the trade, but the only one that was out of the loop of her *real nature*. But when he failed with your friend, I knew it was only a matter of time until someone would put their bid on you." He pauses for a deafeningly long moment. "Two-hundred thousand dollars you're worth. First it was Antonio but—well, I imagine you know how he ended up." He chuckles again, and I desperately want to sever his vocal cords. But his mention of the man Dex and I killed springs a wariness inside of me. "Now that the big man wants you, I was definitely not passing up on the opportunity to present you to him. Because if *I* offer you up to him, I'll not only get the respect but dibs on my pick of bitch."

Fear and understanding freezes over me.

"The big man would frown upon me having my way with you, but what he doesn't know won't hurt him." He glances back at me again and I want to burrow myself into the seat.

The fear that flashed through me quickly subsides, no longer staring at him with alarm but vengeance in my gaze. Even though I have no control or movement over my body, the moment the Nettleshade wears off, I'll paint this vehicle with the blood of his insignificant life.

I will not be offered up to anyone like fucking cattle auctioned up for slaughter.

Blinding headlights of a vehicle crest themselves over his face. He lowers his visor down to shield his eyes from it, then rests his hand on the top of the steering wheel. "He'll never even know I was inside—"

His repulsive words are interrupted as something collides with us head-on, causing his head to fling backwards into the headrest. His body then jerks violently to the right as the car begins spinning out of control. The car loses its balance and flips over, propelling my body forward and around in the backseat.

My head slams into the roof as the car lands upside down, metal screeching across pavement. The sound of a pained groan is the last thing I hear until my vision turns fuzzy, and everything slows down.

Where I can do nothing but succumb to the darkness as it swallows me whole.

The sound of a man's voice pulls me out of the darkness with just enough strength to listen.

"Cynthia, it's me. Levi." Rough hands gently caress my cheeks, enticing me with their warmth to pry my eyes open. But I'm still too weak to open them.

I slip back under until the sound of something heavy being dragged against the pavement draws me back in. A thud sounds before I hear a rough voice that promises bloodshed. "You deserve to die."

I know that voice, I—

I hear the brunt wet smack of something against pavement. Again, and again. "But I'll leave you alive for her to deal with." He snarls.

I feel those hands on my face drift away as voices continue to slither in and out of consciousness with me.

"Stop, we've got him. We need to finish..."

I fall back under, drowning in the darkness of my mind until I feel my body being lifted up. Calloused, damp hands cradle me up against a warm chest, heavy breaths stirring the strands on the top of my head. When I smell the familiar scent of pine and citrus, I know that I'm safe, and allow myself to fall back under. But not before his vow catches me before I drift off.

"I'm right here, Cyn. It's just you and me."

CHAPTER 53

I become conscious once more, feeling the steady rise and fall of my chest. The soft sheets beneath my back—

My eyes spring open as I try to move my mouth. My lips successfully part open as I flex my fingers at my sides. I tilt my head to the side, wiggling my toes beneath the sheets.

I jolt into an upright position, my breathing ramping up as I scan the room around me.

"Hey, you're okay." My gaze jerks over to see Levi sitting in a chair beside the bed, Amelia standing next to him. His brown eyes stay alight on mine as he calmly assures my racing mind. "You're safe. You're back with us."

I force myself to take a slow and measured breath as I calm my sudden nerves. The adrenaline spiking my blood slowly easing to a simmer. "Where am I?"

Levi must sense my decline in anxiety because he slowly releases his hand from my arm. "You're in Dex's bedroom."

I work on a swallow, trying to ease the lingering tightness in my throat. But at the sound of his name the remaining unease whooshes from my body as I lift the covers off of me. "Where is he?"

Amelia nods to the doorway. "He's downstairs."

I lower one foot to the ground, a tremor working through my leg at the fact that I can move my body again. I lower my other foot down, standing up from the bed on a patterned rug. My legs shake a bit, and my body is still mildly sore, but nothing that won't clear up within a handful of minutes.

I lift my gaze up to Levi, then Amelia. "Thank you."

He nods, flashing me a striking half grin. "You're welcome."

The sentimental moment doesn't last long though. "We need to talk." I glance over at Amelia. "I know why we're being targeted, and I fear it's not over yet."

Something fierce and protective flashes in Levi's gaze. Amelia's brows knit together, understanding failing her.

"Give me a few minutes and then meet me downstairs." I say nothing more as I leave the room.

I descend the steps, feeling more and more of my immortal strength flow back into my body. I elongate a claw from my finger, feeling relief when I'm able to have full control over my body again.

I reach the bottom landing and turn the corner to the living room. Halting, I see Dex standing with his back facing me. Staring out at the dark night sky through his living room window. At my approach he quickly turns around, and I take in the man that stands before me.

Splattered blood dots his sharp cheekbones, staining his grey shirt crimson. My gaze lowers to notice the bruises peppering his knuckles on his right hand, the skin around them mildly swollen. I slowly track my gaze back up to his, and witness the darkness settling in his stare.

He closes the distance between us, his brows knitting close together as he looks me over. "Are you hurt?" The slight tremor in his voice is no match for the calm exterior he's trying to maintain. The potent worry behind his words tugs on my heart.

I nod. "I'm okay now." I take a shuddering breath in, exhaling slowly before I bring my hands up around his neck, pulling myself flush against him.

Without hesitation he wraps his arms around me, pressing gentle kisses to the top of my head as he holds me close. His lips brush against my forehead. "I'm so sorry. I turned my back for two seconds, I should've—"

"Stop." I interrupt him as I pull away. Those beautiful, glacial eyes frantically meet mine. "Don't blame yourself. This was not your fault."

The unsettledness in his eyes tells me that he doesn't believe me, that this will haunt him for longer than I'd like to allow it. So, I'll be here to bring him back when he gets too lost in his own shame.

I'll be here to remind him it was he who saved me.

I shake my head. "How did you even get to me? I..." My words trail off as I try to recall the events leading up to the crash. The stench of the cigarette smoke, the blinding headlights—

My eyes widened slightly. "It was you."

He lifts his hand up to my cheek, pushing my hair away and tucking it behind my ear. His silence is all the confirmation that I need.

"You were the one who hit us."

He finally nods. "If you were mortal, I wouldn't have done it. I would've chosen a different method than to put you in so much danger." He shakes his head slowly. "But I needed to act quickly. I knew putting him out with force would be the quickest way to get to you."

He lowers his hand to my jaw, caressing his thumb over my no longer aching skin. Such devotion lines his gaze, and it ensnares me in his hold. Right where I want to be. "I would never, *ever* forgive myself if something happened to you, Cynthia. I—"

The sound of Levi and Amelia coming down the steps interrupts whatever Dex was about to say to me. His gaze lifts to them as he lowers his hand from my cheek. And I immediately miss the grounding warmth of his skin.

I turn around, locking eyes with Amelia and meeting her halfway. I bring my arms around her neck as we close the distance.

She hugs me back as she whispers into my shoulder, "Are you okay?"

I nod as I step back. "Yes," I hesitate before speaking the next words. "He injected me with Nettleshade."

"What?" Dex comes to stand at my side.

Amelia doesn't need to ask for clarification though. The horrors of what I've just said are written all over her face, the realization of what this means for both of us.

For all entities alike.

I turn to face Dexter and Levi. "Hundreds of years ago, there was a revolution orchestrated by mortals who somehow figured out how to recognize demons. There was a penalty of complete execution for any that traveled up here, using a deadly herb called Nettleshade to incapacitate us." I look over at Dex. "Within seconds of administering, a demon will go completely paralyzed. Leaving them fully vulnerable."

"After we found the source of where mortals were getting it from, we burned it. Every last ounce of it." Amelia continues on. "We then killed off the founding families who held the knowledge of our only weakness, wiping them clean from existence." She lifts her gaze to me. "Or so we thought."

"When I was still paralyzed in the car, Jerome told me he knew about me." I glance up at Amelia and Levi. "He knew who you were, too. That Adrian guy you told me about that you both handled? He wasn't just a private investigator."

Levi steps forward but it's Amelia who speaks. "What do you mean?"

I loosen my breath. "I think he was part of a sex trafficking ring. And he tried to get close to you because he wanted to bid you off to a potential buyer."

The anger in Amelia's gaze flashes brightly, her amber eyes churning vividly. But she isn't the only one seething with rage.

I look over at Levi and can see the calm fury about to push through the surface. He runs his hand through his dark-blonde hair, clenching his jaw as Amelia rests a hand on his shoulder. He meets her gaze. "And suddenly the amount of times I stabbed that motherfucker doesn't seem like enough."

She gently grabs his face, making an effort to quell that storm raging within him. "He doesn't matter anymore. He's dead." She reminds him.

Whether it's at her words or her touch—or both, Levi takes a slow breath out until that fury licking the flames inside of him simmers.

"Is that why he took you? This whole time, that's why he had his sights on you?" The utter despair in Dex's words pulls at my heart once more.

I hesitate before I nod my head. "But he won't get to me. Or maybe he can't even." I shake my head, disappointment fueling my next words because I would've greatly wanted him to suffer an agonizing death. "I can't imagine he survived that car crash."

Dex watches me in silence, and I tilt my head in confusion when he remains silent. He glances up to Levi in some sort of unspoken exchange.

I ask no one in particular. "What aren't you guys telling me?"

A faint smirk curves up Levi's lips as he says, "We took him from the crash scene." He nods to Dex. "He's hurt badly, but he lives. He's yours to have your way with."

CHAPTER 54

Dexter

The four of us disappear down to my basement, reaching the bottom landing and walking across the clear tarp laid out beneath us. I alternate my gaze from Cyn to Jerome, who I've strapped down into a wooden chair.

Cyn walks around him like a vulture eyeing up its next meal. Words he tries to spew out of his mouth turn muffled behind the tape covering his lips.

She stares him down, vengeance and retribution simmering in her gaze. And by her hands, she will have both.

A sharp tearing noise follows as Cyn rips the tape off his mouth. Jerome jerks his face away but Cyn grips his jaw with both hands, her thumbs digging into his cheeks.

I watch as her fingers elongate into sharp talons, her skin molding into the color of ash. The sharp talons on her thumbs lengthen, piercing into his pale cheeks as he hisses out in agony. She only smiles down at him as her eyes glow like twin pools of bright jewels, streaks of blood running down his skin.

She tsks at him, shaking her head. "What am I going to do with you?" Her voice full of sinister smoke.

Jerome—with every last bit of strength he has left, tries to spit at her. She only digs her talons in deeper, blood dripping down his neck and staining his beige shirt to a crimson hue.

She laughs at him. "A for effort."

Actually *laughs* at him.

Goosebumps pimple over my arms and the back of my neck. She doesn't need me to do her dirty work for her. She's capable of doing bad all on her own.

And I'm here for all of it.

I feel her power reach out, the energy thickening the air around us as compulsion grasps onto his mind. "Who is the big man?"

I look over at Levi and Amelia. They both shrug their shoulders, neither of them knowing who she's referring to.

Jerome's face slackens as he's forced to reply, but not giving her the information she wanted. "I don't know. He's only known as the man in charge, he shares his name with no one out of complete privacy." He blinks at her. "He runs his operations from the sidelines, letting other guys take the lead to keep his identity hidden."

"And what exactly are his operations?" She asks.

"He runs a trafficking ring. The Denizens—they call them, three men closest to the boss who go and recruit girls online, usually through fake profiles or job offers. They round them up, bringing them back to either be bid on, or if they have already been auctioned off to a buyer, they get delivered right to their doorstep."

My stomach churns at his words. "Ask him how long it's been going on for."

Cyn asks him, his answer shocking me. "Around four years."

"Fuck." Levi curses beside me, shaking his head. This development is not good for several reasons: for one in particular, our girls are being hunted. Which means if they are able to be targeted, then any other woman in the city is at high risk of being targeted as well.

Sawyer will need to hear about this.

"And I was auctioned off to whom?"

Everything inside of me freezes over. It feels as if the tarp beneath me has been swept right from under me. Someone already *bought* her—

I have to turn around so I don't do something like punch him straight in the face. Or wring his neck until I snap his spine.

He's her kill, not mine. She gets the honor of taking his last breath, no matter how badly I want to take it myself.

"Originally to Antonio. But when he was murdered, you went to the next bidder. To the big man, of course." I whip around to see a soft smile form on Jerome's face. "He originally wanted Amelia but gave up on trying to get her when Adrian failed his task."

Amelia steps forward, anger blazing violently in her gaze. Her fists curl inward at her sides.

Pieces of the entire puzzle congrue themselves together in my mind. The chatroom exchange between Jerome and Antonio wasn't just about sharing a leaked photo of Cynthia, he was sharing a sneak peak of what he *purchased*.

And those other women—has he been planning on taking them all this time? Who else in this organization is keeping tabs on women like this?

"Finish your interrogation." Levi rumbles out, his hard gaze set on Jerome. His next words are laced with a calm, deadly promise. "Before I decide to take matters into my own hands and kill him myself."

Cyn takes a breath, gathering herself for a minute before asking one last question. "Who are the Denizens? And where can we find them?"

"I only know the name of one. Roger Farren. He's the youngest of the three. He mostly stays to himself, preferring to keep himself under the radar. But it's rumored he can sometimes be found at Nyte."

Cyn's gaze widens. "That's a club right in The Pleasure District."

"Yes." Jerome responds.

She stands there for a moment as I wonder how she'll enact justice on her behalf. But before I can wonder much longer, she simply draws her power back. When I think she's going to drag his pain out, possibly tear him limb by limb, she strikes at him like a viper.

Twisting his neck and killing him instantly. A quick death he certainly did not deserve.

She walks away, heading upstairs as Levi looks over at me. "So, I brought a tarp for nothing then?" He looks over at

Jerome, his head now hung limp to his shoulder. "We're not gonna get at least a little dirty with his punishment?"

At any other time I'd probably laugh at the genuine disappointment in his tone, but too much has been said in the past ten minutes for me to find an ounce of humor to share.

I rest my hand on his back. "You guys got this from here? I'd like to have a moment alone to speak with Cynthia."

Levi nods his head. "We got you, man." He claps his hand on my shoulder before walking over to Jerome, kicking him off the chair as his body falls limp to the floor.

I turn away and walk up the steps, not seeing her in the kitchen or living room. I almost walk upstairs to check if she's up there when I see my patio door cracked open.

A moderate rainfall splatters down on my wooden deck as I slide the porch door open. Cyn standing a few feet in front of me, her back facing me as rain dampens her from head to toe.

"Cyn." I say quietly. When she doesn't respond, I step out of the awning covering me. Submerging myself into the rain.

I stand in front of her and find her gaze staring absentmindedly ahead. I notice her hand clutching the other close to her stomach, as if to settle the nausea churning beneath.

Rain droplets fall down my forehead as they drip off my brows. I reach out for her, cradling her hands in mine as I caress my thumb over her skin as I bring her back from her thoughts.

She finally breaks her gaze, looking up at me. Her chest rises as she takes a deep breath in, shaking her head. "I didn't expect this. This is—" She shakily releases the breath she was holding in. "This was just supposed to be us taking care of him because he stole my content. Distributed it."

"I know." I try saying gently but an edge is still laced with my words.

She squeezes my hands. "He had me in a vulnerable position where I couldn't defend myself. I was, for the first time in my life, *weak* to a man instead of stronger than him." She bites her inner lip as I feel a tremor racking through her body. "I was scared."

I nod as I pull her into me, hugging her close. "I know."

I held her for several long minutes. During which she didn't shed one tear, didn't scream or rage against me. She just leaned against me, and let me hold her.

I am angry for her, for every woman that has to suffer at the hands of vile men who prove time and time again that being treated equally is the furthest motive from their minds. I am disgusted by the threat that now lies at their safety—at *her* safety. It stirs a frenzy of feelings I've never known capable of feeling before.

They cannot have her. I will give my life before she's ever at the hands of those men again.

I pull her face to look up at me, trying not to get the raindrops to fall into her eyes. "We will handle this. I won't let you live your life feeling unsafe."

She wraps her hands around my wrists. "That's the point. *I'm* supposed to be able to protect myself." She pulls away from me, stepping back as that anger inside of her bubbles up to the surface.

Good. Show me how you really feel. *Let me help you.*

"They've managed to find Nettleshade and now have a surplus of it. How will I protect myself from them?"

"Because you will not be alone in this. *I* will also be here to protect you." I say roughly.

Her frustration at the situation causes a broken laugh to escape from her mouth. "Right, because you care about me."

"No, because I *love* you!" I yell out.

The frustration in her face quickly washes away as she stares at me silently.

I bring her face closer to mine, needing her to hear me loud and clear as I speak the words I've held back on expressing. Rain drips down my lips as the truth pours out of me like the rain gathering at our feet. "I *love* you, Cynthia Monroe. Not the concept, the idea or the illusion of you. Not because of the power of seduction you wield, but the magnitude of who you are *beneath* all of that." I pause. "I have loved *you* through your moments of kindness and savagery. Through the moments of playing and being carefree, and the ones where you found safety in sleeping on my chest. I always lived my life keeping people at arms length, but then—" A harsh laugh bursts out. "Then you came into my life and shook everything up in the best possible way. And yes, I'm terrified to love you, but nothing in this life makes more sense to me than loving you."

She continues to stare up at me in silence as I pour my heart to her. I lower my hands from her face as I take a step back. "So fine, I'll let myself be afraid. Because the truth is? I've never allowed myself to have real intimacy with another woman before because the first time I did? She violated my trust by touching me while I was asleep."

And there it is, the big secret for my abstinence.

"We were both really drunk one night, and I passed out. Woke up to her giving me a handjob and I didn't want it. I tried telling her stop but I was already hard and it felt so good that I—"

I turn my gaze away, taking a breath. But she doesn't rush me. When I'm ready, I force my gaze back onto Cyn.

"It was my senior year of high school. She was the first girl I had really liked enough to date, but I always said I wanted to take it slow. Growing up with extremely religious parents who forced the mentality of *having sex before marriage is a sin* really colored my beliefs, until I was able to form my own morals and separate myself from theirs. But when it's been shoved down your throat since you were ten, it's initially hard to deprogram it from your subconscious." I pause. "She thought she was pleasing me and a part of me does believe her. But it still wasn't wanted, I told her I wanted to wait prior to that. I felt a lot of shame after that and the words of my parents haunted me for a while." I loosen my breath. "It made me feel like I was to blame. That I couldn't properly protect myself by not letting how good it felt sway me in that moment."

I bring my hand to her cheek again. "But I met you, and fell for you hard, Cyn. You make me feel safe, even through my fears of intimacy. I'm amazed every single day how someone who deals with so much can still stand so strong, so powerful amidst everything that has been thrown her way—*is* still being thrown her way. Your carefree nature, your courageousness, it inspires me every single moment. And I'm—fuck, I'm rambling now." A nervous laugh slips out of me.

Cyn blinks back the rain falling on her lashes, a moment of silence passing between us. The look in her eyes both makes me want to melt into her embrace and hide from the nerves spiking inside of me. But I don't back down, not this time.

But before I can open my mouth to continue, she finally graces me with that beautiful smile of hers. The kind that comes around after she's taken a bite of warm strawberry pancakes, or when she's singing her heart out in the passenger seat of my car. The kind of smile that brings every detail of joy on her face into focus.

Brings my whole entire world into focus.

Everything I expected to come out of her mouth falls to the wayside as she says, "I love you, too."

CHAPTER 55

Those four words hit me like the truck I hotwired to subdue Jerome's vehicle. Slowing my heart rate to an almost nothingness as I keep my gaze on her.

"I am so sorry that happened to you." She says, bringing her hands to mine. "You were not to blame in that situation. And I never want you to feel pressured to do anything with me."

I stare down at the woman I've watched for months before I even approached her, observing her silently in the crowd. A woman who doesn't own me a lick of kindness, an ounce of her time but still blesses me with it anyway.

Something takes over me, melting all of the fears I once had. Vanishing the restraints that shackled my willingness to be vulnerable. All of that slips away. "You've never made me feel pressured." I bring my hands to her face, cupping her jaw. "Every single moment I shared with you was out of my choice, because *I* wanted to. I wouldn't have done any of it with you had you not made me feel safe enough to explore that part of myself I've long protected."

I bring her face to mine, sealing my words with a kiss. She parts her lips open for me as I urge her back, moving us under the awning.

She pulls her lips from mine as I begin lifting her shirt up her belly, my fingers pressing into her skin. "Are you sure?" She looks at me with both a yearning and a conviction. A seriousness to her words.

I glide my thumb across her cheek, smiling. "I've never been more sure of anything in my life."

I yank her shirt up over her head, it drops to the ground with a loud smack. She laughs as I bring her close to me, kissing her deeply as she reaches for my shirt. I pull away long enough to let her take it off me before clashing my lips with hers again.

We both move at a feral pace, running our hands over each other's skin as I push the patio door open, our wet pants dripping onto my hardwood floor as we step inside.

"These are in my way." I say before yanking her pants and underwear down. Baring her completely naked before me. I waste no time yanking mine off before I pick her up, her soft moan getting trapped against my lips as I wrap her legs around me.

Letting her feel what's been waiting patiently for her, what belongs to *her*.

Her fingers intertwine themselves through my hair as I carry her up the stairs. I turn the corner to my bedroom, laying her out on my bed as I hover over her.

Her chest rises as I press my lips to her neck, my pulse thrumming with anticipation. My hand skims up her thigh, gliding my thumb along her wet center. She writhes against my touch in response. "Eager for me, little jewel?" A grin curves my lips as I press a kiss between her breasts.

"Yes." My cock aches at her breathy response.

I twirl my tongue around a hardened nipple, reveling in the tiny jerks her body produces in response. I lift my gaze up to find her watching me. "I'm not so convinced."

I lower a finger through her wetness, slowly sinking myself inside her pussy. I lift myself up until my face hovers above hers, descending my finger out at an agonizingly slow pace. "You have to really want it." I lower a second finger in, her gasp trapped between my lips. "Want me as badly as I want you."

She moans in response, filling my head with dizzying need. "I do." She cries out as she goes to lower her hand down to mine.

I snatch her wrist, tsking at her as I slowly shake my head. "Get comfortable, Cyn. I'm going to take my time with you tonight."

I raise her arm above her head, pinning her wrist down as I descend my fingers out of her. I pin her other arm up, gripping both wrists down with one hand.

I slowly drag my finger down her mouth, leaving a trail of herself on her bottom lip. Her eyes shine like vivid spheres of jewels as she watches me lean down to lick it off.

I lower myself down her body until I'm kneeling before my bed. I grip her hips, pulling her to the edge of the bed before pushing her legs back, spreading her wide open for me.

I glance up to see her arms are still high above her head, and a grin curves my lips at her obedience to listen to instructions. "Good girl." My mouth is on her not a second later.

She cries out as I run my tongue along her center, devouring every sweet drop that belongs to me. She squirms beneath me as I close my mouth over her clit, sucking her into sweet oblivion just like she taught me before.

Anticipation drips from my cock at the sound of her crying out my name, and I have to fight the urge to fill myself deep inside of her. Gods, she's soaking wet and ready for me. I could take her right now, but I won't be satisfied until she's coming first on my lips.

She writhes against my mouth before soon enough she's cresting against my lips, crying out her release. I drink every last drop before I stand myself up. Pushing her up the bed as I lower myself down between her legs.

She lowers her hands back down, her beautiful face sated with release as she looks up at me. "Are you sure?" Her words hardly above a whisper as she asks me one final time.

I nod. "I'm positive."

A soft grin curves her lips as she lowers her hands to my waist, her touch sending maddening sparks through my body. I lower my hips, angling myself so my aching cock is positioned at her center.

Fuck, is it really this low?

I lower a hand to my cock, palming myself before rubbing the head along her pussy. A sharp hiss slips through my teeth as I curse, trying to contain my reaction.

If I'm already cursing from just rubbing my dick along her pussy, how the fuck am I going to act when I'm actually inside of her?

I exhale a ragged breath as I lower my cock down, slowly pushing myself inside when I feel resistance. My hand trembles as I try to rub my way in, trying to find my opening.

Where the fuck is it?

Those nerves from earlier ricochet to the surface, my chest sinking as I try to loosen a shaky breath. Willing myself to relax—

"It's okay." Cyn says as she lowers her hand down to mine. "Look at me."

I lift my gaze up to her face, working on a swallow.

She smiles, and it's enough to bring me back again. "It's just us." She urges my hand lower until I feel the opening. Her words are a reminder to the oath I spoke to her once before.

That when we're together, there's no performing or hiding from one another. It's just us.

She removes her hand as I slowly descend myself inside of her, releasing a harsh breath as I feel her for the first time.

"Fuck," I curse as I plant my hand down next to her head. I clench my teeth as I halt from descending deeper inside.

"Further." She instructs softly.

I shake my head. "I can't. I—" I groan as she urges my hips further down, sheathing me deeper into her. Gods, this feels *fucking amazing*. "I'm not gonna last."

She grins up at me. "We have all night."

Her words light a fire in my veins, causing me to thrust all the way to the hilt. I bark out a curse again, lowering my head down to her neck as my lips tremble against her skin. "Good boy." Her words laced with wickedness.

The restraint I've been trying to keep a lid on snaps right off at her praise.

I descend myself out of her just to thrust into her again, the euphoria of how her soft, wet pussy feels clamped around my cock blurs my thoughts along with that self-imposed restraint. I watch her face distort in pleasure as I find my rhythm, consumed with watching her take me as I fuck her harder.

I bring my lips to hers, parting her mouth open with my tongue. Our shared moans get lost between our lips as I ram into her, my cock straining inside of her.

She lowers her head back, her eyes glistening with need as she bends a leg down to her chest. I quickly lower her leg over my shoulder and—

Fuck, I didn't think I could get any deeper.

"Fuck, I'm gonna cum." I groan out against her neck. "I—"

I jackhammer into her as I bite down on her neck, humping her like a fucking animal as I spill myself into her. I feel her gush around my cock, her screams through her own release only intensifying my orgasm.

"Fuck!" I bark out as I tear my lips from her neck. The harsh wave of my orgasm goes on and on and on as I drown in her silken walls. "I can't stop coming." I whimper out.

She is not my reward. She's gods damn my salvation.

After several moments, I finally feel my climax dwindle. I slow down my pace before I finally pull out. My cock—my whole body, tingling with heightened sensitivity.

I lay myself down next to her, staring up at the ceiling as I try to catch my breath. A buzzing sensation travels from my arms down to my legs, followed by a ringing in my ears.

Cyn turns on her side to face me, resting her hand on my chest as the softness of her body touches mine. I wrap my hand around hers, bringing it to my lips and pressing a kiss to her palm. I lean up from the bed, walking over to my conjoined bathroom and fetching a clean rag.

The simple act feels wholly taxing.

I walk back over to the bed, using it to clean her up before wiping myself. I toss it into my laundry hamper before laying back down beside her.

There are no words that are left to be spoken. I've willingly shared both my heart, and now my body to her. And at the reminder of those three words uttered from her lips, I rest in a weight of ease that she feels the same way.

That she *loves* me.

I wrap my arm around her, tugging her close to my chest as I bring the blanket around us. And I let the steady rhythm of her breath soothe me into a deep, restful sleep.

CHAPTER 56

Cynthia

I stir awake to the sound of a tray being set down onto the nightstand, followed by the bed dipping behind me. A grin curves my tired face as he snakes his arm under the covers, laying it over my waist.

"Goodmorning." He whispers as he leans in to kiss my cheek. The tired rasp in his voice makes my skin skitter with heated excitement.

I nuzzle myself closer to his hard chest, his skin warm against mine. "Goodmorning." My words laden with exhaustion.

"I made breakfast," he says, pressing a kiss to my shoulder. "In case you're hungry."

I take in the delightful aroma of coffee, syrup, and breakfast sausage.

I turn around to face Dex, his hand lifting to trail my hair back behind my ear. But my gaze lands on what's behind him.

I lean up onto my elbow, the bedsheet pooling down to my waist as I gaze at the tray behind him. An assortment of breakfast items including coffee and pancakes with cut up strawberries on top. But what's set next to the tray is what keeps my attention.

A glass vase brimming with fresh pink peonies, and white and red roses.

I lower my gaze back down to him. "Oh, you *do* love me."

He laughs. "The flowers are the least I could give to show my enamoration for you." He leans up onto his elbow and kisses my collarbone. The touch of his lips at my neck, and his hand at my hip, causes wicked warmth to pool low. The need for more only intensifies when I feel his hard length press against my belly. "I could name a few other ways." He says through heated promises.

The hand at my hip lowers an inch as his thumb traces idle circles along the crease at my thigh. I chuckle as I say, voice lowered, "Such a horny boy."

His lips at my neck raise up to my jaw, my breath hitching. "I thought I wanted to constantly be near you before. But now," he kisses the corner of my lips. "I don't know how I'll ever stop touching you."

His hand at my hip lowers, his thumb now sweeping over my pussy.

His hand grips into my skin, demonstrating his neediness for me. His urgency. "Please," he pauses before he kisses me on the lips. His voice lowered as he whimpers. "I need it. I need to feel you again."

My blood thrums like violent waves crashing at sea at his plea. "Begging, are we?" I smirk.

He presses another kiss to my collarbone, and I feel his hard length press into me as his hips jerk forward. "Always for you."

Without hesitation I lay him down onto his back, clashing my lips with his. He doesn't even have to beg to be inside of me. I want him—*need* him, just as badly.

But watching him beg for me just makes it all that much more fun.

I straddle him as his other hand moves to my hip, gripping me down onto his shaft. His groan gets trapped against my lips as I rub my pussy along his aching cock. "Tell me what you would do for it." I whisper against his ear.

"Anything." He says with no hesitation.

I hum my appreciation as I bring my hands to his chest, my breasts hovering above his face. "I want you to tell me how badly you want it." I lift my hips until his cock is positioned right at my entrance.

He blows out a harsh breath. "Fuck, I want it so bad." He glances down to where our hips meet, jerking his hips up and sliding the tip along my clit. "I want you to put that pretty pussy on me and fuck me." He leans his head back into the pillow, clenching his teeth as he positions himself at my entrance again.

I lower myself down an inch. "Like this?"

He locks eyes with me, his hands on my waist still gripping on. He could just as easily pull me down onto him, but he doesn't. Instead, he lets me set the pace. Allows me to have fun with teasing him.

And I can tell from the fire lit in his eyes that he likes it. A lot.

"Keep going." He forces out.

I lower myself down another inch, his cock spasming as he whimpers his neediness. The way his body reacts to me touching him, how vocal he is when I pleasure him. Gods, it sends me blazing with fucking need.

"All the way." His words hover above a snarl.

I slowly lower myself all the way down onto his aching cock, a ragged breath escaping his lips as he curses. I lean forward as I ride him, slowly to start.

He raises up to close his mouth over my nipple, my back arching into him as he sucks the hardened flesh. His mouth releases a few seconds later as he pleads, "Please, please, *please* go faster." A moan slips out of his lips. "Harder."

I lean up and lift myself up onto my feet, rocking my hips into him as he meets my pace. I cry out my own build of release as he grips my hips into place, and pistons in and out of me.

When that isn't enough he leans up, pulling me flush against him. I cry out as he lifts me up, bringing me back down onto him *hard*. Over and over again until I'm cresting around his cock, gushing my release onto him.

He follows me only moments later, spilling his release inside of me. Whimpering as he trembles beneath me, bringing me down onto his cock over and over again.

When both of us are spent he lays me back down onto the bed, pulling himself out several moments later. At some point after, we finally do eat breakfast.

After we both finally showered, ate again, and got ready for the day, Dex informed me that Sawyer wanted to meet with all of us to discuss the situation at hand. When I told him that we could either stay at his place until then, or we could stop back at mine, he offered a different alternative.

"How about I take you shopping?" He'd suggested.

I'd raised my eyebrow at him, even though my interest was immediately piqued. "Shopping?"

He'd shrugged his shoulders. "Are you suddenly opposed to me spending money on you?"

I'd laughed. "Not at all. It's just..." My voice trailed off, trying to think of the proper way to convey what I was thinking. "I'm beginning to feel like I'm being rewarded for taking your virginity."

He'd looked confused. "Is this not the standard for all men when they lose their virginity? How else do they show women their gratitude for sharing something so special with them?"

My heart had felt like it was going to swoon right out of my chest. I couldn't even come up with a solid remark at his response, his expression was so serious and he was truly baffled that more men didn't do something similar. I could only give him a soft laugh before I said, "Similar to a push present."

He'd tilted his head. "Come again?"

"A push present. You know, when a woman gives birth the man gets her a push present. For going through the trouble of delivering an eight-or-so pound baby." I'd tilted my head as I shrugged my shoulders. "This is kind of like that."

He'd pondered over my words for a few moments before a grin slid up his face. "Yeah, exactly."

So, here we are.

I push the black velvet hanger down the gold mounted clothing rack. The lacey two-piece I pull out matching the one being showcased on the half-mannequin on the black hanging shelf above. I hold it out in front of the dusted pink wall, admiring it.

Cute, but not practical for work.

It was actually a perfect idea for Dex to suggest shopping before we met up with Sawyer. Since Janice agreed to let me host the fundraiser to help raise money for Pauline, I thought it'd only make sense for me to buy a few new outfits for it.

Dex hovers close behind me, looking over my shoulder as I pull out another hanger. "That one's nice."

I roll my eyes. "You said that about the last four I pulled out."

His breath dances along my shoulder as he speaks. "Correction, I said that about the last *three*." He pauses. "The pink and black one prior to those you already own."

I turn around, looking up at him. "No, I—" I tilt my head as my memory surfaces. "Okay, I take that back."

I continue rummaging through racks of exotic dancewear and lingerie. Pulling out hangers ranging from leather two pieces, to satin slingshots. Each time I add a new one to the bunch, Dex takes it out of my hands and carries it for me.

When we finally make it to the fitting room, he has well over fifteen hangers in his hands.

I step beneath the mulberry heart-shaped awning, the hot pink LED light tracing the edge around it highlighting the row of dressing rooms inside. The floor transitions from hardwood to plush pink carpet, the smell of some floral perfume heavy in the air. I step into the largest fitting room, drawing the amethyst curtain as Dex follows me inside.

He hangs my items on a long clothing rack before he seats himself down into a black chair. Widening his legs as he watches me undress.

"So what do you think Sawyer is going to say?" I adjust the halter over my breasts.

Dex exhales. "Honestly, I don't know. We've never dealt with trafficking before, so I assume this will be as new for him as it is for us."

"And you think he'll want to get to the bottom of who is behind it all? Truly?" I look in the mirror, seeing how I like the lingerie.

"Sawyer can be a cold man. Closed-off is probably even an understatement." He chuckles. "There are many things that we do business wise that are to our benefit, but he has always had a soft spot for protecting and taking care of women." His eyes soften as a faint smile curves his lips. "I think Priscilla being born really melted away some of his bitterness."

"And Priscilla is his niece, right?" I look over my shoulder at Dex.

His gaze remains fixated on me for a moment before he nods. "His one and only."

I turn back around, lifting my hands around my back as I unclasp the tiny hooks. "Well, if he's going to get involved, I don't think Amelia and I need to tell either of you that this will get brutal." I look at him through the mirror, lowering my voice. "If it is the same as last time, and there are entire families involved that know our secret, they won't live to tell any future offspring."

I set the halter back onto the hanger, grabbing a green and blue V-shaped, sling-shot piece off a different one. I slip the polyester over my body, fixing my breasts inside the scrunch-trimmed cups.

His gaze tracks my every movement. "If their deaths ensure your safety then it's a necessary sacrifice." A moment of silence stretches between us as his hungry gaze continues to gawk. "I am definitely buying you that."

I turn around, showing him the complete bare back design. "Yeah?"

He nods slowly, lowering his gaze further down. "Yes." The intensity in his gaze when he lifts it back up to meet mine makes my skin suddenly feel on fire.

I face him again, tsking at him as I remove the teddy down my body. "Don't give me that look."

A grin curves one side of his face, that damn dipple making an appearance. "What look?"

I hang it back up on the hanger and pull a two piece off another. *"That* look." I fasten the leather belt around my waist before adjusting a smaller one at the top of my thigh.

He chuckles. "I don't know what you're talking about."

I fasten the strap to my other thigh, adjusting the leather strips over my ass.

"What is that?" He asks.

"A leather harness." I slip the matching halter to it over my breasts, loosely fastening the collar around my neck. "Do you like it?"

When Dex remains silent I look over at him to see his gaze cemented on my body. For several seconds, he doesn't even blink.

Finally, he responds, and his words are laced with venom. "You're not wearing that to the club."

I knit my brows together. "And why's that?"

He slowly trails those glacial eyes up to my face, and when I meet his gaze, the air in my lungs whooshes right from my chest.

He stands up from the chair, stalking over to me like a predator more possessive than the demons residing in Hell. A ruthless determination in his gaze.

He lowers a hand to the collar at my neck, tilting his head as he loops a finger through the silver ring. A low rumble gets trapped in his throat as he says, "This one is strictly for my gaze."

He tugs gently on the ring, pulling me closer to him. At the sound of the low peep I make, a wicked grin on his face widens, revealing the other dimple.

He steps back from me as I exhale the trapped breath from my lungs. And as I continue trying on the rest of the outfits, an anticipation blooms inside of me at all of the wicked things he'll do to me in that harness.

CHAPTER 57

As we walked through the front door I immediately tilted my head up at the crystal chandelier above. Noting the intricate ivory molding surrounding it.

Dex gently guides me away from the main foyer. "This is his *house*?" I nearly shout.

He chuckles beside me. "I hardly think you can call this a house."

At the far wall ahead of us is a set of double-doors, sunlight filtering in from the clear glass and drenching the polished floors. We turn left down a hallway, passing an open archway.

My mouth drops as I turn my head, catching a glimpse of a massive, pristine kitchen before Dex urges me forward.

We approach a set of tempered glass french doors, golden filigree swirling up the sleek surface. Voices filtering from the other side snag my attention.

I step inside to an all-season room adorned with cream colored couches surrounding a matching ottoman, a black tray placed on top. Colossal ivory pillars embellish the cream-colored walls as sweeping ornate windows garnish the rich, chestnut glass double-doors beneath. The entirety of the room drenched with natural light.

A familiar red-head catches my attention as I finally lower my gaze back down from admiring the coffered ceiling.

Amelia wraps her arms around me as Dex goes to talk to Levi. "How are you?" She asks, pulling away.

I nod. "I'm fine now."

"Good." She says, a faint smirk lifting up one side of her red lips.

At the sound of someone else entering the room, I turn to see Sawyer striding in. His all-black suit draws the light to him like a bottomless void siphoning the sunlight. "Thank you all for coming." He goes over to a bar cart and picks up a glass decanter. "Let's get right into it." He pours some amber liquid into a glass before joining us.

As soon as we all take a seat, we start from the beginning and explain to Sawyer everything we know. As his amber gaze roams from Dexter's to mine, I feel the sting of his stare. As if he's reaching into the depths of my soul, pulling everything he finds of interest out of me, and cradling it into the palm of his hand. As if he has the right to do so.

His energy is chilling and dark, his sheer presence alone commanding a certain level of attention. His title aside, it's easy to see why mortals fear the man.

He takes a slow, measured drink. "Have we breached their systems yet?" He lowers the glass back down to his knee.

Dex shakes his head. "They're keeping their organization as discreet as possible. I'm working on targeting cracks in their foundation so I can slip through their defenses as we speak."

Sawyer nods slowly. He doesn't say anything for a long moment until he trails his gaze back to me. "How were you able to track them last time?"

I glance at Amelia. "We didn't. The founding families back then were discovered by someone we know."

"Who?" Sawyer asks.

"Anastasia." Amelia finishes for me. "She's one of the oldest, most ruthless Succubi there has ever lived." She glances over at me. "Once she sniffed them out, we helped her dispose of them."

Sawyer's finger taps the side of his glass, drawing my gaze to the silver rings adorning his fingers. "I'd like to speak with her, then. See what more she knows." He downs the remainder of his drink. "For now, both of which remain top priority. I want to know who the Denizens are, and who their boss is." He stands up from the couch, walking over to the bar cart. "Any developments come straight to me."

"Yeah, that's the thing." I begin as Sawyer turns back around to face me. "Anastasia doesn't get summoned, she gets *intrigued*. Only then does she make an appearance to the upper world."

The lines in his porcelain face harden briefly as he gives me a chilling stare. "Well, she may just want to come out of hiding for this." He glances up at Dex and Levi before heading towards the glass doors. "You are all excused."

He leaves the room as I look at Dex, mouth parted open as I raise an eyebrow. "He sure is a bossy little thing isn't he?"

Levi chokes back a laugh as Dex approaches me, trying to keep the grin on his face from showing. "Yeah, you may not want to say that in front of him."

"I'd like to see him try." Amelia mumbles, rolling her eyes at the lack of a threat.

"Well, looks like we have work to do." Levi chimes in.

And as we all silently agree, I wonder just how large this organization is.

CHAPTER 58

Dexter

I bring the hammer back in a controlled arc before swinging it back onto the nail's head. I do this a few more times until I've hammered the nail almost fully into the wall.

I set the hammer down on my nightstand, lifting the canvas and hanging it onto the nails. Tweaking it to the left a smidge, making sure it's aligned perfectly straight.

I step down, assessing it as a grin curves up my lips.

The buzzing sound of my phone against my wood nightstand draws my attention. I pick it up, reading the text from Levi.

I'm ten minutes out.

I send a thumbs up reaction to his text before returning my tools back down to the basement.

After I dropped Cyn off last night back at her place, I came home to do some more work until about one o'clock in the morning. I was determined to find out more about Roger Farron, to find any trail that might lead me to the other two men closest to the leader of their underground organization. And while I had to do quite a bit of digging, I was able to find out enough to help steer me in the right direction.

Aside from getting expelled last fall from Whitland University for disorderly conduct with a professor, nothing else about him screams troubled. No juvenile record, hardly even any speeding tickets. Which could mean he either had his record expunged, or there's some other reason why he's got himself caught up in this line of work. Some other correlation for why he turned out so disturbed.

And for a twenty-one year old kid, that's...concerning to say the least.

His last phone record with a large in-service provider dates back to two years ago. After that the trail goes cold, which means he's been taught how to keep a low-profile.

Charges on his bank statements show purchases being made to convenience stores for new prepaid cell phones every so often, his last purchase made six days ago. And while they offer some level of anonymity, he failed to realize one key factor in tracking someone down: the phones he's purchased are all equipped with GPS, making him still traceable through his location.

What a dummy.

I grab my keys from the counter and head over to my front door, slipping my shoes on. At the loud music blaring up my driveway, I look up to see Levi's headlights shining through my front door. The song gets louder, more clear to understand as he crests the top of my driveway.

I sigh audibly to myself, pinching the bridge of my nose to stifle the embarrassment of this man.

I JUST HAD SEEEEeeeeeEEEX. AND IT FELT SOOOO GOOOOD.

I open the front door, stepping outside as Levi rolls the passenger window down. A wide, foolish grin on his face as he lowers the volume down on the song.

"Is that really necessary?" I open the car door, sliding into the passenger seat.

I knew that when I spoke with Levi before leaving Sawyer's place yesterday, that he'd known right away what happened between Cyn and I. It was probably my fault for the way I kept glancing over at her, for mentioning that we had just come from my place. Call it a man's knowing or hunch—or maybe the word sex was just written all over my forehead, but he'd smirked real wide at me.

I instantly knew I was going to hear about it today.

He pats me on the shoulder, hard enough to jerk me forward. "My man lost his virginity! Of course it's a big deal." He laughs like he's just won the damn lottery. "So, tell me all about it." He backs out of my driveway, turning down it as we leave my place.

"I'd rather not." I say, looking out the window.

"Oh, don't be a prude. What was it like?" He all but nearly purrs. "Did you find it on your own?"

I look over at him. "Find what?"

He lifts his free hand up, his words full of sarcasm. "Her fucking fingernail." He barks out a laugh. "What else would I be referring to?"

A chuckle slips out as I shake my head, letting a moment of silence pass. "I may have needed assistance."

He laughs again as I roll my eyes. "Bro, it's okay. I had the same thing my first time."

"Really?" I ask, looking over at him.

He shrugs his shoulders. "You go in thinking it's way higher and have a moment of panic when it's not." He barks out a chuckle. "No amount of watching porn prepares you for that."

He turns down Boulder Street as the afternoon sunlight paints the busy sidewalks. My attention is drawn to the hustle and bustle of people out today.

I JUST HAD—

I quickly push Levi's hand off the volume knob. "Don't you fucking dare." I warn.

Humor dances across his face as he says, "My boy's a changed man. I'm just trying to celebrate." He shrugs his shoulders, feigning an innocence.

I give him a look. "That is not what you're trying to do." I slowly lower my finger and thumb from the knob, watching him closely.

He raises his hand up. "Fine, I won't embarrass you. I'll leave it be."

I give him a side eye before I finally trail my gaze back to the road. In a flash, the volume is turned up full blast as people walking along the sidewalk look at us as this damn song blares out of Levi's car.

—SEEEEeeeeEEEx. AND IT FELLLT SOOO GOOOOD.

A man walking with a woman gives me a thumbs up, nodding his head and laughing. I lock gazes with a middle-aged woman who's glaring at me, as if I've committed an adulterous sin.

I look over at Levi, shaking my head. Unbeknownst to myself, I can't help the chuckle that rises up my throat. Because he's right about me being a changed man.

Everything changed the second I laid eyes on Cynthia.

Can I see you tonight? There's something I want to show you.

My heartbeat quickens at her response. *Of course, love. Can't wait to see you. Xoxo*

A quirky grin curves up my face as warmth blossoms in my chest. She called me *love.* If it weren't for Levi standing next to me, and us about to walk into this business meeting, I probably would've giggled like a little girl reading that.

I'm not too proud to admit that this woman makes me swoon for her.

I text her back, adding a black heart at the end of my message. *I love you. I'll see you later.*

I slip my phone into my pocket, glancing over at Levi to find him staring at me with a smug grin on his face. I roll my eyes. "It's not polite to eavesdrop on other people's conversations."

He chuckles, a moment later the elevator dings its arrival to the fourth floor. The tall, steel doors open up to reveal a realty office inside. We approach the front desk as a woman with dark brown skin greets us with a warm smile. "How may I help you gentlemen today?"

"We have an appointment with Mr. Dawsten." I say.

She picks up her phone, dialing a few numbers before several seconds later she says into the phone, "Your three o'clock meeting is here." She nods before hanging up the phone, meeting my gaze. "He will be out shortly."

"Thank you." I say before Levi and I go to seat ourselves in the small waiting area. Not even three minutes pass before a man dressed in a navy suit comes out.

He lowers his hand out as I take it in mine. "Thank you for reaching out to me. Let's go ahead and take this back to my office."

We follow him down a long hallway, turning right into an office decorated with monochrome accents. The wall behind his desk painted a charcoal grey, the floor to ceiling windows facing the towering buildings of Lilitu City and lighting the room. Gerald goes to sit himself down behind a beige desk, my gaze lowering to the glass plaque on top that says *success is possible through the belief of self.*

Corny, but okay.

"So, you both are looking to acquire the property on Willa Avenue?"

Neither Levi or myself take a seat in either of the chairs in front of his desk. This won't take long anyway.

"Correct." I responded.

Gerald lightly chuckles. "Well, I hate to disappoint you boys but that property isn't up for sale. In fact, I'm currently looking to remodel it into a new commercial build."

"Is that so?" I ask, having known full well of his plans to do that already.

His gaze glances from me to Levi, his expression turning nervous as Levi turns the blinds down over the small mirror on his door revealing the inside of the office. He works on a swallow as he forces himself to remain neutral. "There are plans for the business currently occupying that space but none of which involve me selling the property."

I nod slowly as Levi turns around to face us, inching his way closer to Gerald's desk. "Even if I were to offer you a generous deposit on it?"

He scoffs at me, glancing between both of us. "What kind of game are you two playing here?" He goes to reach for his phone when I slam my hand onto his.

"I wouldn't do that if I were you." When his gaze darts up to the camera in the corner of the room, angled to face us, I lower my voice as I whisper, "Don't count on it. I've already cut the feed."

He lets out a harsh breath. "What do you want?"

I release my hand as I go into my pocket, pulling out a wad of cash. "Backpayments for the last six months, plus an additional twenty thousand to revoke your ownership over the property."

He knits his brows together, barking out a laugh. "You're out of your fucking mind if you think I'm going to sell you my property for twenty-thousand dollars."

I shrug my shoulders as Levi inches himself to stand on the other side of Gerald. "I think you will because the building is hardly worth forty." I pause. "And because I don't think you'd want your wife finding out about the affair you've been having for the past year now."

His gaze widens as his chest rises. "You're bluffing."

I pull out my phone, showing him a picture of surveillance footage of him and a blonde realtor meeting at a motel one night. "I think you look pretty recognizable in this photo. What do you think?"

He exhales raggedly as he clenches his teeth, anger rising. He remains silent for a long moment before he glares up at Levi. But before he can open his mouth, he lowers a hand down to the desk, his half-buttoned up shirt revealing the tattoo on his chest as he leans down.

Gerald's gaze widens, shock and terror exploding over his face as he recognizes the mark of The Deimari. "Please—" He stutters as he shakes his head vigorously. "I don't want any trouble."

"Good to hear." I open up his lower filing cabinet, shuffling through the documents inside until I get to the one I want. I plop it down onto his desk, wringing a gasp from him. "Then let's go ahead and make that deal then, shall we?"

CHAPTER 59

Cynthia

"You both spoil me." I say, tucking the money beneath my garter.

Renaldo chuckles. "We are only doing our part as paying customers." He glances over at Jessica with amusement in his eyes. "Besides, it was her idea to come out tonight. She all but nearly dragged me out to—as she put it, see her favorite girl."

I make a pouty face as I grab her hands, squeezing them. "Ugh, you're amazing."

Jessica gives me a warm grin. "It's the truth. But let's talk about the real discussion at hand." She leans in closer to me as I kneel down in front of her chair. "You have a certain glow about you girl."

I fight back the grin curving my face but fail. I tilt my head to the side, smirking. When I say nothing, she gasps as she playfully swats at my hand. "Please tell me it's that dreamy dark-haired man who's been watching you dance."

I shrug my shoulders, looking over her to see a man walking towards us. I fix my gaze back onto her even as tension rises in my shoulders. "Maybe." I tease.

I lift my gaze back up, locking eyes with the man in the blue baseball cap and dark navy jeans. His gaze mostly shielded by his hat, causing nerves to work themselves up over my skin. But just when I think he's about to approach me, he walks right past our section. Joining a group of guys in another.

"Well, I do hope you plan on giving me the details because I need to know more." She says, humming with anticipation.

I focus back on her, winking. "I promise another night." I stand up again, laughing when Jessica huffs her frustration. "It was good seeing you guys."

Gods, I'm grateful my shift is over. Aside from the innumerable amount of lapdances I've given tonight, I found myself on high alert. Observing every man that looked at me for too long, never allowing my back to remain facing anyone for longer than necessary.

"Get home safely, dear." Renaldo says as he lifts his drink to salute me.

I make my way to the locker room and change out of my dance clothes, slipping on a pair of cotton shorts and a matching shirt. I hike my bag over my shoulder and head over to Vivianne's office to pay her, giving her an air kiss before I leave the locker room. I do my nightly tip outs with everyone else before exiting the club.

I step outside and Dex is waiting for me with a grin on his handsome face. He opens the front passenger door. "Hi."

"Hi." I say before he swoops in and steals a kiss from me. I giggle in his embrace before he lets me go, and I seat myself down into the car.

He comes around, getting into the driver's seat before driving away from the club. "How was your night?"

"It was decent." I say.

He lowers a hand to my thigh, his thumb sweeping over my skin. "I'm glad to hear it."

My gaze lowers to his hand, fixating on the unique scar there. "So what are you going to show me?"

He chuckles. "Where would the fun in the surprise be if I told you?"

I roll my eyes as I hum my nosey displeasure. "I suppose." I take his hand in mine, sweeping my thumb over the circular mark.

His hand briefly flexes beneath mine as I trace the pinkish skin, lifting my gaze up to see him staring straight ahead. It's not long after the moment of silence that he breaks it.

"What I said the other night, about—" He takes a moment before continuing, his voice soft yet clear like the moonlight shining above Lilitu City tonight. "When I went to tell my parents what happened, I had hoped that they would've put their rigid beliefs to the side and console me. Like any other normal teenager would've wanted from their parents."

A weight of stones settles on my chest.

"But instead, they saw me as impure. My mother, particularly. She didn't believe me that it happened against my will, and said I was trying to distract myself from the fact that I had *sinned*. That I had disobeyed *god's will*, and had to deal with the consequences of my pre-marital infidelity." He pauses, and those stones sitting on my chest fall down to the base of my belly. "I still remember the smell of the cigarette smoke like it was yesterday."

I lean my head up against the seat as I continue sweeping my thumb across the scar.

He finally looks over at me, but turmoil is not what I see in his gaze. "It took a very long time for me to even handle being in a room where cigarettes were being burned. But the scar," he lifts our conjoined hands up. "Is just that now. I've made peace with the fact that my parents will never be who I needed them to be. Which was just loving and accepting."

My gaze roams over his face. "That doesn't mean it hurts any less."

"There are times I wonder what I did to deserve parents who treated me that way, and it does sting. It's a wound that will never truly be gone, not until my final breath." He lifts our hands to his lips, pressing a kiss to the top of my knuckles. "But I don't need them to know what real companionship feels like. To experience real, unconditional love and acceptance." He looks over at me, grinning softly. "And it doesn't mean I have to love another any less. You are a testament to that."

The stones in my belly melt at his words like wax dripping down a taper candle. I bring our hands to my lips as I press a kiss to the scar, watching a softness blanket his blue eyes before he's forced to train his gaze back onto the road. "I believe you." I say quietly. "And you never need to ask me to treat you with love and respect."

I cradle his hand to my chest, wanting to take the burden of his past away but I know that I can't. And when he continues caressing his thumb over my skin again, I know that he believes me when I say, "You already have it."

He curses under his breath as he reaches for his phone, pulling it out. "I'm sorry, I have to take this. It's Levi—"

"It's okay." I lean up onto my toes as I kiss him. "I'll go put my things upstairs and meet you up there."

He nods. "I'll be just a few minutes." His gaze lowers to my bag. "You better have that harness on by the time I'm finished."

I snort a laugh as I walk up the steps, turning the corner and shuffling into his bedroom. I flip on the light switch, my attention drawn to something hanging over his bed.

Did he always have that there?

I notice it's covered with some sort of protective cloth, and I almost go to inspect what's under it when the weight of my bag on my arm becomes cumbersome. I plop it onto the ground, zippering it open and pulling out the harness. A wicked grin curves my lips as I put it on.

After I've put it on I begin snooping around his room. What else is a girl to do while she waits?

I poke around in his closet, at all of his neatly hung shirts and jackets. I become bored and walk back into the bedroom. I go over to his nightstand, opening up the drawer when I spot what's inside.

Heat dances along my skin as I go to pull the sex toy out when I feel a presence sneak up from behind me.

My breath catches in my chest when Dex steps closer to me, towering over me. "You weren't supposed to see that." He lightly trails his fingers down my shoulders, goosebumps pimpling along my skin.

I loosen my breath. "Do you think of me when you use it?"

He lowers his head an inch, his breath coasting along the side of my face as he brings one hand to my chest. Tracing his fingers along the leather material at my neck. "Yes."

I shudder at his touch. "Do you want to use it now?"

He trails his fingers further down, my back arching into him as he taunts me with his slow exploration. "I want to use you instead."

I work on a swallow as I glance up at the frame above his bed. "What is it?"

He chuckles deeply. "Your surprise."

He steps away from me, taking the heat of his touch with him. He raises up, taking the cover off and revealing what's beneath.

I stare at it for a long moment, taking in every striking detail. Every thoughtful attention that has brought his drawing to life.

That has brought *me* to life.

He steps behind me again, lowering his head down to my neck. He presses a kiss against my heated skin. "Dex it's..." My words trail off.

His hands move to my hips, playing with the harness belt around my waist. "Do you like it?" His voice hardly above a rough whisper.

I shake my head slowly, feeling overwhelmed with the adoration he so freely gives to me. "I love it."

One of his hands remains at my hip while the other lowers down, snaking his fingers down the inner junction of my thigh.

A wicked grin forms along my lips as I whisper, "What do you think of when you use it?"

Without hesitation he responds. "I think about you on all fours, playing with your pussy while I stretch and fill you." His hand moves to the right as he starts to touch me.

I moan against him. "And you like how your toy feels on you?"

"Yes." He says gruffly. His lips move to my ear as he nips the skin beneath. "But *nothing* feels better than you."

He goes to lower his finger inside of me when I say, "Show me."

He pauses as I turn around, bringing my hands to his waist. I lower them to the bulge pressing against his pants, and watch as his chest rises as I rub him, slow and tortuously. "Don't just tell me what you'd do. Show me."

The yearning in his eyes intensifies as he lets me unbutton his pants and lower them down his legs. I kneel down, freeing his pants from his legs before I pull his boxer briefs down. Freeing his erected cock as it hangs in front of my mouth.

I slowly stand myself up again and he tracks my every movement with a razor sharp focus. He lifts his shirt up and over his head before laying himself down onto his bed. He lowers a hand into the drawer, pulling the toy out as I kneel in front of his legs.

He goes to grab a bottle of lube when I lean forward, wrapping my mouth around his cock. He groans out as I suck him, getting him wet enough before I pull back.

"You could just keep going." He purrs.

I shrug my shoulders as I lean back, sitting on my ass and spreading my legs open. His gaze lowers to what's between. "But I want to watch you play."

He exhales as he lowers the silicone toy down onto his cock, palming it in his hand as he works himself. I watch him as he pleases himself, the toy making wet suctioning sounds with each measured thrust of his hand.

"Good boy. Now keep going." I encourage him.

He does as I say and masturbates with the toy, pre-cum beading at the tip. I lower my finger to my pussy, teasing myself as he watches with a hunger in his gaze. "Does it feel good?"

He nods, not taking his gaze from my hand. "Yes."

I slip my finger inside, a moan slipping out.

In an instant he's pulling the silicone sleeve off of his cock and hovering over me. Flipping me over until my belly is laying on the bed.

"You like the way I please myself, don't you?" He says as he hikes my legs up, bending my knees into the sheets. He inserts himself in between my legs, spreading me wide for him as he presses himself against my ass. "How my cock drips with need for you."

He grabs my neck, pulling me up until my back is flush with his chest. He keeps his hand at my neck, playing with the silver ring at the center of my throat. He slips his finger through the ring, gently tugging on it. "This little pussy is begging to be fucked by me."

He grinds himself against my ass before lowering a hand to position himself at my entrance. I arch my back deeper into him, moaning at the feel of him slipping between my wetness.

"Wet and aching, for me."

He thrusts himself to the hilt, wringing a gasp from me at the sheer fullness of him. His hands move to my waist as he grips me, driving into me over and over again.

I cry out as his body cages me in, using me as he promised. He lowers his lips down to my spine, pressing kisses there as he fucks me *hard*. As if he's both punishing and rewarding me, and I greedily take every inch of him.

He lifts a hand to my neck again, anchoring a finger to my lips. He urges my mouth open as he curls his finger over my bottom lip. I close my mouth over it, sucking and swirling my tongue as he groans his satisfaction.

He stops abruptly, wrapping an arm around my chest as he lays us both down onto our sides. He pulls out long enough to insert his leg between mine, and I cry out in protest.

"Don't worry." He bends and lifts my leg up, exposing me completely as he brings me flush to his chest. He leans his lips against my cheek as he repositions himself at my entrance. "I know you need it just as bad."

He fills me in one hard thrust, his hand moving to my thigh as he grips me. I cry out as he slowly descends in and out of me, torturing me with his slowed pace.

"Look at you." He moves his hand down to my pussy, my back arching into him as he rubs my clit. "So damn beautiful."

He captures my lips with his as he quickens his pace, my release building wildly within me. My moans get trapped against his lips as his tongue snakes out to glide along mine. His other arm snakes under my shoulders, and he lifts his hand to my breast.

He pulls his lips away from mine as I cry out, louder this time as he gently pinches my nipple before tracing it with his thumb. His hands at my hardened flesh, my clit, and his cock thrusting into me, it's agonizing in the most pleasurable way possible.

Tears brim my eyes. "I—" I cry out his name as I cum against him, rocking back into him into oblivion as he keeps his same pace. But the crippling wave of my orgasm doesn't settle.

"I can't—" I cry out when the tears brimming my eyes trail down my face, dampening my cheeks.

"I know, baby." His tongue reaches out as he glides it up my trail of pleasure-soaked tears, amplifying the thrill coursing through my blood. "I know."

He keeps rubbing my clit and tracing my nipple. "You can do it, though." His voice is a rumble when he says, "You can do anything."

I scream out for him as the crescendo of my orgasm keeps going, my ears ringing as my skin buzzes. A few seconds later Dex is whimpering his release behind me, fucking me until both of us lay limp in sweet completion.

My heart races a mile a minute as I feel his race against my back. We lay there in silence for a long while, unable to form words until Dex breaks the silence between us. His words laden with exhaustion, and awe. "You are the reward I never thought I'd earn, Cynthia." He presses a trembling kiss to my cheek. "You are everything I ever wanted."

CHAPTER 60

Dexter

"I learned something interesting today."

Her head on my chest rises and falls in tandem with my steady breaths. My fingers snake themselves through her soft blue hair, finding comfort in her arm laid over my waist. "What's that?" I ask, exhaustion evident in my voice.

She lifts her head to look up at me, mascara smeared beneath her eyes. "I called Pauline to tell her about the fundraiser. That I was confident I could raise enough money for her to keep her shop open." She pauses. "She told me her past due balance had actually been paid for by an anonymous donor."

I nod slowly. "That is interesting."

She gives me a look. "She then told me the owner suddenly sold the building to a new investor, and met with him earlier today to discuss the future of her business."

A faint grin curves up my face. "Sounds like she's getting a fresh start."

She hums softly. "She said the new owner wants to invest in expanding her shop, making some renovations that will help bring in more customers and expand the adoption center." She raises a brow. "What was most interesting was when she asked if you had mentioned any of this to me yet."

My grin deepens as I lean down to kiss her forehead. "The message may have gotten lost in translation."

She chuckles, letting a long moment of silence pass between us. She shakes her head slowly as she asks, "Why?"

I push her bangs away from her eyes as she leans up onto her elbows. "Because I don't like to see women fail in a world unfairly dictated by men."

She stares at me, silently.

"I'm in a position to help others financially." I glance down at her lips, swollen from the amount of time I've spent kissing and worshipping them tonight. "Now she gets to keep her business."

A grin slowly creeps up her face before she leans in to kiss me. "Thank you." She says as her lips hover above mine. "But I'm still hosting that fundraiser."

She goes back to resting her head on my chest as I bark out a laugh. Smoothing her hair away from her face as she curls in next to me. "I expected nothing different." I lean down, kissing her forehead. "The money can still be used towards her business."

"How are you going to find willing contractors to work on her building?"

I grin. "I have connections."

I turn onto my side, facing her. I cradle her head into the palms of my hands, bringing her lips to mine. I feel her body melt into my touch as she snakes her hands up my chest.

I pull away long enough to whisper, "I love you."

Her face lights up as she whispers back, "I love you." Sealing her words with a kiss.

We spend the next long while kissing, touching, doing everything that I once forbid myself to explore. The safety of her love lulls me into her depths, safely drowning into her embrace. It isn't until we've both found ourselves too tired to move that we finally allow ourselves to drift off to sleep.

And it is in my dreams where thoughts of shame do not plague my subconscious, but the reward of rest.

CHAPTER 61

Cynthia

A loud screech penetrates the silent space as I push the heavy door open. My heels click on the dusty concrete floor as I slip inside the abandoned building.

I glance up to see he's already here, waiting at the top of the staircase. I walk across the dimly-lit room, following the shine of the moonlight illuminating the second floor. I gasp as a mouse skitters across the ground, collecting myself before I continue up the rusted metal steps.

The moonlight casts through the large round window, highlighting his short auburn hair with his feathered, large jet black wings on full display.

I approach the demon, standing to his right as I look out the window. "It's been awhile, Lucifer."

His gaze remains facing forward, upturned eyes the color of whiskey stare out the window at the towering lit buildings of Lilitu City. His deep voice is a mixture between silk and smoke, and his words collide together like an eather of power. "Indeed it has."

The Prince of Hell finally turns to face me, his height surpassing mine by an entire foot. His gaze lowers to mine beneath thick brows. "You requested to see me."

I nod. "We have a dilemma up here."

He tilts his head to the right, revealing his sharp, angular jaw.

"The mortals know of our existence again." I pause. "And they've somehow come into possession of Nettleshade."

He straightens his head, exhaling a soft breath. "Anastasia told me that you were nearly at the mercy of one."

I nod again. "Thankfully, I was not alone and was able to get out. But the man who captured me works for an underground trafficking ring. It is safe to assume that more people are aware of how to incapacitate us."

His stern gaze searches mine. "You mean yourself and Amelia."

I roll my eyes. "Just because you don't visit the upper world doesn't mean other demons don't. The mortals' knowledge of this makes us vulnerable, and I want it dealt with." I loosen my breath, following his gaze to the expansive oval-shaped window. "Besides, I don't think I have to remind you that while you prefer to remain below, another Prince frequents much of his time up here."

Lucifer is quiet for a moment before he turns his gaze back to me again. "What do you wish for me to do?"

He may have some sort of authority here, but damn does he really make me have to spell it out? "Warn the others. Tell them there is no room for careless mistakes while they're here. To be on alert."

Lucifer nods his head. "Have you told her yet?"

I blink, nodding my head. "I don't think she has any interest in leaving Hell though. A part of me wonders if that might actually be in the best interest for everyone involved."

He chuckles as he runs his hand through his auburn hair. "Possibly."

The Prince of Rebellion, Truth, and Knowledge, graces me with a handsome grin. Reminding me that other than being a stern demon, he sure is handsome.

A few moments later it smooths out as he says, "Keep me updated on this. I'll intervene if necessary."

I exhale. "Thank you."

Without another word, I watch as a void of darkness appears behind him, forming an oval as tall as him. Tendrils of shadows snake out to latch onto him as he steps back, allowing the darkness to swallow him whole.

Portaling the Prince of Hell back to our domain, our home.

CHAPTER 62

Dexter

Two weeks later

"Unless you want to have the bones in your wrists broken, I suggest you tip her more than two dollars."

The man in the plaid polo T-shirt turns to look at me, eyes widened by my threat. It takes him only half a second to register that I'm the same man who threatened him weeks ago when he tried to put his hands on Cynthia.

He makes the smart decision not to ask questions, and digs into his pocket. Pulling out his wallet and shelling out three crisp twenties. "That's all I have." A slight tremor working through his hand.

A devious grin curves my lips. "Much better."

He steps away from me, moving closer to the stage as Cyn glances over my way. She smirks at me before she continues her stage performance.

He throws the money on stage, quickly stepping back and away from me. I have to stifle the laugh that bubbles up my throat.

Cyn made a wise move holding the fundraiser on the busiest night of the week. From getting the other dancers to participate, to even adding a raffle for a free thirty minute VIP room to the patron who donated the most money, she's put so much effort into making tonight a big hit.

And from the amount of people here tonight, I'd say that she more than succeeded.

As soon as the doors opened up, sections were filled and the remaining patrons left were either forced to stand around on the main floor or crowd around the bar. Every time I glance over at Ace he's busy pouring another drink.

I know he's making good money tonight.

The moment Cyn got on stage men were just lining up to throw her cash. Maybe if I were a different man, I'd find myself a little jealous at the amount of men whistling and littering the stage floor with bills. Maybe I'd even feel my ego bruise a little at all of the attention she's getting.

But to see the stage floor covered in bills only makes me happy to see her getting her well deserved flowers for the night.

It might also make my dick hard to know that while they all throw her money, feigning for her attention, that I'm the only one who actually gets it.

She glances over at me again as she lowers herself down the pole, the men around me going crazy when she lowers down into a split.

Such a flexible little goddess she is. I'll have to remind myself to ask her to do a split on me later tonight.

She does some floorwork until the end of her stage performance, the bouncer bringing up a bag to stuff all of her money into. She carries it in one hand, her halter in the other as she descends down the steps. She winks at me before walking to the locker room to freshen up.

I make my way back over to our section, seating myself down next to Levi with Amelia perched on his armrest. His hand roams up and down her bare back as the other balances a glass of whiskey on his knee.

"I guarantee she made at least four thousand." Amelia says, sipping her cranberry vodka.

I lean back into the leather seat as a waitress with black hair comes around. Moving to stand closer to me. "Can I get you anything to drink, Mr. Lacroix?"

"A shot of tequila, and a bourbon, please."

She nods her head. "Absolutely." She passes a strange glance over at Levi before hurrying off.

I look over at him, raising a brow. "Is there a reason why she's looking at you like you're the plague?"

He barks out a laugh as Amelia giggles beside him. I get the impression I'm missing something here, but all he says is, "I have no idea."

Sawyer joins us, seating himself down while he curses under his breath. His brows furrowed together as he clenches his teeth, downing his whiskey in one full sip. His usual stern face appears even more harsh.

"What's the matter with you?" I ask.

Sawyer shakes his head curtly, setting his empty glass down onto the low-table in front of us. "I just had a rather *pleasant* experience with a wretched woman."

I raise my brows, glancing over at Levi. "Oh, do tell."

One thing Sawyer and I have had in common is that we've both been abstinent, him far shorter than I. Unlike me being a prior virgin, Sawyer's had sexual relations with women. But that's it. Nothing that ever lasted, no further commitment other than for the sake of pleasure. But it's been years since he's last been with a woman.

I find myself wondering if that's why he's extra grumpy now.

"I'm leaving the men's restroom and as I walk out, I bump into this woman. I apologize and she snaps at me, saying—and I quote, *watch where you're going dickhead.*"

Levi coughs next to me, stifling the laugh I know wants to erupt from him.

"I grabbed her arm, turned her around and asked her who she thought she was speaking to. She looked me dead in the face and asked if I had a hard time hearing at my old age." He pauses as he visibly stifles back his anger. "She then yelled it loud enough for even the people nearby to hear us, then walked away."

Old man? Oh, she definitely got under his skin.

Sawyer's only forty, and takes good care of himself. Meeting him for the first time, you'd probably think he's no more than thirty-five. But he's definitely the oldest out of Levi and I, surpassing us by at least a decade.

Sawyer curls his hand inward. "I had to walk away for my own sanity."

The waitress comes back over, handing me the drinks then leaving again. "Maybe she's just having a bad day."

Sawyer scoffs. "That wretched woman can kiss my ass."

I take a sip, hiding my wide grin. A few moments later Cyn joins us, lowering down to grab the shot of tequila. "You know me so well." She says before slamming it back.

I chuckle as she seats herself onto the armrest, my hand lowering to her back. "Anything for you."

She lowers the shot glass back to the table, fixing her halter top as she looks at Amelia. "Have you seen her yet?"

Amelia scrunches her brows together. "Who?"

"The new girl. Viv just told me that a new girl is supposed to start tonight."

"Weird, I had no idea." The red-head says as she pushes her hair over her shoulder.

The five of us enjoy each other's company, laughing and talking as the club music booms around us. The simplicity of the moment is soon interrupted.

"No fucking way." Cyn says as she straightens her back, looking at someone across the way.

Striding towards us is a woman with long, platinum blonde hair that travels below her breasts. Her hair is reminiscent of the moonlight, and those eyes—

Even through the headlights on the ceiling shining around, anyone would find themselves momentarily ensnared by those bright amber eyes.

She walks straight over to us, keeping her gaze on Cyn as she stands up from my seat. Rushing towards her and giving her a warm hug. "What are you doing here?"

The woman pulls away, smirking as she shrugs. "I'm bored." She pauses. "And I hear you're in need of some help." She locks eyes with Amelia before she greets her with a warm hug.

"I really didn't think you'd come." Cyn all but nearly squeals, her excitement adorable.

"Excuse my rudeness, but who are you?" I ask.

Cyn turns her head around towards me, smirking. "Everyone, meet Anastasia."

Anastasia's gaze roams over me then Levi, taking us in as if she's examining the threat that we could pose to her.

"You've got to be fucking kidding me." Sawyer mutters under his breath.

The woman snaps her gaze over to him quicker than a viper striking its prey. Her chest sinks as she exhales an exaggerated breath, rolling her eyes. "Who is this annoying mortal?" She asks Cyn, ignoring Sawyer.

She bites her inner lip. "That would be Sawyer. The one I told you about."

"*That* thing? He's the boss?" Anastasia remarks coldly.

Sawyer glares at her with hatred in his eyes, and when she looks at him, she shares the same disdain in hers. "Are you always this dreadful to be around or are you just on your monthly?" He seethes.

My eyes nearly bulge out of my head as I look down to the floor. This man is treading very dangerous water with a being that can quite literally dismember him.

Anastasia only laughs at him, entirely unaffected by his crude remark. Before she can open her mouth, Amelia steps in. "I think what we are all *trying* to say," she says, pointing a hard glance at Sawyer. "Is that we are surprised to see you here, and appreciate you coming to help us."

Sawyer says nothing as he adverts his gaze elsewhere, Anastasia doing the same.

"Wait, you're the new girl?" Cyn asks.

Anastasia nods her head before striking a sultry pose. "You're looking at the newest dancer of The Playground. Silver."

Cyn claps her hands together, Amelia sharing her same excitement. The girls huddle together as they catch up while I look over at Sawyer.

His hand grips around his new glass of whiskey, his finger tapping against it annoyedly.

Levi on my right leans in closer to me. "This will be interesting." He says quietly.

I shake my head, grinning. Interesting would be an understatement.

For the rest of the night, aside from the girls getting called away for lapdances and things of the like, we spend it reveling in each other's company. Our drinks stay full, and the laughter remains consistent.

Anastasia and Sawyer remain as far away as possible from each other, her paying him no mind while he acts like she's invisible. The awkward tension from the two of them is palpable, but I find it's easy not to dwell or focus on it when I have my whole world sitting in my lap.

My beautiful, constant reminder that life can be really good. That pleasure can be safe, and rewarding.

I look over at Levi, catching a big smile on his face as Amelia playfully scruffs up his hair. He leans in, melting into her touch. The sight makes me grin, and serves as a vital reminder.

While we may not have an idea on what we'll face the further we dig into who is behind the trafficking, and where the source of the Nettleshade is coming from, there is one thing for certain.

That there is no price great enough to keep our girls safe. No matter what it takes.

The trilogy continues in its final installment:

SILVER

Deal With A Succubus, Book 3
Available for pre-order now!

AUTHOR'S NOTE

A heartfelt thank you to you, the reader! This series was something I started writing back in 2024, and it has been a pleasure creating these characters and this storyline. When I wrote book one, CHERRY, I knew this story was going to be different from anything I've written thus far. I wanted this series to be a fun read, filled with banter and spice, but to also incorporate real-life themes into it. But most of all, I wanted to create strong FMC's that took the word *strong* to a new level. Because creating an independent character just wasn't good enough for me. I needed these female characters to not give a single fuck, and embrace it proudly.

Thank you for taking a chance on me and reading this book, and please consider leaving a review. Reviews really help indie authors. :)

ABOUT THE AUTHOR

Michelle Rossa is the author of the *Shadows and Fire &
Deal With A Succubus* series. Her work centers around
Adult Romance and Fantasy. From writing poetry to
daydreaming fantasy worlds inside her head, Michelle has
had a vast imagination since she was a child.

When she's not writing, she's most likely time out in
nature, snuggling with her cat Diva, making edits of her
favorite fandoms or re-watching The Vampire Diaries for
the millionth time. Outside of her passion for writing, she
practices as a psychic medium and tarot reader. She is
greatly passionate about all things astrology, the left hand
path, occult studies, mythology, non-conformity to societal
standards, and advocating for women.